GRANT'*d*

A NOVEL

Edited by Jared Austin

Cover Art by Dak Lyons

Ron,
Two of the purposes of this novel are to transmit hope and to connect families. These are two ideas you have fertilized in me. You have accepted me as family, and you have given me hope in some of my darkest moments. I hope I can return the favor.

For all the Grants out there

Thank you for allowing me to join you and your family in the hope cycle.

Michael P. Dale

GRANT'*d*

Chapter 1: Hate

There is always some heat in hate. Repulsion, rising up, becomes anger, which morphs into a hot rage of fear and indignation. For the first time, Grant felt desperately alone, and anxiously afraid. At first sight, he felt repulsion and rage, and as the saying goes, it "made his blood boil." But not with anger—with hate.

Hesitantly, and with great caution, Grant rapped his knuckles on the two-ply, paper-thin door of the dilapidated trailer. Flies buzzed around the flypaper that hung from the tattered roof of the makeshift porch. The flypaper, suspended gracefully, stared back at Grant brown and sticky, while an odor reminiscent of the smell of rotting carcasses wafted into his nostrils. A marble, if placed upon the porch, would have rolled quickly down and to the right through a puddle of filth just out of reach of the reptiles and rodents that called the area underneath the house their home. The dogs that slept under the porch didn't seem to mind the carcasses, so why should Grant? The atmosphere was thick and heavy, like an oven full of sweat, and Grant covered his mouth and nose with his hands, while his intestines heaved in protest as he assessed the scene.

The lone trailer sat on the mountainside surrounded by the ever-growing piles of trash. From above, the trailer appeared to be a small sliver cut into a great mass of green. Dead on, it was a massive wasteland, repudiating order. Cars rusted and bikes grew useless in the yard. Foliage was destitute. A nearly worthless shed or barn slanted down into the ashen mountain wall. Piled underneath this original structure was more waste: trash cans, gasoline cans, paint cans, random rusted wire, and a crowbar.

And to the right was a caged animal frantic in the pen. The pen couldn't be called a dog house because there wasn't a roof, and it couldn't be called a cage because that name was much too sophisticated. Inside the pen was a female dog, obviously, in heat. Her erratic pacing, the rubbing of her body against the rusted barrier wire, and her irritated body roll tantrums were a live give-away. The fact there was a male dog on the exterior of the cage—howling and humping everything in sight—also provided Grant with some clues. The odor was pungent, the lattice trailer skirt was coming undone, and nothing in the place was right. Before Grant could indulge his eyes anymore to the degradation of the earth, the door slowly opened.

The man who opened the door uttered some unintelligible greeting, but Grant was nearly capsized with sensory overload.

What smelled like cigarette smoke laced with sweat and pinto beans—cooked for hours—molested Grant's nostrils.

"Ew ya hyear for?" the man grunted near Grant's face.

Grant made eye contact. The old man hunched forward.

"I sayed, ew ya hyear for?"

He blew a breath of stench so horrid that Grant's eyelids fluttered, but through the wavering lashes Grant saw a mouth—a mouth with several teeth cracked and broken, others missing, all dingy, black and yellow; and worst of all was the loose flesh dangling in the form of gums between the gaps. Grant grimaced and attempted to speak. In that moment, between attempting and speaking, a chicken bolted out the door and began attacking him. The chicken, a red molten torpedo, flapped furiously as it slammed into Grant's right thigh. Grant swiftly circled left and booted the chicken with his left foot into the corner of the universe. *This has to be hell.*

After the welcome on the porch, Grant regained his bearings and asked, "Does Jacobi live here?" Without an answer, the old man dragged him inside and chauffeured him to a seat, stopping just shy of an old pleather recliner, brown, with cracks in the covering that Grant traced with his fingers once he sat down. With his gag reflex hemorrhaging, Grant asked again, "Does Jacobi live here?"

As the words left his mouth, he saw it: through the back window, he saw the beginning of the end.

A man walked by, shirtless, tattooed, wearing black jeans, boots, and a black baseball cap. An old hatchet bounced against his left shoulder while he carried a gray cement block in his right hand. Following behind him were two children: one a boy, no older than five, sauntering in a pair of dingy white underwear and brown moccasins, and the other, a barefoot toddler girl, in a loose diaper. Grant wondered if this nightmare was real. He wanted to rescue those children from their life sentence, but he only stood and unabashedly walked to the window.

"Naa, Jacobi lives clear cross over der in at other holler with hes mama," the old man replied, interrupting Grant's thoughts.

Transfixed, Grant stared out the single rectangular pane window in the door at the back of the "home."

Passing in front of Grant's eyes with brood in tow, the man in the black cap swaggered out to the cage next to the dog pen. Howling, the male dog clanged against the fence, desperately searching for a weakness. Grant saw plenty. The man threw down the block in disgust and cursed the dog. He swung open the makeshift gate to the chicken coop and encroached on his prey. His shorter right leg thumped harshly as he swiveled on the bowed and bent left leg he nearly dragged behind. Grant's heart raced; he needed to move—quickly.

"Them chickens got diseases; cain't eat 'em," the old man explained.

Grant nodded in understanding as he glanced quickly at the old man who fiddled with his pipe. He didn't seem to be bothered by Grant standing at the back door, watching. Since they hadn't been fully introduced, Grant assumed this was not the first of the family's odd visitations. He turned his burning eyes, the bulbs of scorn, back to the window.

Chickens do not give up the ghost easily. Hatchet, the name Grant gave the shirtless man, backed a chicken into a corner with a piece of torn fence. Then he snatched the chicken from the earth as it fluttered and squawked, flapping its wings at a maddening pace. He showed no pity. He stretched the chicken across the concrete block, placed his foot on its body while holding its head in hand, and with one swift movement chopped straight through the chicken's neck. Sparks flew. The hatchet blade ricocheted off the block, splintered and slightly curled.

Blood sprayed everywhere. Hatchet laughed, but the toddler girl shrieked in horror. The headless chicken chased the girl, spewing blood as it ran. Nearly cemented to the ground with fear, the girl cried in terror. But she screamed without sound, as it was lost in the cacophony of dog howls, chickens squawks, a man's laughter, and the earth's own revulsion. Inside the house, Grant stood petrified as if he were a fear-stricken child watching his first horror movie.

After a few moments, the scene quieted and Hatchet continued with the poultry revolution. Chicken after chicken was captured, laid bare across the stone, and severed from reality. As surreal as it seemed, the children eventually quieted, the dog returned to his noisy rut, and the executioner set about his work as if it were daily business. He worked in a pool of chicken remains: bodies, heads, blood, and feces. The children played and laughed as the bodies and heads of chickens piled up. With each execution, the blade tip dulled. Hatchet wasn't too sharp in the first place.

Grant was broken. His righteous indignation burned within, scolding him to put a stop to this massacre immediately. *Children should not be exposed to this psychosis! Who lets his children watch him massacre chickens and then lets the kids play in the blood? Maybe the world is flat*, he thought clenching his jaw, as he wrestled with his heart. He stood alone and cold as the show came to a close, but the heat still burned.

Bloody and frustrated, Hatchet finished executing. The blade was as dull as a mallet. He had hit the chickens two, three, four times before he completely mangled them, cursing as he went. Grant wished he could vomit. The kids began to hold fast to their dad as if he were a war hero while he gathered the bodies into several black trash bags, along with the heads, and threw them one by one onto the trash pile. *He should have bagged himself*, or so Grant thought, but it wasn't over yet.

Grant returned to his seat, his anguish lost on his host, and stared blankly at the wall. This was a world he never knew existed, and somehow he still didn't quite believe it. Startled, he turned his head and squinted at the host's wife, who had joined them while the scene outside had captivated Grant. She grinned with her toothless smile and offered him some water in what Dale, whom he just met the day before, had called a Mason jar. He wished Dale were with him now—to help him navigate this mess.

The water fizzed. Bubbles rolled from the bottom of the glass to the top. Grant noticed the color was wrong; the glass did not seem dirty, but the water appeared a murky yellow. The old man waved his cane through Grant's appalled gaze.

"Ya gotta let dat werter sit a minute before ya drank it," the old man said. "Some sulfur's in der and it makes da werter all bubbly-like. Jus' give er a minute cheer and it'll quiet right down. Then ya can take ye a swig."

Lost in a parallel universe, Grant's automated responses began to take over. His years of training in etiquette went into overdrive. "Well, thank you so very much for the water. You are too kind. I appreciate your inviting me in on a hot day like this. I am sorry that I haven't introduced myself: I'm Grant Erlosung." Grant mentally excoriated himself for not completing introductions at the door; his first words had been a direct request of his host. He grew warm as he thought of his failure—again.

"No need for all da smoke and mirro's, boy. Ima Chester Combs, but I spose ya already know that, seein' ya came a knockin' on my door. I guess ya's lookin' for da boy, but he ain't hyear right about now—don't live hyear noways-- he's done gone up to da court wer he always be."

"Oh, well thank you," Grant responded wisely. He noticed a small glass globe atop the television. Inside the globe was a single red rose—fake, of course—and the wooden base of the globe had the words "Family is

Forever" printed on it. Grant continued, "I am pleased to meet you, though, and thanks again for your open hospitality." Grant glanced at the untouched Mason jar. He didn't dare. "It was gracious of you and your wife to invite me into your home. I had a terrible time finding it, but you have made the prize worth the struggle."

"Boy," Chester chortled, "manure is meant for da field, not da house. I 'preciate da manners and all, but I'm old, and I knows better. Ya's here for da boy . . . and not to meet us."

The man's candid reply took Grant aback, but it was well received. Business—this was a game Grant could play, so he cut the crap. "You're right. I am here for Jacobi, but I'm not sure why I'm *here*. This was the address I was given, but you say he doesn't live here, so where do I find him?"

Chester wheezed, coughed, and spit into a tin receptacle. Imagining the contents of the can, Grant closed his eyes and shuddered. "Mr. Combs?" Grant prompted, "I have—"

"Don't cha call me Mr. Combs. That was muh daddy, not me. I'm Chester, plain and simple. . . don't need none of dat mister stuff righ' cheer anyways. Now, you can see da boy, just like I told ju . . . he's done gone up to da court— where he spends most his time."

"Thank you. Now, where's the court?"

"It's dun up ayer a fir piece. You just go 'cross Gomer's Creek, up dat next holler, turn left at da switchback, and go round in circles a few times and yer der."

"Can you give me the address, please?" Grant retorted.

"Now why'd ju need da address for? I jus' gave ya the de-rections. Listen to wut I say. Over da creek, up da next holler, left at da switchback and foller the road 'round till you git to da top. Then, you'll find da court, and Jacobi with it."

Sweat dripped off Grant's forehead and rolled down his cheek. His shirt stuck to his back, and his belt felt uncomfortable at his waist. He could see the steam rising off something cooking in the kitchen. The smells assaulted his senses. He closed his eyes and counted down from five to zero. His eyes met Chester's. "I appreciate your patience. I am new to this area, and I want to be certain before I go, so I don't waste time—"

"Waste time!" Chester challenged. "That's all we dun got 'round hyear is time! And lots of it. You ain't wastin' no time if ye get lost, yer just discoverin' a new path."

Grant disregarded the platitude. "Look!" he exclaimed, now standing. "You may have time, but I value mine. I'll see myself to the door."

Chester's wife followed Grant to the door politely, but Chester just sat and rocked with a sly smirk on his face as he held his pipe. Halfway out the door, Grant turned and thanked Mrs. Combs for her hospitality. As he pivoted and stepped out onto the porch, he walked smack into a piece of fly covered fly paper, catching his eyebrow. He batted away the paper furiously, and it ripped away from his face, sticking to his arm hair. Hot and frustrated, Grant tore away the fly paper—and the arm hair—threw it down on the porch, and walked off hoping never to see that trailer, a chicken, a hatchet, or those people ever again. *Poor kids*, he thought as he escaped, *they'll never know what they're missing.*

Chapter 2: Finding Out

The dining room table was a dull mahogany; transparent swirls of overly buffed polish arrested its surface and the sunlight gleamed through the lacy white curtains and refracted atop the glossy wood. Small glimmers of particles swam in the haze created by the streams of light while Grant waited for his father to return to the room. With his elbows propped on the table, he set his mind quickly to work. *If I exchange the total number of loads I accept for only the more lucrative, easily scheduled ones, I will be able to offer my customers the increased visibility and reassurance that kept them happy. This strategy results in less revenue, but could increase profit and customer satisfaction. What's more important for long-term gain, more or satisfied?* He chewed his bottom lip for a moment, pondering.

Mr. Eric Erlosung, Grant's father, was working steadily on a birdhouse project. An hourglass stood nearby, draining the last bits of sand being siphoned down by the ever-present pull of time. His dad preferred the pressure applied by an ancient chronometer over a newer, more exact timepiece. As far back as Grant could remember, exactitude of time was not his dad's goal or measure; rather, it was the slowly increasing pressure of watching the time disappear before his very eyes that drove him. He waited for the last piece of sand to slip to the bottom, and he put down the sandpaper.

Grant sat back and scratched briskly behind his right ear. He shifted in his chair from left to right to left. Mr. Erlosung took his time, his precious time, cleaning up and storing the last of his tools. The light pouring into his workroom illuminated his beautiful blade. He caught his reflection and admired his remaining gray hair and dark eyebrows. He paused for a moment, to reminisce, and put away the last saw. Grant was waiting, again, in the dining room.

Mr. Erlosung walked into the room and slowly closed the door behind him. It swung on its hinge easily—never creaking. His belongings didn't creak. They shined, glistened, slid, secured, undergirded, and performed, but they never creaked. He walked toward his son, so he could sit with him at the table while Grant stared intently out the window. The sunshine was nearly blinding. Mr. Erlosung pulled up his chair and resituated himself on the firm cushion. He leaned forward, eyebrows raised, and asked, "How are you, son?"

"Oh," he muttered, clearing his throat, "I didn't see you come in, Dad."

"I noticed," Mr. Erlosung replied. "What did you see, Grant? Right then?"

"Where? What are you talking about?"

"In your mind's eye, Grant. What did you see right then, right there? You were obviously looking at something— something had your attention. But it wasn't something in this room; it was something in your thoughts."

Grant's primary focus was his success. Others often caught him daydreaming about his next right move with the transportation company he owned. He often disengaged at dinner or at the gym; he was present in body, but mentally unavailable.

"Dad, eh . . ." Grant sighed forcefully. "I saw . . . well, I was distracted and you know how I—"

"What did you see, Grant? Tell me right now, what did you see?" Mr. Erlosung demanded.

"Dad, I saw the same thing I always see!" Grant huffed. "I saw nothing. I didn't see anything. I let my mind get distracted with ways to improve my business, but I didn't *see* anything. I am not a visionary like you. I'm a doer. I just think, and then I do. Just like I've always done."

"I see," Mr. Erlosung replied, with a half-smirk. "You look, but you see nothing. But when you *do*, you see something. I wish you could see what I see . . ."

"And what's that?" Grant inquired, confused.

"The same thing I see every time I look at you, Grant: a young, brilliant, talented man who has taken the world by storm and beaten it like a dirty rug. You're strong, smart, and swift to make decisions. You're good, true, and honest with your customers. You're kind, gentle, and loving to your mother. I have told you before: if you could see what I see, then you wouldn't be looking, you would have found!"

Grant turned his head away from his dad and looked out the window. He clenched his jaw, closed his eyes, and let out a small sigh of exasperation. Then he turned his gaze back upon his dad.

"I look every morning, Dad. Right in the mirror, I look myself right in the eyes, and I say the words you taught me to say, and I believe the ideas you taught me to believe, and then the day comes—"

"Grant."

"Let me finish, Dad! The day comes and I get tired, and sometimes I get tired of believing."

"Grant, have I ever told you how much I love blue jays?"

"Yes, Dad," Grant replied, incredulously.

Slowly, cautiously, Mr. Erlosung continued his explanation.

"I love blue jays because they are beautiful. I love to watch them fly, and dance, and just sit on fence posts. I love them because they are glimmers of light shattering the transient wind as they streak across the yard at low altitudes. I love them for their dark humor and compelling candor."

He began to wax eloquent, but Grant just waited, as he always did for his Dad. He knew something either silly or profound would be spoken, so he held himself in anticipation.

"But you know, son, the blue jay is not really blue at all. The feathers appear blue due to their structure. If broken, the feathers are no longer blue, just crushed. When their feathers are crushed they lose what makes them unique."

"Dad . . . what's your point?" Grant asked.

"Grant, if you are going to go around making deposits all over the place, then make sure your deposits count. Make sure they represent you, and only leave deposits if they are not going to get crushed. You're worth it, and you're unique. Only leave a trail of the work for which you want to be remembered. If the transaction isn't worth it, then don't roost in that tree."

Mr. Erlosung had an ability Grant had witnessed in only a few men. Not only was he sage-like, but he could speak without mitigating or hesitating. He didn't pause often, or say "um" or "you know." He just spoke, and Grant listened.

"Thanks, Dad. I need to hear this stuff sometimes. I tell myself these things, just like you taught me, but the busyness of life and the demands of my never-fully-satisfied customers can be overwhelming."

"Surely you know, son, that people always want more, and they are never fully satisfied. That is a truism if I have ever known one."

"Okay, Dad, I know . . ."

Grant was a good son, but then again, he had a great father—a father who had shown wisdom and tenderness daily when Grant was a boy. He always tried to compare himself to his dad, but it never worked.

"Grant, Grant . . . what do you see?" his father asked again.

"Okay, Dad, you caught me again. Do you want to know what I see, now? This is what I see. I see a future where I sell my transportation company, retire to some island, build birdhouses just like you do, and relax in the sunshine. That is what I see. Are you interested?" Grant got up and meandered about the dining room.

"I'm interested, but for now, I am checking your vision. Now, why did you come see me today? Did you want to take me to get breakfast?" his dad said, lightening the mood.

"Not exactly. I was hoping you would have breakfast made when I got here," Grant replied, smiling.

"I don't have breakfast, but I do have some hot coffee. I'll make some tea also, and then we can talk."

Grant agreed and joined his dad in the kitchen. *Didn't we just talk? I've got to get to work. I'll stay for a few more minutes, but then I've got to get moving.* While his dad heated the water for the tea, Grant filled his cup to the brim with hot coffee—his fourth cup of the day. Mr. Erlosung wiped down the counters while they waited for the water to boil, and they made small talk of birds and feathers and homes and the weather. And then Grant's mother entered the room.

The Letter

That night, Grant lay in bed ruminating over the day's happenings. He flashed back to his conversation with his mother early that morning, only a few hours ago, but seemingly a lifetime away. Now, covered in sweat and anxiety, tossing and turning in a bed that offered no comfort, he thought back to the morning. He saw his mother walk in the room of his memory.

His mother had beautiful dark hair, dyed that way of course, and startling blue eyes. They pierced his. Her kind smile, rosy cheeks, and white teeth completed his image of her as the most endearing woman he had ever known—that and the fact she was his mother. As always, Janice welcomed Grant with a warm embrace.

Grant thrust the covers back. The heat was miserable. He had left his parent's home that morning, but in his mind, he was still there. He heard his mother speak in his thoughts.

"You look great today, son, just great!" she exclaimed. "Have you had breakfast?"

"Thanks, Mom, but no, Dad and I are just in here getting some coffee and tea. Maybe we'll have some toast, too," he said, winking at his dad.

"I'll not have my son going without breakfast," Grant's mom said, and that was that.

As Janice set about making eggs, toast, and oatmeal as well as carving up some fruit, Mr. Erlosung and Grant went back into the dining room to finish their conversation—only after staying in the kitchen long enough to help Janice get everything started and feel appreciated.

Settled at the table, Grant began a frank discussion. "Dad, look . . . I want to do something with meaning, and I appreciate what you said a few minutes ago. It's just, well . . . I don't really know what I want."

"Good, I don't know what you want either, but I know how to find out—the same way we have been doing it all these years. You have to ask yourself, 'What is it I want? What do I *really* want?'"

"I have, Dad. I want to be happy like you and mom, but I also want to be rich and comfortable, and able to fish or run or ski or swim whenever I want. But I don't know if I'll enjoy it. I have this burning inside me I can't extinguish. I can't sit still. I can't settle. I want a penthouse and a mansion, an estate and a farm. I want too many things, Dad; I want it all. I know that sounds selfish, but I do; I want it all."

"Well," said Mr. Erlosung, "you had better set about determining what 'it all' is. I can tell you this: you will not be happy, like your mother and me, if you are constantly searching for what will make you feel better. You have to realize, you *are* better. I have a sneaking suspicion that you are afraid of finding what you want anyway."

"Now, Dad, look, I am not scared, I just haven't found it yet. By the way, I think you're afraid of arm-wrestling me," Grant said teasingly. They had a long history of arm-wrestling, but they both knew that Grant was avoiding any further patrol of his conscience. Before they could begin their match, though, Grant's mom walked in with breakfast. Before Grant could replay the rest of the morning, he was jarred back into his current reality—lying in bed frustrated, at the end of the same day.

Grant winced at the pain in his mind. He had left his parents' home much earlier, but he was stuck replaying the day in his memory. In a mess of sheets, Grant lay with his hands covering his face as he remembered the moment, the second, the sound. His eyes were bloodshot red, and his heart pumped in his throat. He couldn't get away from it, that feeling. That fleeting feeling that everything he knew to be true was a lie. It was a paradigm shift—that's for sure—and he was scared witless.

The memory played in his mind: the ride from his parents' house to his first client meeting, the meeting, the handshakes, the contract signing, the task list depleting, everything leading up to stopping at his office. *I shouldn't have stopped,* he thought, *I wish I wouldn't have stopped.*

Grant usually never stopped, but today he had. His schedule was to check his mail on Thursdays, but for some reason he checked his mail today, on Monday. His whole day was off anyway. He could still hear his mom's voice etched in his mind, repeating her oft-given encouragement, as he opened the third letter on his office desk: "You're a great son to your father; I can't wait to see what kind of father you're going to be when you settle down."

I can, Grant thought, as he ripped open a new life.

The sound of the envelope tearing mirrored the anguished untethering Grant felt in his chest. Inside the envelope was a short letter, but a long history:

Dear Grant,

I haven't spoken of you in years, nor have I spoken to you. I don't even know if you will remember me. We met while we were at university. We dated for a short while and things became intimate quickly. We shared a night or two of passion and then you left. You left for your internship that summer and before you could return a month later to visit, I disappeared into what I hoped would be oblivion.

I am not sure if you tried to contact me. I know we planned to visit throughout the summer, but once I found out, I left. Grant, I am writing to tell you that all those years ago I found out I was pregnant. I was embarrassed and humiliated, or so I thought, so I absconded with my life and returned home. Out of shame, I told my family I was raped, and I have lived here ever since.

Grant, I don't know what you feel at this very moment. I am not asking you for anything, but I am informing you. You have a son. His name is Jacobi, he's thirteen, and he plays basketball. I am writing you, for I have finally told Jacobi the truth. His father didn't leave; his father didn't know.

I hope your life has turned out well and that you are happy and fulfilled. I had someone make an inquiry into your whereabouts and your address. My return address is on the envelope, and the choice is yours.

Katie

Katie! Grant thought. The girl who had stolen his heart and faded into the blackness of his memory—he'd loved her! *How could she? How evil . . . I hate her . . . I have a son?* For a moment, Grant bathed in disbelief, pacifying himself by repeating, "She's lying, she's lying," but then a deep sense of longing and a feeling of being defrauded exposed itself. Grant looked to the sky and held out his tensed, shaking hands and screamed, "I have a son, and I didn't even know about it! He's thirteen and nobody tells me! I fight to build my life and this, now this . . . God! No! I didn't do this . . . I don't deserve this," he roared as he slammed both fists down on the office table. He sat down in his chair and stewed in great waves of anger and anguish, grief and despair, hopelessness and fear, while he felt the pain of one who has had time stolen from his hands.

Like a tree branch in a windstorm rapping against an old window pane, Grant mindlessly knocked his head against the desk. *Why? Why? Why?* He looked through the window, but in the glass, he caught his vague reflection. His dark hair was slightly mussed from the repetitive drumming and his habit of running his hands through his hair when he was stressed. His reddened eyes sagged under the weight of his new knowledge, and his brow was slightly furrowed. A sharply handsome man, his reflection did not bear witness to his normal appearance, but nothing about this day was normal. He laid his head back on the desk and wished for death.

Eternity never seems longer than when in the valley of indecision. For a few hours, that is where Grant resided, in the depths, in the cesspool of that valley. He didn't know how to climb out. His customers wouldn't wait, his schedule wouldn't wait, so he raked his face with his hands and stood up on trembling legs. His heart beat in his temples, his fingertips, his clenched jaw. He walked out of the office into the day ahead. Alone.

As the sweat pooled on his sheets now, Grant knew his tormentor. The racing in his mind held him captive to his bed. In business, he was a quick draw, a decisive man who could trust his instincts and training. In this new life, he was an invalid . . . he couldn't even decide whether to sleep or wake, so he suffered. As his introspection tortured his body and drained his spirit, Grant slid back into semi-consciousness. He remembered leaving the office . . .

Grant quickly rushed back to his parents' house. He had told his assistant, Molly, that he would not be available for the remainder of the day. After some convincing, Molly acquiesced and agreed he was not to be disturbed, but it was too late. Grant raced back the direction he had come; he wasn't sure what he was racing, or from whom he was running. His mind was a jumbled mess when he arrived to his mother's embrace. *I'm running home to mama*, he thought, as the self-condemnation began to mount. *Here I am, a grown man, running home to mama*!

He laid the letter before his parents. In a flush of anger Grant had never realized before, he told the story to his parents. He told them of the weeks before his summer internship, Katie's disappearance and the change he experienced during the internship, his suspicion something was missing, and his fears validated all these many years later.

Grant felt as if someone were stepping on his heart. Like his chest had been cut open, his rib cage peeled back, and his heart pulled to the surface. A man stood over him, a man who held his fate, and slapped Grant's heart on the ground and stepped on it. All Grant could do was writhe in pain and call out for mercy, but the man kept pushing and grinning. His heart was on the floor, the man's big black boot atop it, and the man leaned forward, pressing with so much force Grant's heart felt it would explode like a grape. He couldn't breathe. Through his hazy vision he saw his parents weeping for him, sharing his pain, and he pulled himself from his trance.

The day was done. The sun dropped over the western sky and shed its last bit of light before escaping into the night. The house went cold. Grant's dad went to start the fire in the fireplace. It was unseasonably cold for this time in the spring, but today it seemed especially so. Grant's father returned to the room, and he, Grant, and Mrs. Erlosung shared a final cup of tea. In the silence, Grant's mother slipped out of the room, through the swinging door, into the kitchen. The door swept back and forth, one, two, three short strokes, and then came to rest vertically upon its hinge. It did not squeak.

"Well, it's been a long day, and an emotional one at that," commented Mr. Erlosung. "I suppose you know what to do?"—insinuating that the answer was obvious.

"No, Dad, I am not sure what to do. This changes everything, or nothing. I don't know, I'll figure it out. I always do. I'll just go figure it out. I am spent. I need to sleep; I'll know what to do tomorrow. I can't believe this, it is only 9:30 and I'm exhausted. Usually, I am getting my third cup of nighttime coffee and cranking out some work right now."

Grant's dad smiled. "Son, you think about it. Think about it tonight. Think about it tomorrow. Ask yourself one question: What story do I want to tell?"

It was a heavy load to bear, so Grant chose to ignore the question and head home. He hugged his parents, thanking them profusely for spending the day with him. He would have to talk to Robert, he knew, but for now he just wanted to get home, so he stepped out into the cold evening air.

And he lay in his bed. It was now 4 a.m. and he couldn't breathe. *What story do I want to tell? What story do I want to tell? What story do I want to tell?* He mused over and over. Grant hadn't had such a battle in his mind in more than fifteen years. Sleep was not only evasive, but it taunted him, so he gave up and slugged through the early morning.

The Advisor

Grant hit Robert's office door at 8 a.m. They hugged, as they typically did, and got situated with their coffee. Robert's button-down blue shirt bunched under the stress of his stylish suspenders pressed against his muscular frame as he leaned forward in his office chair. A lifelong friend, Robert was also Grant's financial advisor. They had started many ventures together in their early adult years, but as Grant began to become more and more successful with his transportation business, Robert had settled into family life and a job where he could work standard hours. Robert had a great income, wife, two children, and home. Part of the income he owed to Grant because the percentage he made off Grant's investments was substantial. In spite of Grant's earnings, both found it to be an equal partnership, and they both had the ability to speak candidly.

Grant hunkered down for the barrage of questions. Robert had a great listening ear, but he was full of questions, too. Choosing his words for maximum impact and shock appeal, Grant looked down, then up at Robert through the top of his eyes, and said, "Robert, I have a son!"

Robert smirked—sort of—and turned his head slightly to the left and looked at Grant out of the corner of his translucent, blue eyes. He straightened his face, raised his auburn brows, and then asked, "Are you sure?"

Grant dumped the story, then the letter.

"What are you going to do? I mean, what do you want to do?"

"I don't know . . . find out, is he my son, what's he like, go there" Grant exhaled sharply. "I always know what to do when I am at work. It's simple. I ask, what makes sense? Then I do it, but here with this, and my life . . . I don't know."

Robert looked at Grant. "Grant, I know what you're feeling, but this *is* pretty simple. You go meet him. You have some tests run. If he is your son, then you take responsibility. You don't worry about what you're going to do; you just do it."

"No, I don't think you know what I am feeling . . . You know what it's like to be a dad, but on your terms. You don't know what it's like to be asked to be a dad to someone you've never met. It's simple for you, because you don't have any skin in the game."

"I do have skin in the game," Robert said poignantly. "First off, you're my friend. Second, you're my client, and third—"

"I'm not talking about business here, Robert. I am talking about my life. I don't know this kid. I wasn't even given the chance to be part of his life. Will he want to meet me? Am I supposed to be his dad now? Heck, I don't even know if I know how to pronounce his name right! How am I supposed to know what to do when I don't even know who I am supposed to be? I-I-I've got to go to the restroom. Give me a minute."

Grant walked out of Robert's office and into the restroom. He felt like a weak child. He placed his forehead against the mirror in the bathroom and looked into his eyes. He slowly let himself lean against the wall as his head flopped to the right side and then fell forward against the mirror. *All these emotions*, thought Grant. *I am so tired. It's 9 a.m. and I can't keep my eyes open. I've got to tell Robert I am not going to do it. I'm not. She's lying. Never in the past did she say anything. Never was I given a choice. She just wants money. She probably looked me up, found out I have some, and now she is trying to take it. I need some coffee. Stop it! Don't let your emotions control your thoughts . . . don't let them. Choose to be content; choose to be happy. But I don't want to be happy! She's lying to me!*

"Stop it, Grant!" he whispered. He looked back into the mirror and said, "You can do this. You're a strong person. You've failed before and overcome. You have to keep moving. Don't drown in your emotions. Don't do it! They are valid, but you can choose your response. Choose wisely!" And with that, Grant pushed away from the mirror, washed his face, and walked out of the restroom.

"Look, Grant," Robert said, "I want to help you choose wisely. Take this pen. Make a line right down the middle of this paper."

Grant stared. "I know what you're doing," he said.

"So do I," said Robert, "now make the line. Write the pros on the left side and the cons on the right. Let's do it!"

Grant made the list.

Pros	Cons
I am a dad.	I don't know if he is my son.
I have a son.	
I can teach someone what I know.	I have a business to run.
It's my responsibility.	I don't have time.
It is what I would want someone else to do.	This could be a fraud.
	I don't want to deal with Katie.
I have the money.	
I may be his only hope.	My business needs me.
My dad.	There is too much risk

My mom. I am good at what I do. I will make this world a better place. He deserves it.	involved.

"Okay, let's look at the list," Robert said. "Good. Notice there are more pros than cons, and your pro statements are bold statements."

"Bold statements?"

"Yes, bold statements . . . Listen. I am a dad. I can teach. I am good at what I do!" Robert said emphatically. Then Robert slouched forward, his rounded shoulders just slightly smaller than Grant's, and read in a weaker, whinier voice that came from his nasals, "I don't have time, I don't want, this could be, I am afraid…"

"That's not on there," Grant snapped jokingly.

"Yes it is," Robert retorted. "Now listen. You could retire right now and live comfortably the rest of your life, but you didn't get here by living comfortably. You got here by taking chances. That is who you are. Now, take your chance. It's yours. Take a week, and go meet this kid. Find the truth. Make it right. Look at the list. Read these pros aloud: I am good at what I do."

"I am good at what I do," Grant replied.

"Put some bass in your voice," Robert chided. "I will make this world a better place."

"I will make this world a better place!" Grant replied.

"I am a dad."

"I am a dad!"

"I am a dad."

"I am a dad!" Grant shouted.

"I am a dad!" Robert read sternly.

"I am a dad!" Grant repeated, determined.

Then Robert put the paper down and asked, "What do you want to do?"

"I want to meet my son, learn all about him, change his world, teach him about life, give him what he wants and needs, and be the absolute best dad there is! I want the world, and I am going to start by changing someone's world." Grant's eyes narrowed, and his jaw jutted slightly.

Grant knew that exercise felt less than authentic, and that it was somewhat forced, but he also knew, wisely, that eccentric actions spur results, while fear and conservation only maintain what already is.

Grant looked through the window and noticed the sun. An hour had passed and the sun ascended much farther, casting long rays of light that glistened blindingly off the city. A new day had awakened, risen, and begun with fervor. This was a new beginning, the death of the night before, and the resurrection of a once dead dream into a vision, a fantasy, a moment in time to be captured. *This time has never before been and will never be repeated . . .* A shadow broke Grant's gaze. He was staring at a broken writing pen in his hand.

Grant exhaled deeply, inhaled, and said, "Thanks, Robert. This was a tough one. I couldn't quite make the decision on my own. For the first time in a long, long time, I was baffled completely." He ran his hands through his hair. "Thanks," he said sheepishly.

Robert met Grant's gaze with his clear, penetrating eyes. He adjusted his small-rimmed glasses, and quickly scratched the top of his neat auburn hair. He looked every bit as smart as he was. He glanced away, raised his brows again, and said, "Don't mention it." And that was it.

Grant finished his second cup of coffee—Robert had refilled it while Grant was in the restroom—and stood. The men embraced, and Grant walked out of the office and back to the restroom. Something made him jittery. Once he finished, he washed his hands meticulously and walked out the door, stepped out of the Ark, and began a new day.

Chapter 3: Change

Grant had a massive day ahead of him. His business, the transportation company, was a money-making machine, and he wanted to keep it that way. He had spent years building it, refining it, cultivating it to get just the right mix of personality and business. Many times Grant had passed over the deal that would have allowed him to expand the company just to keep the ethos he had created: the ethos of a quality-driven culture. Grant did the hiring, firing, and coaching. An entrepreneur at heart, he struck gold with his business this this time. His transportation company was the first start up that began making money in the very first quarter. But now he was leaving, at least for a week, so he had to make plans, and quick.

The best advisor in the world for his company was Grant; the worst advisor in the world for his company was Grant. At times, he was his own worst enemy; although he had trained and motivated many, he still struggled to delegate the most important assignments. Keeping them close to his chest, he felt he must make the decisions in order for them to be made correctly. He was hesitant to trust.

Grant spent the day talking, listening, ordering, and meeting. His team was keenly aware something significant was happening, and his right-hand woman, Robin, knew the bulk of the weight would be on her shoulders. Ever ready for a new task, Robin assured Grant she could handle being at the helm for at least a week.

"I have been, in fact, working in my current capacity for five years now. Five years," she said as she looked out at him reassuringly.

Young, beautiful, and eager, Robin stood nearly as tall as Grant. She had red hair and deep brown eyes, and was a woman that most men looked on with intent. Married for six years now, she had been the perfect hire for Grant. She was able to present a pleasant, reassuring, intelligent figure to Grant's most dependable customers, and a sharp, biting wit to his more volatile ones. Grant should have been reassured.

Just as importantly, Robin and Molly were great friends, which made the flow of communication to Grant positive, poignant, and purposeful—Grant should have been reassured.

"The weekly update?" Grant questioned.

"It will be out on Thursday," Robin replied, and then added, "as always."

Grant smiled; he knew she was giving him a hard time.

"Hey!" she said, grabbing his attention. "We're going to be okay without you. We all know what needs to get done and we have our execution plan. We'll be working even harder with you gone because we all have something to prove to you when you return. If you can't trust us by now, then you should have replaced us long ago."

Her curt comment made Grant trust his long-time intuition over his short-term panic.

"You're right," he said. "I've made good decisions with each of you. I trust those decisions." Looking Robin right in the eyes, he said, "And I trust you."

That was the ultimate compliment for Robin, so things were settled. Grant could walk away, guilt abated, and feel reassured—almost.

After meeting with several customers, a few employees, and making travel plans, Grant decided to head home. Upon arriving, he opened the door, and looking directly ahead said aloud, "This is the earliest I have been home since I moved into this place." As if expecting a response or a reaction, he stood looking, listening, and let his arms drop to his sides. There was no audience, no fanfare. Now, he needed to pack. He decided against flying. He would need more time to prepare his mind—this was a whole new territory.

He wouldn't pack too many of his business clothes, suits, ties, jackets, etc. That would be a waste. The casual clothes he owned for meeting with the "mom and pop companies" probably wouldn't do the trick either. He packed jeans, t-shirts, athletic shorts, socks, shoes, shirts, and a few business and causal outfits. *Seven days*, he thought, as he packed enough clothes for three weeks. Succinctly, he packed the clothes, and then went for a run. He had missed his run in the morning, and his body ached for the action.

Feet pounding the pavement, arms pumping, and knees high, Grant traveled his six-mile route with precision and speed. His feet grew lighter with each step, and his figure was taut and controlled. His heart rate flattened at the apex of his run, for a few minutes, and slowly decreased as he rounded out his last mile and a half. Feeling better and more in control already, Grant had a thought—*What if he's fat?*

He knew this was stupid, but he built his life around fit people. Sure, some of his friends were overweight, but not much, and they were not his children. He didn't have any children—before yesterday. Now he had a new child, one who might be fat, or grouchy, or lazy, or weak. What if his son didn't like him? What if Katie was remarried and her husband hated Grant? What if his son was disabled? No, she had mentioned basketball. What if . . .

After a shower and clean up, Grant swung by his parents' home briefly to share his intentions with them.

"This may be the most important decision of your life, son, and I am glad it is you who gets to make it. You are a hero for what you are doing. Forget the past mistakes, forget how you got into the situation, and do the right thing now," Mr. Erlosung said, wiping a strand of silver hair from his forehead. "You are doing a great thing, a great thing," he said, and he embraced his son fully. He then clapped Grant on the back and walked him to the door.

Janice met him there and gave him one long, lasting hug, put her hands up to cup his face and said, "Be gentle, Grant, he's just a boy and he doesn't know you. Oh, I know you will . . . I can't wait to meet my new grandson." And with that, he was gone.

I'll never be able to sleep, he thought, but when he arrived home, he collapsed on the couch and welcomed the darkness, fully dressed.

Traveling

Alarm awakened the apparent heir to the title of "World's Greatest Dad," —at least that's what Grant told himself. Up before the actual alarm sounded, Grant stripped off the previous day's outfit, showered, changed, brushed his teeth and hair, and left the home, the status, and the busyness behind for a week. *One week*, he thought, *one week*. He stepped out into the darkness of the predawn light.

The wind whispered like a storefront mannequin just moments after passing by—calling him to turn and look again. Grant looked behind him. He saw nothing, but he felt the cold that had been so unseasonable. In the darkness, the leafless trees swayed in the wind, and the moon lit up the world. Grant looked again, certain something or someone was following him. Nothing there. He continued on, and his premonition faded to a vague memory.

Traveling brought clarity. It was a moment, or a series of moments, to allow the mind to wander and dream and remember. The leafless trees passed by, as did the concrete jungle gyms. Lights and flashes and signs and wonders came and went, came and went, but Grant pressed on. Stopping occasionally for restroom breaks and coffee refills, Grant began to notice the landscape—what he could see of it in the darkness. There was more space here, more empty space, and the wind blew unabated by enclosures. The sound of the wind was less ominous, and more melodic.

He thought of his parents arising this morning, and of the pressures at the office. He began mentally calculating the losses he could suffer from his week away. Some intangible loss of confidence could exist when his customers couldn't reach him. These things couldn't be measured by numbers, but only by feelings, and then decisions, which resulted in a change in numbers. Grant hoped the numbers didn't change—didn't decrease. He began to sneeze.

Every time, every time. Every time I change climates this happens . . . His nose began to drip and his eyes watered. It wasn't long until one nostril was stuffed and the other free, and then it switched. It was as if his body had reacted viscerally to his leaving home . . . or he was just allergic to something.

The sun came over the hills and greeted the new day. The trees had begun to have leaves, change shape, and bud again. Evergreens were everywhere and the hills were alive with music. A thought, a passing memory came to Grant, a line of verse once spoken: "*And wander we . . . and wander we . . . and wander we to see thy honest son, who will of thy arrival be full joyous . . .*" He couldn't place it, but he remembered. The time spent traveling allowed Grant something he desperately needed—time to slow down, time to think, and time to be. He thought of love and loss and games and friends, and he thought of nothing. For a time, he just enjoyed being.

As dawn turned to dusk, Grant turned in. The feeling, whether external or internal, was much warmer here, and thick. He stepped into the atmosphere of the mountainous range. Full-bodied and green with rolling hills and treble clefts, the landscape was unlike anything he had seen in years. His legs and back ached with the stiffness that came from a fourteen-hour traveling adventure. Stretching his shoulders by placing one arm across his chest and pulling, he then turned his head sharply the other direction to stretch the muscles in his neck. His blood began to flow more freely, and the tingle in his feet intensified to being almost painful. He was stimulated by change.

And change he would, later. He had spilled some cold coffee on the crotch of his pants about an hour before arriving at the restaurant. Untucking his shirt to cover the now dry stain, Grant was only moved by the scenery, and his hunger—a deep, abiding hunger. The inner turmoil between hunger and fearing judgment over walking in untucked and unkempt lasted a brief second. Hunger won.

He slowly stumbled forward as his muscles began to unfurl, and he looked at the restaurant ahead.

Coal Miner's Fodder

Coal Miner's Fodder, that's what the sign read: Coal
Miner's Fodder. Grant gazed at this rustic brown building
hidden in the lush green of the mountains. The dirt was
black, the sky a hazy purple as the sun set over the hills,
leaving streaks of amber and orange against the violet. The
clouds were frayed like torn cotton balls, ending in wisps.
Painted into this beautiful picture was a lone, tattered
building named Coal Miner's Fodder.

After a few moments, Grant recognized the building
wasn't tattered, but made to look tattered. The tin roof
appeared to have shades of rust, and the darkly stained
wooden plank siding had been intentionally scuffed in
places. The ambiance was set externally, and Grant
absorbed it as he walked from the black coal lot onto the
gravel path to the front porch. *A front porch*, Grant thought;
*I haven't seen one of these in years either. The owner must
be trying to do something with this design.* Grant saw too
much intentionality just to accept this place as
happenstance. It had been carefully crafted; he was sure of
it. His attention flares exploded in his mind, and he forced
himself to pay attention, even though his body screamed for
rest.

A hungry man is not easily distracted; he is driven. Grant got distracted. He walked through the double doors into another world, as if the front doors were a portal into a time past, a season unremembered. Greeted by wonderful smells his nose had never before entertained, his eyes widened. The entryway was dark and warm, but hard. Grant looked through the darkness at charcoal-colored walls, which appeared jagged, and brushed his hand against a brown beam that resembled a railroad tie but ran up the wall and adjoined ceiling support beams of the same color and same rough hue—until he received a splinter. Pulling the shard from his hand, Grant recognized the smell of baking bread and frying bacon. He felt a pastiness settle on his forehead—some kind of texture and odor filled the atmosphere—but it was not smoke. He took another step and dropped the bloody splinter into his pocket.

His shoes scuffed across the earthy floor, and a dull, wooden board creaked under his step. This first room was small, almost claustrophobic, and intensely dark. *Why would the owner keep it so dark in the entryway? Wouldn't that ward off patrons?* He mused on this until he saw the light. The little light on top of a hat, or affixed to a hat, or a helmet . . . it was a bit blinding.

"Hey there, honey," came the voice. "Are ya dinin' alone?"

Clear and beautiful the tone sounded in Grant's ears, but the strength of this awkward accent startled him. The hat, dark and plastic, jostled slightly as the voice approached. As the light came nearer, Grant thought the hat might be even steel-covered with linen or leather. It was hard to ascertain in the dark, beyond the approaching light. The wearer of the hat was a young girl, between sixteen and eighteen if Grant had to guess. He told her, yes, he was dining alone.

As she turned her head, Grant was able to make out more of her appearance. The room was just dark enough for the ambient light from her hat to illuminate the outfit she donned. She wore a stark white, button-down shirt—*not much of a coal miner's garb*, Grant observed—bright red suspenders, khaki-colored pants, and brown boots. The suspenders accentuated the girl's figure, which again, Grant found odd in this setting so hard and dark yet warm. *Maybe that's it*, thought Grant, *maybe the warmth and the bright white and the young girl are supposed to be in contrast to the rest of the restaurant.* He was wrong—sort of.

As she guided Grant through the front room into another adjoining room, he noticed the deeper he went into the building, the more spacious and illuminated it became. A few wisps of hair with blond highlights, probably from the sun, hung loosely beneath the girl's helmet at the nape of her neck. "How opposite from a coal mine, I would suspect," Grant said.

"Pardon, sweetie," the young girl replied. "Did ye say somethin' to me?"

Grant laughed. "No, I was talking to myself. I was commenting on how this building is constructed. The farther we go into it, the more spacious and well-lit it becomes. I thought that would be the opposite of a coal mine—darkening as you get deeper. Considering the name, it caught my interest."

"That's nice," she replied, without much interest, or even awareness. "Here's your seat, honey. Gracie'll be right with ye."

She ran her fingertip atop an unbleached muslin cloth that covered the brown, wooden table. On the walls hung pickaxes, mattocks, shovels, hand picks, and a few assorted tools Grant did not recognize. He turned his head slowly from right to left, gazing up at the lighting from the lanterns that hung from the ceiling support beams, and then back down at a few wall lamps, then nearer still to the lamp directly in front of him on the table. He tried desperately to understand the lighting pattern.

Grant found himself comfortably sitting on a hard bench attached to the table and watching the quivering flame in the lamp. *The tablecloth would require extra work, extra laundering*, thought Grant. *That's not too strategic. Nor is the lack of a menu.*

Oftentimes, Grant's attention to the minutiae irritated his friends and family endlessly. Every scene, every event, presented itself to him in some form of strategy, or something to analyze. He tried to stop, but he couldn't, or he didn't really want to. What drove some people crazy was the same quality that made him unique—successful.

Gracie arrived rather quickly and with a smile. She was dressed like the hostess, but she was wearing shorts, mid-thigh, not pants. Grant guessed she was about twenty-two. Her skin and hair were darker, and her eyes were very brown and very sharp. Still, she smiled.

"Are you ready?" she asked.

"To order?" Grant asked politely.

Eyeing him with understanding, Gracie said, "Ye ain't never been here before, have ye? Ye ain't from around these parts, I can tell it." She looked at Grant for an acknowledging response and then began her explanation quickly. "Here's the menu," she said, but didn't hand Grant anything. "Eggs, gravy, biscuits, sausage, bacon, pork chops, ham, water, tea, lemonade, and honey for ye biscuits."

"No coffee?" Grant asked without missing a beat.

"Of course coffee . . . sweetie," she said a bit hesitantly. "It's ona house, as always."

Grant knew she was smart. "May I have egg whites and pork chops," he requested, "with a coffee and a water?"

"Sure, I'lla get you the works," she said as she set down a thick, clear glass jar with a screw top and the word *Coal* beveled into it. The glass was full of ice, and Gracie took a pitcher of water and poured until Grant's glass was full. The water was a bit opaque; Grant thought maybe the glass was dirty, but in about five seconds, it cleared up. She then placed a tin cup on Grant's table and poured coffee from a tin pitcher. Steam rose from the pitcher and the cup. *She must be strong*, Grant thought, *to hold that tray with two different pots and remove one or the other without spilling anything.* She handed Grant a linen napkin and said, "I'll be right back with your biscuits." Before Grant could protest, she was gone, walking through the double doors into the other side of the wall.

Mesmerized, Grant visually investigated. The guests seemed to be from all generations, but very similar. The men, talking of work and "aught tos," wore overalls, and the women wore both lengthy, dark dresses and faces. Thoughts of the letter and his son interrupted Grant's inspection. Suddenly, one of the plenty plump women passed through his blank gaze, blocking the light, and stripped Grant of his momentary thought kinesis. *None of the guests seems to be in dire straits, but a few do need some cleaning up: a shave, a haircut, washed hands, fingernail trimming, a shower, and a comb for their hair would be sanitary.* He noticed most of the men had a cap or a hat, either in their lap or on the table next to their drink. That explained the mussy hair.

A fly landed near Grant's forearm. He once had a friend who used to torture flies. He would tear off one wing at a time, slowly. He was obsessed with pain, and death. *I can still hear their screams in my mind.* He couldn't really, but he lied to himself to keep entertained. The war between the senses and the mind continued to rage. Grant chose to focus on the setting; it would help him concentrate.

On the tables were tin pails and tin plates and tin coffee cups. The air moved easily about the room, despite the great number of guests and tables that filled it. The room felt comfortable, but Grant wasn't. He felt like an orange in a pile of potatoes. He didn't fit, but he was so enthralled with the makeup of the restaurant, it didn't matter.

This large dining area led into another grand area through an open entryway. The brightest light shined from that third room into this dining area. A sound, a low rolling sound, then a high-pitched sound, a banging, and some laughter came from the other room. Grant had to investigate, and as he stood, he bumped into a great man before him.

Ruddy-faced with fading blond hair and a rotund belly, this impediment offered a large, meaty hand to shake. His hands were rough, but his eyes and smile were kind and put Grant at ease.

"My name is Dale, and I wanted to come over and introduce myself to ya," he said. He stood a good five to six inches taller than Grant, and surely weighed sixty to eighty pounds more.

"Pleased to meet you, I'm Grant," he said as he squared up and inched closer, looking directly into Dale's eyes.

"You ain't from—"

"Around these parts, no sir," Grant finished the statement for him. "No sir, I am not. I have come this way to meet my son."

"Yer son?" Dale questioned. "What's yer son doing here? Yer no older than thirty-five or thirty-six if I had my guess, so what's yer son doin' here so far away from 'is daddy?" he asked, jokingly.

"I don't know . . . I have never met him."

And with that, they were seated. Grant and Dale began to talk about Grant's trip, and the reason why he didn't know his own son. Dale displayed compassion and a familiarity that made Grant wonder about Dale's own experiences as a father. During the discussion, Dale explained that he was the owner of Coal Miner's Fodder.

"You are the owner?" Grant asked suspiciously. "This was your idea?"

"Yes," Dale said, "twenty-five years now. Started it out of an old log cabin with a barn out back. We had some chickens, a pigpen, a few cast iron skillets, and a dream, Ma' and me did. I was injured 'bout two years before it, in the coal mine, and we was runnin' out of money. My best figuring told me that hard-working folk required two things: friendship and good food. I set out to give'm both in one spot, and it worked."

"So tell me," Grant inquired, "why the outfits for the wait staff?"

"That's easy son. Everyone likes nice girls with good manners who are beautiful. Men get all puffed up by another man who intimidates 'em, and since these men are intimidat'd by ever-thang but good hard work, I knew I couldn't hire men. I had to hire young women. Well, school ain't as 'portant as money 'round here, so I can help out some families by hirin' their daughters when they's fourteen or sixteen or so. My wife teaches them the manners for dealin' with customers; I train 'em on how to be friendly and appropriate—can't trust some of these dirty men round here—and I keep a close eye out. The women folk, on the other hand, just love 'ese girls. They come in and dote on 'em and tell 'em how pretty they are and how when they was younger they used to look just like 'em. So, it's pretty simple. The young men and old men all like a pretty girl to greet 'em and help 'em. The young women and old women all like a sweet girl to smile and talk to and dote on. The coal miner's life is a hard 'un, so there's got to be some beauty in it somewhere. This is how I give 'em beauty, but I'ma careful. I've got daughters of my own, so I know . . ." and he trailed off.

Meanwhile, Gracie had already been back to the table, placed a huge tin pail full of biscuits, refilled Grant's coffee and water, and given Dale his drink. She brought out a massive tin plate full of eggs, over easy, bacon, sausage patties, and pork chops. Atop the plate was another tin bowl brimming with a gray, speckled mass that Grant assumed was what they called "gravy."

Kindly, Grant started, "I didn't order all this food, only egg whites, pork chops, water, and . . ." he began listing.

"It's on me," Dale interrupted. "My treat."

Grant eyeballed the food. The smell was tremendous, especially the scent wafting off the "gravy," but he wasn't sure he could handle all this. Dale sensed the tension and questioned, "You ain't never had gravy and biscuits have ye?"

"No," Grant replied, smiling. "No sir, I have not. I have had biscuits, and I have had brown gravy with a roast, once, but I have never had this type of gravy nor this type of biscuits."

"Gracie, set this young man up here," Dale requested.

"May I?" Gracie asked as she took a seat beside Grant and reached for a biscuit.

Grant was hesitant about somebody touching his food with her hands, but he allowed it, either because Gracie was a young lady and he didn't want to be rude, or because Dale suggested it. As Dale talked away about the first years of the restaurant, Gracie began to crumble up the soft, yellow biscuits onto the plate. She took several spoonfuls of the gravy and drenched the biscuits. The gravy was thinner than paste or pudding, but thicker than a pancake batter. It was darker than the muslin table cloth, but not quite as gray. It had been peppered, and Gracie salted it slightly, and it smelled delicious. Gracie even chopped up the eggs for Grant. Some of the yolk, which Grant had never tasted, ran into the gravy. It bothered Grant to see that, but he feigned normalcy; plus, by this time he was starving. Gracie then pried a biscuit open, filled the steaming middle with honey, closed it, and placed it on a smaller serving plate next to Grant's coffee. Then she disappeared into the warm dimness of the lantern-lit room.

The restaurant was eerily silent. The noise of conversation and the clanking and chopping of eating remained—maybe increased—but something was missing, something Grant could not identify. Some rumbling background noise of distraction that wasn't effervescent, but wasn't droning either, just ubiquitous. He looked up at Dale, and Dale looked back at him. "You want me to say 'grace' for you, don't you?" Dale questioned, and the undiscovered missing element was quickly forgotten.

"Uh… yes," Grant said.

And Dale did.

Grant took his first bite of the biscuits and the gravy and knew he had discovered something wonderful. The aroma filled his nose, his palate softened, and it was easy to masticate—*chew that i*s, Grant thought, *nobody here knows what masticate means*—as if he were going to explain his dining experience to the people who had dined there throughout their lives. No, he was plotting, plotting to tell all of his friends and especially his family about this experience. His family—his mood began to shift to a more uncomfortable place as he realized his family wasn't so easily defined anymore.

"You don't like it?" Dale winced as he noticed the sour expression on Grant's face.

"No, I love it!" Grant said. "I got distracted thinking about my family."

"And what that word means, now, I bet ya!"

Grant was stunned, but not overly. He had already seen some of the genius in Dale's behavior. But he switched the conversation away from family back to the restaurant. It was safer.

"You know what I think is brilliant about this place?" Grant asked, rhetorically, "Everything you have here, you can use again. The meat can be fried, refrigerated, and thrown back into the skillet for just a moment to reheat.

The biscuits and gravy both use flour, and if my guess is right, there's bacon grease used in this gravy. The sausage can be reused the next day in the gravy, and the honey is used for the biscuits and the coffee."

"Smart boy, but it didn't start that way. It started with-a what we had, then kinda turned that way when I realiz'd that all the extra stuff was gettin' thrown out. You missed two or three items, though. It takes milk to make biscuits and gravy; we use that pork chop grease for the gravy too, and'a sausage and bacon grease to fry da eggs. But we got one more item you don't know 'bout—dessert: chocolate gravy—only for special."

"What is that?" Grant asked.

"You'll see," Dale said. "Now, you wanna go see what's in that other room you been craning your neck to see this whole time?"

"Yes!" Grant said, smiling as he nodded with approval.

This room was like stepping into a fairy tale—rather a fable. Grant glided across the smoothly polished and reflective floor, passed the newly painted white walls interspersed with dark-brown support beams and headed straight for the rear. Above his head, multiple lanterns illuminated the room, creating a halo of light. The light and the warmth and the reflection and the shimmer so deeply contrasted the other rooms that Grant unknowingly smiled. Then with his mouth open and eyes squinted, he saw a strange thing. On the back wall, as unexpected as butterfly drool, was an acting stage.

Set upon the stage, which was about six to eight inches above the floor, were two wooden rocking chairs, one on the left and one on the right, and in the middle was the entrance, a gateway from a childhood dream, exactly eight feet wide. A curtain, like a dressing screen hiding someone's secret lies, covered what must have been a tiny backstage. Fascination imbibed Grant; who or what was behind the curtain?

From behind the curtain walked a second great man, a great little man.

B.G., as Grant came to know him, was a storyteller. His remaining white hair blew about as he walked hastily across the stage. He smiled genuinely through a white, scraggly beard, squinting the deeply tanned skin around his eyes, which was accented all the more by the steely blueness of his eyes. Cloaked in an overly large, dark blue-gray suit jacket with patches on the elbows and wearing olive-gray pants and tanned moccasins, B.G. didn't seem to fit here either, or anywhere else for that matter. He was a small man, but highly animated and charismatic, and he wove his masterpiece. As he told his story, both young and old sat in smoothly polished rocking chairs, anticipating the next sound. He paused, and with a twinkle in his eye, he looked right at Grant and said, "Then Dynamite Red hit a home run all the way over the mountain!" and the crowded room erupted. A few whoops and hollers could be heard saying, "That's my boy," and "I knew it. I knew he'd hit it, boys!"

B.G. continued, "A grand slam! Not just a home run, but a Grand Salami, all the way into the clouds. And then, Ms. Sizemore, Dynamite's arch nemesis, came crumpling down on the pitcher's mound and wept into her hands, great sobs of anguish and grief . . ."

The room let out a feigned "Awww" in response, while a young boy whispered, "Serves her riaght, I hated her anyways!"

B.G. jumped up and with an air of finality announced, "And when that ball splashed through the clouds, the sky went black." The eyes of the room widened. B.G. started up again with a low baiting voice, "And the wind gusted down and around in circles." At that, a few of the men in the room made whistling noises like rushing wind and began rubbing their rough hands together. "Then the thunder rolled, and billowed, and boomed!" B.G. yelled with great gusto and vibrato. The ladies began to clack their heels on the floor, and the men stomped their feet, the boys pounded their fists on the floor, and the girls patted their hands. "The thunder clapped," and in unison, the group clapped, deafening Grant momentarily. "The lightning cracked," and the boys and girls picked up their tin plates and began clapping them together; "and the rain struck down," so the kids began to rub tiny tin pans together violently. "And Dynamite rounded first, and then second, and then third, and he slid over the muddy home plate like lye soap 'cross the bathroom floor! His schoolmates picked him up on their shoulders, and . . . and . . . and . . . they carried him home chantin', 'Red, Red, Dynamite Red! Red, Red, Dynamite Red!" The room chanted along with B.G. He paused for a moment and scanned his intimidating eyes over the room, and in a whispered exclamation revealed, "Then all the Quietuses, and Quiguzzards, Wampus Kats, and Boogaroos came out and gobbled up Ms. Sizemore!"

The room cheered, and some of the boys and girls chanted, "Red, Red, Dynamite Red!" As B.G. tried to exit the stage in the commotion, a small voice darted through the noise begging, "But, Mama, where da ball go that went into da clouds? Did it never come down?"

B.G. whirled around and said, "It never came down . . . but the angel Gabriel caught it, and gave it to Dynamite." He paused momentarily, then continued slowly, "And my friend Dynamite, he gave it to me." Into the jacket pocket nearest his heart he reached and pulled out a dingy, lop-sided baseball, then spun it dramatically on the palm of his left hand with his middle finger and thumb. The signature, *Dynamite,* appeared on the lop-sided bulge, between the faded red stitching. B.G. held the ball out as the mother stood up from her rocking chair, her son on her hip, and read the signature aloud. He handed the boy the ball, to a warm reception of laughter and smiles. With her other arm, the boy's mother reached out and hugged B.G. close, and then she gave him a quick kiss on the cheek. Even with the tan skin and white, scraggly beard, his blushing could not be hidden, and he rushed off stage, away from the loud applause.

Grant instinctively knew there was something more to that hug, something more to that gift, and although he couldn't explain it, he knew . . . that young boy didn't have a daddy.

Dale

"Incredible," Grant exclaimed, "I would have never believed you could get people so excited just to hear a story!"

"You have to have da right storyteller . . . and da right people."

Grant looked around: he had seen the right storyteller, but not any of the right people—just kind of dirty, gullible ones—except Dale of course—and maybe Gracie.

Grant and Dale sat down for a last cup of coffee, and Gracie brought out the chocolate gravy in two small tin bowls. Wisps of heat rose from the bowls, distorting Grant's exhausted vision, but enticing his taste.

"So how'd you meet B.G.?" Grant asked. He noticed a deep, endearing expression on Dale's face. His face was a reddish hue already, but it grew almost amethyst. The hazel in his eyes grew dark and piercing as his emotions shifted from endearing to intense. Grant took a bite of the gravy to give himself a reason to look away. It melted like warm chocolate pudding, running away from a fountain, over his tongue and into his heart. He was hooked. He looked back at Dale and knew that would be another story for another time, if they ever met again.

Dale cleared his throat. "Where ya stayin' tonight?"

"I have secured a place about fifteen miles from here, in Pine Bosom."

"No, yer astayin' right cheer tonight . . . right cheer!"

Grant noticed that Dale's colloquialisms and accent grew much stronger after B.G.'s performance. He accepted Dale's offer, with some reservation, and had his arrangements canceled in Pine Bosom. He spent the remaining hour in the dining area, just watching and drinking coffee, as Dale helped close the place down. Grant then followed him into a room adjacent to the kitchen; it was like a studio apartment: it had a twin bed, a couch, a table and chairs, a bathroom and a kitchen area—it was separate but connected.

Dale had someone from the restaurant fetch Grant's suitcases and bring them.

"I really appreciate this, Dale: the dinner, the conversation, the stories, and everything. Thank you for letting me stay here, too. I have plenty of money, I'd be happy to pay you, again, as I said before."

"No," said Dale. "Yer my guest, and now yer my family, and family don't pay."

Grant let the family remark pass almost unnoticed. "If that's your offer, then I accept—and appreciate it!" They shook hands, and Grant closed the door. He walked to the restroom to undress and noticed on the night stand a black book with gold-gilded pages and the words *Holy Bible* embossed on the cover. The name *Dale* was etched on the bottom right corner of the Bible, but the last name had been scratched out—not from wear, it was intentional. Dale . . . Dale . . . no name.

In the middle of the night, Grant knew he had made a mistake. With a deep rumble and cramp in his lower abdomen, he ran to the restroom and sat down just in time. Fire exited, and his eyes welled up with tears. He flushed and flushed and flushed, and after a few minutes he was done. Sweaty and disoriented, he climbed back in bed. A few hours later, he was back at it. This time there was more spray than substance, but it was just as painful, if not more. *What have I done to myself?* he thought. *I'll never eat like that again!*

Still drowsy from the lack of sleep, Grant got up at dawn to find Dale had gone to another town, and the restaurant was already bustling. Feeling a bit uneasy and out of place, Grant quickly packed his things, showered and dressed, slid some money under the Bible, flushed the toilet a few more times, and walked out of the room. Not exercising yesterday and sleeping two hours later than usual today made him feel depressed.

Before he could leave, one of the breakfast ladies talked him into staying for breakfast. Grant thought, *My will is iron clad*, as he ate, then he rolled his eyes up and to the left. Against her insistence, Grant paid, left a big tip, then walked back out the little dark entryway, away from the light, and stepped into the mountainous clean air.

Omen

As he left the parking lot, he felt this visit had been some strange occurrence, maybe even an eventful moment in his life. He couldn't quite decipher it, but he knew it was special. If nothing else, he'd learned something about people from Dale and B.G. People are not all logic and sense; emotions and attachments are involved, and a myriad of other factors must be considered. If he could determine how to cause people to have emotional attachments to his product, to himself, he could establish a customer base for his company that would never leave. It would be like family, only better, family loyalty with massive dividends. Maybe he could move to some island and make birdhouses as he had jokingly suggested to his dad earlier. He smiled. Just then, a cardinal and a blue jay whizzed in front of the vehicle, and though the cardinal made it, the blue jay smacked the front, rolled under, and spit out the rear, crushed. Grant looked back quickly at the heap of blue jay on the road, broken, gray feathers strewn all about. Blue jays don't bleed blue.

Hours later, he arrived in the most dangerous mountain terrain he had ever seen. Gravel roads rutted deep with the wear and rain, narrowed into nearly impassable corners with solid rock on one side and sure death on the other.

Someone had created a path into the mountain, others followed, and eventually it became a road, a road without guardrails. *Surely this wasn't real; people didn't really live like this, did they?* He shook his head in disbelief.

He arrived in a small, hollowed-out area cut from the mountain. A lone trailer sat on the mountainside surrounded by trash. From above it appeared to be a small sliver cut into a great mass of green, but appearances can be deceiving. From the ground it was a massive wasteland, repudiating order. Cars rusted and bikes grew useless in the yard. Foliage was destitute. A nearly worthless shed or barn slanted down into the ashen mountain wall. Underneath this original structure, was more waste: trash cans, gasoline cans, paint cans, random rusted wire, and a crowbar. Grant dropped his chin to his chest, slowly shaking his head.

Chapter 4: Meeting

Home, Grant thought. *This is stupid. I am going home. This place is sick, these people are sick; there can be nothing good here. I just saw a man massacre a flock of chickens while his children watched! I don't want to go "Over da creek, up da next holler, left at da switchback and foller the road round till you git to da top!"* He took a few steps and remembered Dale and Coal Miner's Fodder from just a few hours prior. He remembered the embrace of his mother when she told him she was proud of him. He remembered his day-dream of meeting his son, and that name—Jacobi—which was seared upon his conscious. Maybe some good could be found here, but he couldn't see it.

He did not look back at the trailer, the wasteland, or the bird carnage, for he knew he would never return. In the silence was an absence of sound . . . he didn't hear the dog barking anymore. He could only imagine. He went up Gomer's Creek, through the next valley, or "holler" as they called it, to the switchback, turned left, and followed the road. Chester Combs and his wife never asked why he was there to see the boy. *They never questioned it. Did they know, or did they just not care? They are oblivious.* On top of the mountain was a wide, sprawling plateau. It looked like a park with pathways and rolling hills, and one large white building that resembled an old church or town hall. In front of the building lay a dirt court for basketball surrounded by thirty to forty men and boys.

The crowd confused Grant. The court was just dirt and gravel with chalk lines for boundaries. *What is the huge attraction?* Dust particles sprayed through the air as the players cut and turned, pivoted and jumped, landed and ran. A fierce game appeared to be taking place, especially since a sticky, black residue covered the players in addition to dripping sweat.

Grant hung back to assess the scene. He had brought some running shoes and shorts with him and decided to change in an inconspicuous place. He had worn finely woven, tan, double-pleated wool trousers, a blue Oxford button-down shirt, brown suspenders, and brown, highly polished shoes, from Coal Miner's Fodder to the wasteland where he thought he might first meet his son. *Her dad, Chester, never even mentioned Katie by name*, he thought. *He only spoke of Jacobi. They're all weird—all of them.*

As he walked back around the side of the building, a quick player shattered his thoughts by crossing over from his right to his left, pushing the ball out in front of himself to gain an advantage over his defender. He took one dribble with his left hand and exploded off both feet, kicking up dust in his wake. He hung suspended in the air momentarily, and then stuffed the ball through the rim with a vengeful authority. The rim buckled, and the semi-circle wooden backboard pulled forward as if it were going to explode into shards of painted white splinters. The man landed lightly on two feet, and pivoted on his toes to the right with little to no reaction.

"Game!" shouted a scrawny, red-haired freckled kid, and he jumped up to give him a high-five. When the victor turned, Grant noticed he wasn't a man at all—just a giant-sized kid who obviously had springs in his legs. Mesmerized, Grant watched the boy congratulate both teams, and then keep moving as they started another game of three-on-three.

This was the stuff of dreams. Grant had never seen someone so young, yet so powerful and graceful. His silent jump shot, from anywhere on the court, always rattled the bottom of the chain net. The ball seemed to be an extension of his hands, of his movements, as he coiled and exploded left and right, ever intent on making his way to the basket, pushing, pursuing forward as if no defender could stop him, and, as of yet, Grant hadn't see one who could. Grant watched him dribble up left, stutter step, spin right quickly, split two defenders, propel off the ground, and tuck his head and himself under the net to lay the ball up on the right side of the rim. Incredible couldn't describe it. *The best ball players make moves like that,* he thought, *but some tall kid from this valley of bones?* He paused. *Actually, it's a mountain of coal.*

There were three of them, kids on this team. The big, unstoppable one, the small, scrappy, red-haired one, and the shooter. The third boy had brown hair, was an average size for being maybe fifteen years old or so, and he could really shoot the ball. He never seemed to miss either, but then again, he didn't need to shoot that much because the enigma was totally dominant.

Their opponents were not boys, but men. One looked to be Grant's age, while the other two appeared to be college-aged. They, too, were good players: swiping the ball from the two smaller kids, blocking their shots, and harassing them physically. But the prodigy just kept scoring, and scoring, and scoring.

When the other team wasn't careful, the man-child, Jacobi, stepped between two of them and swiped their pass from the midair. He took it back behind the makeshift 3-point line, turned, and drove in to finish with a leaping, leaning, left-handed dunk from the right side of the basket, burying his shoulder in his defender's chest. The opponent fell to the ground with a harsh thud and slid backward, as the man-child swung off the rim, landed gently, and walked over to offer him a hand.

The red-haired, freckled-face boy yelled out:

Y'all just got dunked on by Ja-cobi!
But y'all don't know me, so show me
You said | | and I did, it again
My friend, within this'n.

Showin' dirt and dabs and guns and fabs,
As he remunerates those who try to placate
And oxidate the hind ends, of his friends.
To secure a spot, on the court—it's hot—
And make him look bad so they feel good
 About their wanna be lives on da court o' wood.

The adolescent lyricist continued rattling off rhyming metrics as he walked off the court, but Jacobi just shook his opponents' hands and walked the other way. Grant stood dumfounded. The giant boy-man was his son, and his son's friend was some type of lyrical gymnast; both were in the midst of the chronic degradation of humankind in this wasteland. It felt so fictional. Uneasiness crept into his chest as Jacobi approached, leaned forward, and asked, "Wanna play?"

The cosmos tilted slightly in that moment and smiled down upon Grant: as if Destiny and Fate had schemed to arrange a basketball feud between father and son that pitted all of the lost dreams of parenting against all the angst of living without it. But the moment was lost on Jacobi, for he did not know, and on Grant, for he was trapped within his mind. A hesitancy covered Grant like a soft blanket over a naked lightbulb. *What if I lose, or look stupid in front of all of these hillbillies?* The deafening silence was pierced when he heard himself say, "That's why I'm here," and the automated response dictated to his mind and will what he must do. A warm breeze, almost searing, blew across the court and against Grant's face as he made his commitment. It was, in fact, game time.

Grant was assigned two teammates, one shirtless and one in blue. Two dogs, one lame, began to fight on the court as Grant and his teammates greeted each other. Their fur was mangy and filled with stickers and burrs. Unannounced, the dogs had arrived separately, spotted each other, and decided the court would be a good place to settle accounts. One of the bystanders ran over to shoo the dogs away, and

Grant watched as the lame one trotted off, lopsided on three legs. As if that were a regular occurrence, the rest of the group continued business—or lack thereof—as usual. Grant began to stretch. He hadn't played basketball in a few months, but he was still in great shape. But was the boy inside of him man enough for this game?

To Da House

"Game up!" Grant shouted as Jacobi checked the ball back to him. They made eye contact, and Grant exploded right, dribbling once, and then flung the ball, one-handed, on a bounce pass to the open, shirtless teammate standing just underneath the basket. Two points.

Walking back to the 3-point line, Grant felt the temperature cool as if a heat source had stolen into the forest of trees. *Weird*, he thought. *It is warmer here than home, but this area is surrounded by evergreens and mountains, so it should be less breezy* . . . He was jarred back to reality by the feel of the leather ball against his fingertips when he caught the checked pass. Jacobi had backed off just a step. Grant shot a quick 3-pointer and rattled the chains at the bottom of the net.

"Ooohhh," exclaimed a few of the guys on the outside of the court, but Jacobi seemed unfazed. Grant felt energized. On the next check he drove left, with his head down, then jerked quickly back right, crossing the ball back over from left to right between his legs. He flipped the ball to his teammate in blue from his right hand, as he continued to cut up to the free-throw line, precisely turning on the corner and sprinting down the lane. Mid-stride, he caught the ball from the quick return pass and jumped off his left foot for an easy layup. The ball floated—until the layup was disrupted by a skyward Jacobi, who had shadowed Grant and then smacked the ball out of midair into eternity. A few young kids sprinted off after the ball to catch it before it left the mountain.

"Nice block!" Grant complimented Jacobi.

"Thanks," Jacobi replied nonchalantly, and passed a replacement ball to Grant.

Grant's teammates were good players, but an odd-looking duo. The shirtless one wore a backwards cap with the strap right at his hairline. He was tan and had a bit of a potbelly. He looked to be about twenty-two years old. His dark hair hung out from underneath the hat, and the further it extended, the lighter it became. He was missing two teeth, on the right side, but Grant only noticed when he smiled. He also noticed it was midday and none of these guys was working.

The other blue-shirted teammate was rather tall and wiry. His black hair was short, while his nose was anything but. He moved with jerky motions and dangerous elbows. He was too skinny to play a very physical game of leverage underneath the rim, and the appearance of a mild deformity plagued him, too. His ramrod-straight back had little flexibility. As Grant watched him hustle and play, he admired his hard work and tenacity, but he couldn't help but notice something was amiss.

"Take 'em to da house, boys! Take 'em to da house!" the boy in blue advised as Jacobi defended Grant oppressively.

"To da house, boys, to da house," he chanted.

Grant stepped back quickly enough to get some breathing room and fired a two-handed missile past Jacobi to the boy in blue. Bluebird, which was Grant's new nickname for him, turned and shot, left-handed, from the right side and banked it in.

"To da house!" he yelled, "Weeza takin' 'em to da house, boys, da house!"

Grant appreciated the fun commentary, but he felt like he may gouge out his eyes if he heard "da house" one more time.

After Bluebird missed an easy layup, Jacobi's team took possession, and Jacobi scored at will. Grant debated internally. *He's huge, strong, genial, and a phenom—he can't be only thirteen. He can't be my son. This must be some type of setup to get a wealthy guy—probably the only wealthy one Katie knows—to support her basketball-star son. But that didn't add up either. If Jacobi were older than thirteen, then Katie must have had him before we met. I left college eleven years ago, only three years after meeting Katie.*

The score was now eighteen to twelve, in favor of Jacobi's team. Jacobi had scored sixteen of the eighteen points, rather quietly, and Grant felt his lungs begin to burn and his legs weaken like an overstretched rubber band. The other two points belonged to Jacobi's teammate, the sharpshooter, whom Grant heard them call Spencer.

Grant took the checked ball from Jacobi and drove right, but then, very deftly, Jacobi poked the ball so it bounced to the left away from Grant. Jacobi seized the ball, turned around, fired a quick shot over Grant for three, and ended the game with one complete motion.

For Grant, losing felt devastating, like watching a perfectly cooked steak slide off a plate onto a dirty floor. For everyone else, it was uneventful; Jacobi was just being Jacobi.

One of the boys was kind enough to let Grant use an extra bottle for water. Grant filled it up from a gray hand pump beside the building. Unlike the glass of water from Chester's wife, this water came clean, clear, and pure from the pump. Grant hung around impatiently to watch several other games. He answered banal questions about where he was from, and what he was doing in this area. He kept them interested with talk of his transportation company, not because of the business, but because he appeared to have money. Some of the guys broke for lunch and ate, some went home, and some just stayed throughout the day drinking yellow soda and eating snack cakes. Grant looked the other way. He played another game with his team, which they won, but his team didn't play Jacobi. As the night began to fall, and the mosquitoes began to rise, the number of players dissipated until only Grant, his teammates, Jacobi, and the red-haired boy remained.

One on Won

In the cool mountain air, the remaining players made plans for a final game. The flickering lights of fireflies could be seen in the grayness of the backdrop sky. The red-headed boy, named Dynamite, grabbed his basketball to announce his departure. He had turned out to be a great-nephew of the storyteller, B.G., whom Grant had met several hours earlier. He had inherited his name from his uncle's favorite character, and his lyrical talent from his uncle's tutelage.

I best be a-leavin',

'For mom starts a-screamin',

And Daddy starts a-smackin'—

Me around for late.

I've become, undone, under

Duress, the stress,

I can't manage,

So home I must carriage,

The bones that won't break

And heart that won't take

The time, to mend,

But I'll see you

Again, my friend,

Tonight's the end,

But tomorrow's the begin—

Again . . .

Into the peaked sunset Dynamite walked, his hair all but consumed in the flames. He had said his good-bye to Jacobi before shaking hands with Grant and walking away. *He is odd; there is no denying that, but he is also endearing,* Grant mused. *It's getting late, but Jacobi doesn't look tired.*

"Y'all favor," said Grant's potbellied teammate, interrupting his thoughts. "You'ns look alike," he added.

Grant winced. He didn't see it. He was tall, but this kid was just as tall, and only thirteen! *Well, if he really is only thirteen*, Grant thought.

"How old are you?" Grant interrupted his teammate's observation.

"Thirteen," Jacobi replied.

"Why?" Bluebird asked as if he suspected something.

Grant knew he didn't—he didn't suspect much—so he replied, "Because he's so tall, but he looks young."

The boy with sandy-colored hair and pale, translucent green eyes, the boy with chiseled arms and legs but a baby face, the boy with Grant's heart in his chest, commented, "People always ask me that, 'How old are you?' Especially at basketball tournaments. They think I'm older and playing down a league, or that I'm a ringer or something. It gets pretty annoying."

"Sorry for asking," Grant said, and then paused. "Let me ask you another question: Why don't you sound like everyone else here? Are you originally from here?"

"People ask me that all the time, too," Jacobi said with a smile, "usually when we play a new team or someone interviews me. I'm from here. I speak differently because my mom makes me. She always says, 'It's 'I saw, not I seen,' and 'Johnny and he went to the store, not him and Johnny went to the store!' She's an English teacher at the high school. She says I can't have a definitive accent if I want to appeal to the masses—whatever that means."

"Definitive! Now there's a big word. I know what it means," Grant patronized.

"So do I," replied Jacobi confidently, but in a somewhat snarky tone, and he grabbed the basketball. "Are you up for a game of one-on-one?"

"Sure, but don't thirteen-year-olds need to get home before dark?"

"That's what they say, but my mom doesn't care about that. That's another thing she always says, 'If you don't learn to make decisions for yourself now when the consequences are small, you'll crumble when the consequences are great.' She is always saying stuff like that."

"Does that get annoying?"

"No, I know she only wants what is best for me."

"Oh."

"Is you'ns gonna play?" Bluebird asked.

"Yes!" replied Jacobi and Grant simultaneously.

"Well, boys, y'all have a good en' then. Me and Possum's outta hyear," said the potbellied one.

He walked over and bear-hugged Jacobi, then he patted him on the back. Grant shook his hand and said, "I didn't catch your name earlier."

"Melvin, but the ladies call me emmmm!"

Grant rolled his eyes and thought, *I bet your cousin does.* Possum waved good-bye furiously and advised Jacobi to "take 'im to da house!" Then they slowly vanished down the path like a shadow in the dark.

The evening dew had settled on the now murky court. Grant picked up the ball; the court rules dictated the visitor gets the chance to draw first blood. He stepped to the makeshift top of the key and checked the ball. A warm breeze blew. Grant noticed a visitor, an older man with a plastic chair, had come to audience the last game of the day. Jacobi checked the ball back to Grant, and the uneasiness that had weighted Grant's gut vanished like a falling eyelash from a young child swinging on the playground.

Grant crossed over. He was euphoric as the weight of the moment began to settle into his chest. He was playing basketball with his son, his one and only son. From right to left Grant crossed over and pushed the ball ahead. Jacobi drop stepped quickly, but not quickly enough, for Grant blew by him like a train in the night. Two points. Two points for Grant for the direct drive and direct score. No flash, just efficiency.

Grant caught the checked ball again while the past few years played out in his mind. He thought of how he'd closed his first deal to carry intercity deliveries in the back of his vehicle. He drove right, but Jacobi stopped him. Grant did not pick up his dribble. He kept pursuing, adjusting, maneuvering to get closer to the basket. He crossed back left, then back right, but he couldn't get by Jacobi. He pressed in, and he pushed against him as he drove down the baseline. He looked for a clearing to lay the ball in on the left side, but with no luck because Jacobi was on him like a mosquito on a blood puddle. Grant dribbled back out to the makeshift 3-point line on the left side of the basket and took another approach. Jacobi had his arms wide, so Grant picked up his dribble and slammed the ball off Jacobi's chest from just a foot away. The ball stung off Jacobi and right back into Grant's hands as he streaked past his unsuspecting opponent and scored another two points.

As he turned, Grant saw the perturbed look on Jacobi's face. The kid showed composure. He didn't get angry, just determined. Grant, however, grew angry . . . at himself. *He's just a kid*, he thought. *What was I thinking? What grown man hits a kid in the chest just to win a game? I wonder if he'll tell Katie? Will they come after me for some sort of child abuse?* As his mind raced, Grant's posture changed. He became stiff and cold.

After his score, Grant fired up a quick 3-point shot without hesitation, and like that he was ahead seven to zero—he hadn't missed a shot. His mind wandered again. *If she hadn't taken him away, I wouldn't be in this position. I'd know what to do. What selfish animal takes a man's child from him? What if I had a dream for my family?* Jacobi slapped the ball Grant had dribbled while lost in thought. As the ball rolled to the right side of the court, Grant snapped to attention and tried to run the ball down, but Jacobi was too quick.

It was his turn now. Jacobi spun quickly and erupted forward. Although he was on the right side, he raced past Grant dribbling left, and laid it up and in on the left side. Two points. Grant checked the ball, and with raw determination, Jacobi pushed past him as he charged right, shoulder lowered. Jacobi scored again. Grant checked again, and Jacobi pulled out an old trick: the rocker step. He swung the ball left to right to left quickly, and then with a feigned drive right, he dribbled the ball off the floor with a step forward, then back, and he drained a three. It was seven to seven, and Jacobi had matched Grant—bucket for bucket. Sometime in between Jacobi's scoring his next two baskets, Grant felt the temperature cool again, and he saw the old man had disappeared.

It was nearly dark, and the moths crowded the sole overhead light mounted to the white building. It shone down onto the court, pulverized by two unsuspecting players. Jacobi led eleven to seven when he missed a shot. It clanked off the rim, high and to the right. He and Grant jumped simultaneously—Grant had the better position; Jacobi had the hops—and they crashed midair. Their heads and bodies collided, but Jacobi landed unfazed with the ball and spun swiftly toward the basket. Grant tried to catch him, but Jacobi was too quick. Jacobi took one step, leaped from two feet, and high above the dark shadows he rose and rocketed the ball through the rim with both hands. He didn't dare hang; he just landed, stood, and stared. He stared at Grant as if to say, "You can't handle me; I'm too much for you!" But Grant was not bewildered.

Determination consumed. Lost in the competition, the two did not care for the passing time or their opponent's identity—each only wanted to win. Grant settled deep into a defensive posture: arms wide, hips low, weight centered, with his eyes on Jacobi. Jacobi dribbled, and Grant batted it away furiously. Jacobi retrieved the ball. He checked the ball again and tried to shoot a quick jump shot, but Grant was on top of him in less than a second. Jacobi put the ball on the ragged court and moved right, but he couldn't get by Grant, so he crossed over, and there was Grant. Ferociously, Grant stuck to Jacobi, but Jacobi kept pressing, moving, spinning, dribbling, hesitating, and then charging until he saw an opening. He dribbled through, but missed the layup, and Grant snatched the ball.

Grant hustled out to the line, spun, and drove back with furious determination. Another two points. Grant then backed Jacobi down, punishing him by slamming his body into him all the way down near the rim. He put in an easy left-handed layup from a quick spin. Thirteen to eleven.

Back and forth they struck, push and pull, push and pull, until the game was tied at nineteen. The first person to twenty-one would win, and Jacobi had possession.

Grant's legs began to sag; his movements slowed. He had always been a great athlete, but his age was telling on him, and this kid was phenomenal. Grant played basketball all through high school and on the college intramural team, although track had been his main sport. Right now, his mind was willing, but his body was weakening. His shoulders ached, the arches of his feet and his shins hurt, and he couldn't stop the stinging sweat from running into his eyes. He felt his nipples and thighs chaffing from sweaty contact. *Only two points*, he thought, *only two points*.

Jacobi looked him dead in the eye, like a man. He fired the ball off Grant's unsuspecting chest, caught it, and rushed toward the basket. He finished by jumping high in the air and slinging the ball through the rim and off the court. He landed, and the game was over. That quickly.

"Good game!" Grant congratulated him—still stung by the loss.

"Yeah, you too."

"Thanks for letting me play," Grant said as he rested his hands on his knees, head down, panting while sweat pooled at his feet. "I haven't played that hard in years."

"It was fun . . . who are you anyway?"

Scout's Honor

Grant was caught off guard by the audacity of the question. He had already introduced himself to nearly everyone throughout the day. People all knew he was from out of town and that he was there visiting family.

"I already told you."

"Okay, but I've met people like you before. They come here, they watch me play, they try to talk with me one on one—like they want something from me. Sometimes they're just scouts from other schools. Sometimes they are scouts that want me to move to play at their school. Sometimes they just want to see if I am as good as everyone says I am. So what do you want?"

"I don't know," Grant responded. "Look, I'm here looking for my family—meeting my family—and I came up here because I heard this is where people meet to play ball."

"Who's your family? What's your last name? I know everyone around here."

"Erlosung—what's yours?"

"Combs. I don't know any Erlosungs . . . never heard that name before."

"Well, I know some Combses. Don't worry about it; I know who I'm looking for."

"But where do they live? I know almost everyone around here, and I don't know any Erlosungs. Are you sure you're in the right spot?"

"No, no I'm not. I'll have to see."

"So you don't know where they live? You haven't been to their house?"

Exasperated, Grant said, "I've got it under control. I know what I'm doing. Don't worry about it."

"I'm not worried," Jacobi replied.

"It's dark. I've got to get going. Thanks for the game and good luck with your career," Grant said as he walked away feeling awkward.

Jacobi stood looking at Grant, bewildered. He picked up his gear and turned to walk home. He looked back over his shoulder as Grant walked past the white plastic chair sitting courtside, and Jacobi smiled. Grant walked away.

Chapter 5: Katie

Grant grabbed his stuff, his mind racing. *I bet he suspects something. I wonder if Katie told him my name. She only wrote that she had told him . . . she didn't write what she had told him.* He had to find Katie, and they had to talk. Grant had no idea what he was doing or where this was all going. He turned and watched Jacobi walk away from this strange little court, in the middle of nowhere, surrounded by nothingness. *How deceived*, he thought, *how deceived these people are to think this is how to live. How deceived I was—thinking that I could figure all this out with a game of basketball.* With that thought, he realized he didn't have a place to stay for the night, and it was dark. How opposite from his home.

The stars shone brilliantly as Grant arrived at the local motel: Holler Inn. Grant grimaced. The inn was old and white and in disrepair. The black metal gate surrounding it was misshapen, having been hit too many times by drunk drivers. The lot and driveway were gravel with no clear boundaries. The grass sprouted between the gravel, and the gravel lay among the grass. Grant noticed random tire tracks ran through the yard, and he walked hesitantly to the front door over awkwardly loose stones that served as a walkway. To the right of the inn a large piece of coal slid down the face of a massive coal pile, unattended, leaving a puff of dust in its wake.

Grant walked up, opened the front door, and noticed the sign that read, "No shirt, No shoes, No service" —only someone had scratched through the word *service* and replaced it with the word *pant*. Since the perpetrator had written *pant* instead of *pants*, Grant guessed at his intelligence level. Much wisdom can be gathered from bathroom walls and store signs.

A fast-talking young man greeted Grant at the counter. Grant hardly understood a word.

"Ya lookin' for a room for da night or week?"

"For the night, please."

"That's fitbucks if ya wont air ditionen, an fordy if ya don't. Most folk do though cus it get hotter'n a stewed mater some mornin's, plus it keepsa noise down from da other rooms at night."

"I beg your—I mean, what?!"

"I sayed, fiti fo air ditionen an fordy for none. You 'ont it?"

"Fifty dollars for a room with air and dish, and forty-four dollars without either?" Grant spoke slowly and deliberately.

"Fiti for air!"

"Air conditioning's an option?" Grant asked, not sure he had heard correctly.

"Yessir, itsa optional."

"Air conditioning, please," Grant requested, not sure he'd need it.

The man took Grant's money, filled out some innocuous paperwork, and gave Grant the key. It was to room thirteen, of course. Grant walked down the exterior corridor, stepping over broken bits of glass and a dirty diaper. He opened the door, and the stench punched him in the face. It smelled as if two dirty dogs had just mated, urinated, and left. Grant gagged and stepped back. He had no other choice, so he carried in his bag, with his nose and mouth covered, and dropped it on the bed, which squeaked. He opened the window, placed the quintessential stick underneath it—for surely the windows didn't actually work in this place. He left the door open, too, for a moment, until he saw a snake on the sidewalk. It had a small head and a wide body, and it slithered toward the door. He slammed the door and walked to the bathroom, furious.

Upon entering the bathroom, he noticed it didn't smell any better. *Why would it?* The window was open in the bathroom, too, and Grant remembered the snake. He wasn't sure if snakes could climb walls, but he certainly didn't care at this point. He would rather die by snakebite than smell this sewer room all night. He undressed and turned on the shower. The knob squeaked and the wall rattled as the pipes shook with the water pushing through them. Grant waited, and finally water began to trickle out of the faucet and the shower head. It was brown.

Grant cranked the shower knob, slapped the shower head away from himself, and shook his head. He used the restroom quickly, dressed, and walked out into the main room. The floor looked less infested than the bed, so he threw his bag on the floor and flopped down. No way was he lying on that bed. As he sat on the floor considering his plight, he finally grew tired enough to lay his head on his bag. He closed his eyes in hope of maybe falling asleep when he heard a tiny sound.

Stirring up, he saw a mouse run across the floor, and a cat jump through the window. Grant pounced, chased the cat around the room, yelling and cursing, and throwing whatever he could find. Tripping over the power cord to the lamp and ripping it from the wall, he brought the whole lamp crashing down on his back. He smacked into the wall with his head and fell to the ground. *This is hell*, he thought, lying face down on the floor, while the cat jumped out the window with its tail like a flag pole.

School

The next morning, Grant didn't quite know what to do, but he knew he wasn't going to stay in that place again. After the cat and mouse episode, he had commandeered another room, but it wasn't much better. He slept until 5 a.m. and got up. He tried the shower in the new room, and the water was a pale yellow, so he decided to chance it after his quick run in the dark. The run was rather liberating, working off some of his frustration—and at least the air was clear. He returned, showered, and checked out by 7 a.m. The smell of sulfur and egg salad chased him; the shower may have cleaned him up, but he smelled worse for it. The motel didn't have coffee, which gave him a headache. He pushed forward.

Grant couldn't find a real diner around—in fact, there really wasn't any type of city either. He assumed someone had found a valley between some mountains, and people had slowly settled it haphazardly without any real planning. The roads ran pretty much parallel with the creek, winding back and forth, as did the railroad tracks. A lone grocery store stood near the center alongside a refueling station. The atmosphere felt abandoned. Grant couldn't decide if it was the village that had been abandoned, or the dream of a better life.

He still didn't know where Katie lived, or how to contact her. The address on the envelope didn't appear to be her address, just her parents'. *Why did she give me their address instead of her own?*

He went to the refueling station and purchased a cup of coffee and some apples, asking the man behind the counter, "Can you tell me how to find the high school?"

"Turn right outta hyear and head up Bungalow 'bout ten mile. You'll see it right thar on da right."

Grant walked out the door. "No shirt, No shoes, No service" the sign read, and Grant began to notice a trend. Apparently, shirts and shoes were not hot commodities.

Grant arrived at the school around 8:30 a.m. amid a flurry of activity. School buses, personal vehicles, bikes and walkers left and entered rapidly. Parents, in pajamas and housecoats, raced out of the lot as if something very important were waiting on them. Some students walked through the front doors, while many just stood around outside the school. Several people smoked, primarily students, and Grant wasn't sure exactly what they were smoking. It didn't look good.

A few couples were intermeshed, making out, up against the brick wall of the school. The girls were pressed deeply against the boys' crotches, and the boys were groping the girls' fundaments. Their faces stuck together as though they were looking for something in the back of their lover's skull. *Good luck*, Grant thought. *Probably isn't much in there anyway.* He walked past a few jeering teenagers to the front door; it was locked. *I wonder if they're trying to keep people locked out . . . or in.* He pressed the intercom and waited for an answer, but he only heard the door unlock. When he walked through the front door, he found his answer.

On the other side of the second set of double doors, Grant saw a young girl grab another by the hair on the back of her head and smack the blood out of her face. She didn't stop at that, though; she followed with two, three, four, five more blows until they both fell to the ground. Screaming and scrambling quickly, she mounted her victim and dug her nails deep into her face. More students crowded around, cheering, enamored with the violence.

"Rip 'at skank's eyes out! Yeah, hit 'er again!"

"Scratch her face off!"

"Kick her back, Shirley, kick her back!"

Grant stood appalled and inactive as the scene unraveled. The girl on top grabbed the other by her face and began to smack her head against the tile floor. The thuds were sickening; still, no one intervened. *Will she really kill her, right here?* Grant wondered. Then, scuttling from the right a frantic lady charged into the mass of huddled students. She shouted and swam through the sea of bodies to break up the fight, but they pushed her back.

A man arrived next, surely a coach, and barked orders as he began tossing students out of the way like yesterday's horoscope. A few students turned and faced him to protect the fight from being stopped. With precision, he plowed right through them. Before he could reach the girls on the ground, a student sprayed his face with pepper spray. Writhing in pain, he grabbed his face, seized by a coughing frenzy. The crowd, full of blood-lusting teenagers, began to disintegrate quickly, covering their faces and running away gagging. Those who remained just a few seconds longer left with puffy, red faces and swollen teary eyes. A swarm of adults hastily arrived, mouths and noses covered with shirts or rags, and dragged the remaining students out of the area. The front doors burst open as students began to pour out of the school into the parking lot like lemmings. And with that, school was over before it ever began.

Grant had never even made it through the second set of doors. He was now back in the parking lot watching the production. Students made serious ruckus all about. Kids were crying, laughing, cursing, and some just walked away.

The parking lot surged like ants fleeing the anthill just after the boiling aluminum slides down the shaft. Boys with long hair and jean jackets tried to command the scene, while girls with huge hair, wearing tight pants and short shirts, dramatized the stage. It was pandemonium, but everyone thrived off it. One boy continually repeated, "They needa letus go at da house. Why don't tae letus go at da house?"

Finally, a few kids started to leave, and the desire for another day free from school exceeded the desire to stay and glorify the situation.

Rejection

And then he saw her. Among a group of hysterical girls,
patting, calming, hugging, and pacifying, was Katie. He
still recognized her, even after all these years. Beautiful and
petite, her short brown hair pushed behind her ears. She
wore no jewelry, but her face was that of a porcelain doll:
radiant, pure, perfect. How this setting had produced her,
he would never know. In the time it takes for a cool breeze
to blow across a warm face, she was gone. Grant couldn't
find her. He held his hand above his eyes to scour the
crowd, but he did not see her, nor the group of girls she had
with her. So he waited.

Like a child lost in a View-Master, Grant watched for
nearly an hour. It only seemed like a minute since that
almost ethereal experience when he had lost Katie—again.
Parents and children came and went, as did the school
transportation. Everyone lived on the drama, and everyone
wanted to tell his or her own story. Each character played
his or her part in the event: exacerbating the issue,
amplifying the chaos, feigning concern when there was
none. Then they left. Like liquid soap dropped into the
middle of a pool of pepper floating in water, the once
overcrowded lot became abandoned in one quick, departing
drove. The police and fireman arrived and left while fans

exhausting the polluted air propped open the doors to the school. And then he saw her again, but this time she was walking straight toward him.

Grant stood and waited, but Katie kept walking intently until he stepped forward. She stopped abruptly.

"Hello, Katie," he greeted.

She looked up, startled, then rolling her eyes quickly and throwing up her hands, she asked, "When did you get here?"

"When this happened," Grant said spreading his arms wide as if to present the landscape before her. "This morning. I walked in and saw the fight then came back out with the swarm of students."

"So you didn't try to help? Figures. What are you thinking anyway? That you can just walk right into the school and see me, like you did with Jacobi yesterday? What were you thinking then? You ran up to him like some lunatic trying to reunite with his son over basketball . . . You didn't even talk to me—tell me you were coming! Don't get near him again! I'm his mom, you talk to me first!"

The blueness of her eyes grew strained as her mood intensified. Her face reddened and her body exuded anger and disgust. She moved closer to Grant, impulsively.

"I came because you wrote the letter," Grant replied. She rolled her eyes again. "I went to the address on the letter, and Jacobi wasn't there. I did what I thought I should do: come here, find Jacobi, and figure out what's next. You wrote the letter, remember?"

"Don't patronize me with stupid questions," she snapped. "I know I wrote the letter, and I expected you would respond like a man, not a child." She pointed her finger at him. Motioning with her hands, she spoke emphatically, as if to a small boy: "Children don't live in reality; they believe they can rescue any situation just by being there— just because they're involved. They are the focus; they are the answer! They are egocentric, like you. All you care about is yourself . . . and adults can't afford that. Adults care about other people, they consider other people, they know that relationships take time. They do not just show up like some type of superhero, believing that their presence will rectify any situation!"

Grant stepped back, stung, with his jaw set and his eyes clenched. He dropped his crossed arms to his sides, then stepped forward, brought his arms and hands in front of his body again and glared down at Katie. "I didn't ask for this," he said poignantly and with feigned control. "And I didn't run away. I came here to fix a problem, and you want to blame me—"

"You are the problem!" Katie announced, almost screaming, with a flailing arm. She walked past Grant, brushing him out of the way with her left arm, like he was an unwanted shirtsleeve protruding into the aisle of a clothing store.

Grant didn't even turn around; he just walked away, lost.

Where am I walking? He didn't know; he just continued to walk. He walked back the way he came, destroying his shoes with coal dust and mountain runoff. The air was oppressive, the terrain wreaked havoc on his soles. He watched little streams of water running down the mountain pool into larger ones, and then pour into the creek. He wondered if there were more snakes here, as he crossed his eyes in anger. He felt as if his eyes would burst from his head if he held in this raging storm any longer. His body tensed, quaked, his left leg began to tremble in rage, and he balled his fists and yelled, "I hate that—!" The sound of a blaring horn from a passing train mauled his scream. The horn harmonized with his siren's call to Anger, and he felt embarrassed and stupid. Just as she wanted.

Before long, and well after short, Grant found himself at the basketball court again. Players were not as prevalent as the day before. Some of the kids he had seen leaving the school were playing today, but Jacobi wasn't there. After a few moments he realized: *Of course Jacobi isn't here, he is thirteen and in middle school. These kids are high school students—so they are probably around twenty-two*, he thought snidely. *Nobody makes a difference in this place.*

Ronald

A warm breeze blew, and Grant heard the chain net shake. An old man in brown corduroy pants, black shoes, and a white t-shirt had just swished a twenty-five-foot hook shot to end the game. The other players and onlookers gave him high fives, slaps on the back, and congratulatory words of praise as he hobbled off the court to the solitary, white plastic chair.

"You steel got it, Ronald, you steel got it!"

"Nice shot, old man!"

'You da man, Ronald! I can't believe you hit that shot. Everytime, everytime!"

He had a bit of a limp, but he clearly maneuvered about well. He took a seat, looked up over the rim of his glasses, and spotted Grant. He motioned Grant over.

Grant felt like talking to this old man about as much as he felt like getting kicked in the crotch. Actually, a kick in the crotch might be better; at least it would take his mind off Katie and Jacobi. He walked over, regardless, to see what the man wanted.

"How ya doin'?" the man asked, looking up at Grant from his seat.

"I've been better," Grant replied.

"Me too, and younger. Boy . . . back then I could play thirdy to fordy games a day, no sweat. Now, two or three and I'ma pooped. How 'boutchoo? You play any ball?" he asked, leaning forward.

"Some, when I was younger. Anyway, I've got to go. Nice to meet you."

"We ain't met yet," the older man said stiffly, leaning back, cocking his head to the left and placing his hand on his chin. "Name's Ronald, and you's right. You did play when you was younger. You was younger yesterday than ya' are today, and I saw you playin' last night."

A little baffled, Grant took a closer look at this man. He was leaning slightly back and looking right in Grant's face. His glasses were held on with a strap. His right ear was deformed, almost nonexistent, merely a stub protruding from the right side of his head, to which his glasses had been secured.

"When did you see me play?" Grant asked.

"Outcheer, last night, you and Jacobi. I came, saw you two playin' and left. Jus' checkin' on da boy. How a'bout it. Did ye win?"

"No, he did."

"Course he did, can't stand to lose none. He's a good kid, 'minds me of myself when I was younger, 'cept he ain't got no maladies like I had, 'cept no daddy."

Grant felt the sting of the last comment, and it seemed well aimed. "What do you mean?" Grant asked.

"Well, I got dis here missin' ear. Born that way. Had to overcome it, and it made me stronger, but ol' Jaki, he's body's perfect. Jus' his mind is a little diff'rnt. I had my daddy—coal miner, good man—but he didn't have his." Ronald stood up to face Grant.

Avoiding the topic, Grant asked, "How'd you overcome it?"

"Train'n, pure and simple. I didn't have balance, so I practiced. I ran up an' down da mountain on my toes, over an' over an' over. I dribbled dat ball everwheres. Up da mountain, down da mountain, through da creek beds, in da barn, ona porch, everwhere 'cept da house. Mama wouldn't lowit ina house. Da mountain's what gave me balance, though. I couldn't walk straight, ear an' all, but runnin' up an' down 'at mountain day after day after day taught me to balance. Taught me da negotiate when my body started to fall. I don't need no balance now; my body won't let me fall."

"Okay, I'm leaving!" Grant announced impatiently, having heard enough.

"You don't needa go; you need to stay. Now listen hyear. I can tell by da way a man walks, how he plays. If he plays better'n offense or defense, if he'sa physical or mental, if he commits or just makes it look like he does. You needa learn da play defense. You're all offense. You gotta learn to plant yer feet, dig in, and take the charge, or you'll never get the ball back." He paused for a deep contemplative breath, and Grant started to shift his weight on his feet. Ronald continued, "Look right chyear son. I trained Jacobi. For eight years I done trained 'at boy right. I know him, better'n anybody else 'cept his mama. And I see his daddy right in him, and I see you, and I know who ya are."

"I don't even know who I am. How do I know if I'm his dad? She left, not me."

"Getchyer butt low, plantcher feet now, getcher head up, and get ready for this."

Appalled, Grant said, "What are you even talking about?"

"You, boy, you need to stay rightcheer."

"Stay! I don't want to stay! This place is awful. These people are awful. I think people just come here to die. I'm not staying; I'm leaving!" Grant's voice intensified as he railed on. "Since I got here, everybody has been dirty and stupid . . . and you know what? They talk to me like I'm the idiot! They're the—" he grunted a gruff growl of anguish, and then finished, "idiots!"

"Everyone?"

Grant's mind flew back to meeting Jacobi and Dynamite. He remembered the kindness Chester's wife showed him. *Sure, she was repulsive, but she was kind*. He thought of how Dale had treated him—*like family*—before he arrived here. Grant looked at the old man who spoke forcibly to him, but did not treat Grant like he was stupid. He was just direct—something Grant could appreciate.

"No, not everybody. It just feels like everybody, but I know better than that. I have had my feelings betray me enough to know better than just to trust every feeling that comes along."

His breathing slowed, he exhaled slowly, and his face softened.

"How long you here for?"

"A week," Grant replied.

"How long didju say you'd stay hyeer?"

"A week."

"Then give it a week. Doesa boy know yet? Have ya told 'em?"

"I haven't, but I don't know what she's doing. She's crazy."

"Who, Katie? She ain't crazy, boy, she's justa protectin' what's hers. She's a good mama. Only thing that boy had goin' for 'em till he discovered his talent right outcheer. Don't be judgin' her if she gets all hysterical with you bein' round. It's natural. Mamas protect their babies, and mamas protect 'emselves, too."

"Okay, I'll fulfill my obligation. I'll stay for a week, but I'm not promising anything. Nothing seems to work right here."

"Nothing?" Ronald questioned almost teasingly.

"Almost nothing."

"Where ya' stayin'?"

"The luxurious Holler Inn."

Ronald laughed, wheezing all the while. Grant didn't find it so amusing, but then he didn't find anything amusing about this place. Ronald insisted that Grant take his chair and relax for a few minutes. He had one of the boys get Grant some water from the well, and then Ronald offered to help Grant find a place to stay. Grant agreed, and they talked for a few minutes more.

Normally hyperactive, Grant began to feel groggy when he sat down. *I must not have slept well last night; I haven't had any coffee since this morning, and I have walked quite a bit.* Before he could fight it, Grant was fast asleep even though he was sitting up. The last thing he remembered was Ronald walking away and a warm breeze blowing. He wasn't worried, just exhausted; then his eyes closed, and he was lost in the darkness.

When Grant awoke, he was starving. Unsure if it had been thirty minutes or two hours, he was sweaty, disoriented, and in pain. He reflected and realized he had eaten only breakfast the day prior—and a few apples today. The gnawing in his heart had been pushing him forward, but now the gnawing in his stomach brought him to a screeching halt. Several of the guys playing basketball had lunch with them, but he didn't want to ask. He could pay them; surely he had more money than they all did combined, but he didn't want to. Interacting with these people was like a shot of Procaine between the toes: full of pain, and the numbness made him feel dumb.

"Here ya is, son," Grant heard Ronald say from behind him.

He was still disturbed that he had been able to sleep through several loud, whooping boys and men playing ball. Feeling frustrated, he turned to deal with Ronald without

much couth. Ronald stood with his arm outstretched
holding a brown paper sack.

"Oh, well, thanks . . ." Grant mustered.

"Don't mention it, son. Twernt nothin'. I had stopped by
one of my friendses, and his wife offered me lunch. I ate
and brought dis to you. Now, lunch weren't nothin', but
findin' you a good place to stay was like tryin' to pull a
gnat's tooth."

"What?"

"I said findin' you a place to stay was like pullin' a gnat's
tooth. It weren't easy, boy, but I did it."

"How long have you been gone?"

"Bout two hours." He tapped Grant on the shoulder, put
his head down, and inched closer. "And it weren't tough
neither to find ye no place. I already knew of one . . . but
I's tryin' to get you to 'spress some gratitude . . . but dat's
lost on ye."

"Okay . . . thanks," Grant managed. Deeply frustrated and
reflective, he couldn't understand why he was being so
hesitant, such a jerk. He could barely manage a "thank you"
or an interaction with a group of guys playing ball. As if
this place had some oppressive presence over him: pressing
him down, inculcating him with fear and hate, chipping
away bit by bit and thrusting him back into the darkness,

cold and alone. He had been fine until he met Katie's dad and saw Hatchet, but ever since then he was crushed— except for when he saw Jacobi. Ronald was still talking, but Grant hadn't heard a word. Ronald grabbed him by the arm, led him away, and Grant followed without protest.

Cabin Fever

Grant inhaled the sandwich, chips, snack cake, orange, and pear on the way while the sun harkened toward the west. Not his normal diet, but he didn't care too much—only enough to notice. The sandwich kept sticking to the roof of his mouth, against his teeth; in order to dislodge it, he continued digging his finger all the way back toward his tonsils and scraping it off. This was neither the time nor place for manners.

Stunned by the picturesque postcard scene, Grant paused. Hidden in this human wasteland was a natural beauty--an oasis of sorts. Standing in the jut of a mountain was a beautiful log cabin. Its color was that of crème mocha, and the clear pane glass windows shone brilliantly in the escaping sun. Lush green surrounded the entire fixture, and ivy cascaded down the railings of the front porch. Ronald's feet made impressions in the shades of green intermingled with the clover-covered yard, which was surrounded by evergreen trees, crawling with ivy, all of which reflected off the small creek that ran in front of the cabin. The cabin and its location reminded Grant of the fabled waterfall that stood outside the fabled mine in one of his favorite childhood books. The waterfall, as did this cabin, stood in stark contrast to its surroundings, providing a refuge for the miners in its beauty and cleanliness. Out of the mines they would traverse, covered in soot and ash, to be greeted by the blue-white falls and the grotto that lay at the bottom. Home to fish and algae, this sanctuary was a place of refuge and replenishment for the homeward-bound, exhausted miners. A place where they could wash the day away, just like Grant hoped this cabin would be for him—until he went home.

Ronald took him into the cabin and told Grant the fee, to which Grant agreed quickly, it being so cheap. Grant looked at the old pictures, tools, and even cookware on the walls, the great rugs on the floors, the immaculate craftsmanship of the counters, tables, chairs, and the astounding beauty of log rafters instead of a low, limiting ceiling.

"Built it hisself, erething in hyear. He built it all hisself, my buddy Hammond did. Erething you see in this house he did: plumbin', tile, tables, chairs, even the glass in da doors, cabinets, and windows he cut and placed 'emself. He'd do anythin' for ya, that Hammond, but gettin' him to teach ya somethin' is like tryin' to milk a mouse. It jus' ain't happnin'. Now, that's how we differ, me and Hammond. He can do it all, taught 'isself, but he can't teach. I useda be able to do it all, but I can teach anythin', even stuff I can't do myself."

Grant stood looking, not really sure if he was supposed to speak or listen. He didn't have a plan, and he needed a plan. He thought about Jacobi and Katie and what he must do to figure this whole thing out.

"It's incredible!" Grant finally responded. "The whole place."

"C'mon," Ronald waved to him, and they walked out the back door.

As they exited, Grant noticed something eerily familiar: a red rose, encased in glass, sitting upon a wooden base with the inscription "Family is Forever." This one was different than the last, the one at Chester's house, on this one the words were inscribed, not just painted.

On the back of the house stood a small covered porch that sat about sixty feet from the mountain wall. The creek ran against the mountain, then, following the grade of the declining land, flowed from the rear of the cabin back toward the front. Two rocking chairs, handcrafted, sat on the back porch with an upside-down barrel—sawn in two— between them. The chairs faced the mountain, so the occupants could look over the yard, while the barrel sitting between them could hold their drinks.

They sat, and Ronald spoke. He reached over and knocked on the barrel three times with his knuckle and said, "Sometimes you gotta leave somethin' to get somethin'. Truth is, ya' always have to leave somethin' to get somethin', and the bigger the thang is you leave, da harder you'll fight for what you're a tryin' to get. It's like leavin' your mama to learn to walk; you gotta let go of the only security ya know to get da independence you 'ont."

Grant just rocked in the chair, irresponsive, and Ronald rocked right beside him. Dusk cloaked the land, and Grant sat, rocking and thinking.

With that, Ronald stood, told Grant good-bye, and walked off the back porch. Grant watched him fade into the distance, growing smaller and smaller, until his figure collided with the darkness, and then Grant went inside.

He sat down and planned out his mode of attack. He wouldn't directly confront Jacobi or Katie for the rest of the week. Instead, he would accost the local village, listen and learn about Jacobi and Katie and , and then he would know what to do. Surely, in this little village, everyone knew everything about everyone.

After making his list and formulating his plans and goals, Grant stretched out on one of the handcrafted beds. *Dad would love this place*, he thought, and he allowed all the good memories of his father and the smell of woodwork to lull him to sleep.

Investigation

The week was spent like last month's income: whether strategically planned or haphazardly blown, it was gone. Only the future could tell the wisdom or folly of its investment. Grant was not sure he had invested wisely. He learned that everyone loved Jacobi and Katie—at least around here. He learned a lot while he was at the store, picking up some of the week's necessities for the cabin. Apparently, Jacobi was the object of much jealousy in the surrounding counties. Everyone who met him seemed to love him, but the teams that played against him did not. The amount of attention this one middle school kid received astounded Grant, just as the amount of importance placed on basketball in these parts did. Of course, as the week wore on he came to understand it better, but it didn't sit well with him.

One thing he learned was that many people around here did not work. Not only did they not have jobs, they didn't work, period. Vehicles were abandoned; homes and barns were unkempt, deteriorating. People didn't even contribute to their own well-being. They just lived off someone else. It seemed as if the coal miners supported the whole community, and everyone else survived off the labor of the backs of a few.

Since people didn't work, they didn't do much else either, other than consume. Entertainment was like a god. Sports and politics were always the talk of the town. Illegal drugs were rampant among the adults, teens, and even some of the kids. Sex was an unmentionable pastime that was always mentioned, always on someone's lips or mind. Incest was widespread, as was family violence and alcoholism. It was like a cesspool for the breakdown of humanity, and the gene pool wasn't changing.

Katie, on the other hand, seemed to be above the gene pool and beloved by everyone. As much attention as Jacobi received for basketball, she received for teaching and rescuing. She had taken a special interest in teenage mothers and developed a program to help them through their pregnancy, parenting, and the stigma associated with it. As much as she tried to push all kids through school, she would do *anything* to get a teenage mother to graduate. She encouraged the study of literature and history as a way to learn about life outside of the mountains, but that is not why she was so beloved. She ingratiated herself with the people because she helped their daughters, and even the roughest of fathers could be softened by that gift. She was a philanthropist for sure, but one other thing was clear: anyone, anyone who tried to hurt Jacobi was an open target

. . . and if Katie was coming for you, so was everybody else.

Suddenly, lightning struck Grant on the last day of his trial week. The key to the community's heart was Jacobi. The key to Jacobi was Katie, and the key to Katie was Jacobi. They were all intertwined, and he stood outside the locked door. He knew where the key was, but he wasn't sure he wanted it. Could this be the kingdom he was after, this place that made him foam in disgust? Surely not. He only wanted to know what he was supposed to do about Jacobi, but the sand had slid through the hourglass and time had elapsed—it was time to go home.

Jacobi doesn't need a father anyway, Grant reasoned. *He has Ronald, the life whisperer*, and Grant smirked at his own wittiness. Every man from around that area vied to be Jacobi's dad. Jacobi was talented, strong, and respectful, and hanging with him brought instant fame in their little community. And with fame came power, and with power came control, and with control came self-importance. Many men wanted to play the part of Jacobi's dad—for their own sake. From what Grant understood, Katie had been heavily sought after, too, but she had a reputation for being untouchable—unavailable.

Grant tidied up his bedroom, tucked the sheets and blankets around the mattress, wiped down the bathroom and kitchen, and cleaned the huge living area. He left the allotted cash on the nightstand beside the bed, threw out the remaining food, gathered up the trash, and placed it in the barrel outside. He locked the door behind him and began his trek to the home of Katie's parents. Unsure if Jacobi knew Grant's true identity, but suspecting he did, Grant planned to say good-bye to Jacobi before leaving. He now knew where Katie lived, but after their one and only meeting, he thought he shouldn't go over there with a target on his shirt. It would not be pleasant, he knew, and he rolled his eyes and shook his head.

Why do I feel so bad about this? He wondered. *I haven't done anything wrong. She took the kid, she ran, she wrote me the letter, and now she wants me to stay away. He doesn't need me. I don't fit. They don't need me here— don't want me here. I have a business to run with clients and people who need me, so why do I feel so bad? What am I abandoning?* Grant felt the angst well up in his chest and laden his heart. *Again with this indecisiveness stuff,* he fumed, and spoke to himself aloud: "You will leave, go home, and do what you do well. You hate this place, anyway, and you can change the world from home." He paused. "I don't need this place, or these people. I can do this better at home; plus, they need me there. I'm done. I'm out of here."

Then it hit him, the smell that is, it got him right in the gut.

Right in the Gut

Billows of blackish gray smoke rose high into the air, painting tainted streaks across the pale blue sky. Waves of dirty odor settled into the atmosphere and absorbed into the surroundings. Over the hill Grant rose, and around the corner he came to look upon that old, dilapidated trailer again. There he stood, Hatchet, barefoot and pregnant—at least that's what his beer belly portrayed—lighting fires. *He must have run so fast to get out here that it blew his shirt and shoes right off him*, Grant thought.

The smell made Grant want to vomit. That whole area made him want to vomit. What was Hatchet doing anyway, lighting all of those fires? He was burning the trash! The bags with all the chicken heads and bodies had been left for a week to rot, and now he was burning the trash! In fact, Grant did vomit. He turned and his body revolted, dislodging all the contents of his stomach and flushing them out. Gurgling and wheezing, trying to catch his breath, Grant fell to his knees. The one last hurl did it. *I'm leaving*, he thought, *with or without saying good-bye.* So he left both his breakfast and his dignity there in a patch of grass.

Grant wasn't quite sure why he had decided to stop at the home of Katie's parents. He told himself he was looking for Jacobi, but he knew he would find him at the basketball court. Earlier, he had promised he would never go back to that home. *Maybe I had one last itch to scratch with that place, maybe. I'll just leave . . . I'll just leave . . . I'm leaving . . . now, going home to civilization.*

He couldn't do it. He tried, but he couldn't. He needed to go by the court one last time before he left, and there he saw Jacobi again. Some overpowering attraction held him, suspended in time, gazing at his son. He watched him dribble and shoot, laughing and smiling, and Grant couldn't pull himself away. He walked closer to the court, wondering why the kids were out of school again—this time on a Wednesday.

On the other team was a duo of unlikely heroes. The younger, just a boy, was dark-skinned, skinny at best, and full of life. The elder, just a man, was dark-skinned, overweight, and full of laughter. They were fun to watch, but terrible at basketball. Jacobi evidently was taking it easy on them, although they were matched up against him, two on one. As they continued to play, the boy, determined and active, and the man, attentive and joyous, Grant realized what was so attractive. They were a father-and-son team—playing together for the fun of it. It was camaraderie and pedagogy and paternity all in one. What Grant longed for had evaded him like a fog rising off the water.

Watching Jacobi hit a very long jump shot with a smile, Grant turned to walk away and almost ran into Ronald.

"Where you goin'?" Ronald asked.

"Home."

"Good, we don't need your kind 'round here no ways!"

"What the . . . what are you talking about!?" Grant replied, frustrated.

"People 'at run from 'ehr problems, 'ats whut. We got enough of 'em round hyer anyways. We don't need no more."

"I don't run from problems. I fix them; that's what I do . . . that's my job. I'm also smart enough to realize there are some problems that can't be fixed because they don't want to be fixed—like this place—so get out of my face!"

Grant totally lost his cool, and inside he was full of self-reproach. The only thing he hated more than being embarrassed was being embarrassed at his own behavior. It made him feel out of control, and the out-of-control feeling made him angry and self-loathing, which made him feel more out of control. It was a vicious cycle that usually ended in an eruption or implosion.

He brushed past Ronald—when he heard six words that changed everything, that stopped him in his tracks. "Have ye talked to yer daddy?"

At first Grant feared Ronald had directed the question toward Jacobi, intending a last-second, unbeknownst introduction, but he hadn't. Ronald had directed the question toward Grant and found his mark. "No," Grant replied, "I haven't, not since I've been here." But he knew he must.

"Then do it, son," Ronald directed. "Yer bout to walk away from the biggest responsibility of yer life, and ye haven't even talked to your daddy. At's silly. Least you got one to talk to, boy, least you got one to talk to."

A Piece of Mind

Grant spent the rest of the day communicating with people back home. He spoke with his dad and mom, Robert, and even God. He wasn't sure he knew who or what God was, but he figured it couldn't hurt. He had gone to church a few times as a kid, when his dad had read some of the teachings of Jesus and got on a Jesus kick, but they stopped shortly thereafter. The pastor had an affair with a lady in the church and then left his wife and kids behind. Grant's dad was such an ardent believer in faithfulness to his spouse, honesty, and trust that he couldn't stomach it. He said he wouldn't let the followers dictate to him what he felt about the leader, Jesus, but he stopped reading, stopped praying, and eventually it was all but a forgotten memory—until now.

Grant's dad had actually been rough on Grant when he called. Typically encouraging, Mr. Erlosung took a different tact this time. He insisted, "A man does not back away from an impossible challenge. He looks at what he must do to make the impossible possible. Then, if he wants it bad enough, he sets about doing it daily."

Robert hadn't been so curt. He reminded Grant to approach it more logically.

"Just put Robin in charge as interim CEO, and take another month or so to try to get to know Jacobi. Money's not an issue," he reminded Grant. "Time's not an issue either; the business wasn't built in a week or a month and it won' be lost in a week or a month."

"I know, I know, but I feel like I need to come back to make sure things are running like they are supposed to."

"Do you want to see if they are running like they are *supposed to*, or how you want them to run? Grant, the business is fine. Stay there. Evaluate your most valuable relationships. Evaluate what makes them valuable. Evaluate how others have had a positive influence on you, then try to have the same positive influence on Jacobi." Robert paused for a moment.

Grant needed to hear a voice of reason. He knew, internally, that the lies he was telling himself were harmful, but he didn't know how to combat them. He didn't know why they were so powerful when he could clearly acknowledge they were lies. He didn't know why he needed help; he just did.

"You know, Grant," he said, "we experience rejection all the time in our lives. We just do. As men, or leaders, or entrepreneurs, we just do. We can't let the emotions created by rejection dictate our actions. Period. You have money, you have time, and you have a responsibility. You can do this, and if you get rejected, then you persist until you are received. If this goes awry, let it be by their choice, their rejection, not yours."

Grant wasn't fully persuaded. He told Robert about the place, about the people and the lack of drive and desire, about the incest and suicide, the drugs, alcohol, and violence.

"This place is like putting a doormat over a flower and then hoping it blooms," Grant said.

"I didn't know you spoke in such dramatic similes," Robert teased.

"I guess it's from spending time with Ronald . . . although he'd probably say something like, 'It'll be harder 'en curlin' a fly's eyelash, son!'" trying to mimic Ronald's accent and vernacular the best he could.

Laughing, Robert asked, "Who's Ronald?"

"He's this guy who is always up at the basketball court. He said he trained Jacobi, and when I spoke to people around the town, everyone confirmed it. He's a local hero; apparently, he played some college basketball and held some scoring records. This is the same guy I told you about who helped me get that log cabin that's so fantastic, but then he flipped on me today."

"Flipped on you? What did he do?"

"When I told him I was leaving, he shouted, 'Good! We don't need your kind 'round here no ways!' From what I can tell, *all* they need around here is my kind. The kind that actually works and has a future . . ."

"What did he mean when he said 'your kind'?"

"He said something about quitters or something—I don't know. He ticked me off, so I started to walk away until he asked if I had talked to my dad. When he said that, he got me. I did need to talk to an actual 'dad' about how to make a 'dad' decision."

"He also played you. Sounds like he's brilliant."

"What do you mean?" Grant asked.

"Man, think about it. He got you all mad and defensive, and then turned you with a little question. Dude's an athlete and a coach, and he turned you like a screwdriver. It sounds as if he knows how to get people amped up, and how to get them to perform—the way he wants them to."

"He's not a coach."

"Didn't you say the kid's phenomenal? This guy trained him in that environment. How do you create a phenom athlete in the middle of nowhere unless you're a great coach?"

"I don't know," Grant said, beginning to realize his friend was right.

"I'm going to tell you something my dad told me before I moved out. He pulled me aside and said, 'Robert, remember this: a friend who is near is better than a brother who is far away.' I didn't understand it . . . until I met you. You know I grew up with four brothers, right?"

"I thought you had three, but okay . . ."

"And you and I have been through thick and thin together, right?"

"So we're good friends, and I appreciate the compliment, but what's the point, Robert?"

"The point is you were close, in proximity, and we worked together. I couldn't work together with my brothers because they weren't there. I could have built a business with them, if I had stayed back home, but since I moved away I couldn't. Then I met you. When I needed something, you were there with me."

"So now that I'm here, I can help Jacobi, whereas I couldn't when I wasn't here."

Robert sighed. "Yes, you can help Jacobi now that you're there, but that's not my point. This Ronald guy sounds like a smart guy, and he's right there, and apparently he's trying to get you to do the right thing. Now, I'm here and you're there, so I can't help you, and you can't help me like you normally would. So figure out how to become this guy's friend because this is your friend who is near."

"I don't even know if I can trust him; if he's so smart, why is he still here?"

"Because some people are called to stay. Trust me on this one, Grant. I know this is a good guy."

"Okay," Grant said, not fully determined to take his friend's advice.

One More Night

He and Robert finished their conversation, and Grant determined one thing: he needed to stay one more night. Now, he needed to find Ronald to see if he could stay in the cabin again. Grant still hadn't met Hammond; he had only heard of him. Deciding to go back to the basketball court, Grant left the little refueling station where he had spent most of his day. At least this time he had eaten lunch.

When Grant arrived at the court, Ronald was there, chalking it. Grant didn't understand why they didn't just pour concrete or lay blacktop or do something to change this court from dirt and gravel. It seemed like a waste of time, but Ronald didn't appear to mind; he seemed to enjoy it.

"Ronald," Grant started.

"Oh, hey there, man! I thought you was leavin'."

"Was leaving, but I talked to my dad. I'm staying, but I'm not sure how long."

"Then it don't sound like you're stayin'. It sounds like you're visitin'."

"I'm staying," Grant said emphatically.

"Okay, you can stay at the cabin again. How long you want to rent it for?"

"A night."

"A night?!"

"Okay, a month."

"Done."

"Don't you need to talk to Hammond?"

"I already have. Don't worry 'bout that none, ya need to focus on gettin' to know yer boy. Now look hyear, everybody's got their spot, ya jus' need to find yers here, and with Jacobi. Now he plays ball, that's what he does. He eats it, dreams it, sleeps it, all that stuff. Ya gotta learn to play ball with him . . . and I don't mean jus' play ball, I mean learn to eat 'n dream 'n sleep what he does. Then ye can win."

"What about you?"

"I done won the lottery with that 'en, 'n I 'on't mean no Shirley Jackson type lottery neither. He's a best I ever coached. Speaking of, 'at boy's comin' 'round da hill right now. I can hear 'at ball poppin' a mile away. You best git ready, son. It's game time!"

Jacobi stepped onto the court and started warming up by completing his George Mikan and Larry Bird drills like he always did. Bouncing up and down on his spring-loaded legs, he hit layup after layup after layup from both sides of the rim and from underneath the basket. Working up a good sweat, he continued to focus on his form and his finish, not allowing for a missed shot. When he did miss, he made himself sit for five minutes. He hated sitting—it was the worst punishment, far worse than disciplining himself with something physical.

Grant watched and learned. Finally, after about fifteen minutes, Grant approached him.

"Wanna play?" Jacobi asked.

"Sure," Grant said, and took the ball to begin dribbling to warm up.

"You're not dressed for it," Jacobi commented.

"We'll play HORSE, and shoot the long ball," Grant replied.

"I know," Jacobi stated, and then he waited.

"Okay," Grant responded.

"I mean—I know about you. I know who you are."

Shocked, Grant looked at Jacobi, and with a bit of trepidation. "What do you know?"

"I know you're my dad."

"Who told you that?"

"Mom did after she saw you at the school. She was so mad about that pepper spray thing and then you, so she told me."

Grant knew there was so much more to the story that Jacobi wasn't telling him. He knew Katie despised him—so why she wrote that letter he didn't know—and that since she despised him, she didn't trust him. From everything he gathered, she was a protective mother bear, and surely she had warned Jacobi to stay away from Grant.

"Okay, well, I just found out a little over a week ago, so I guess we're both shocked."

"What do you mean?"

"I didn't know I had a son, until a few days ago, and when I found out I still wasn't sure what to do . . ."

"So what are you going to do?"

"I'm going to stay at Hammond's cabin, and come up here and play ball with you."

"Hammond's cabin? Where's that?" asked Jacobi.

"Over near Possum Squat, about fifteen minutes from here," Grant said.

"Oh," Jacobi said, and slapped the ball from Grant's hand and turned to hit a twenty-six-foot jumper.

With the dusk settling, Grant and Jacobi shot and talked—but mostly shot—games of HORSE into the night. There they were, father and son, stroking 3-pointers in the moonlight. As they shot, Grant kept replaying the mental picture of the father-son duo playing basketball earlier in the day—laughing, playing, and enjoying every minute of it. His thoughts triggered a memory, a memory of a time when he was a small child. His dad had placed his large hands over his own while they rubbed a hand planer over a board, scraping back and forth, until they received the finish they wanted. And now Grant was with his son, watching the night sky run its hands over the earth, enveloping it in cool darkness, and finishing the rough-hewn day.

Chapter 7: Turn

As the morning sun broached the mountain range on Grant's eighth day, something was decidedly different. The mystique had fallen and the cynicism had subsided; Grant had experienced acceptance. Up since 4 a.m., Grant strategized his approach to this situation. He would not transfer a portion of his business here, for it would consume too much of his time. He would contact Robin today, though, to let her know she needed to assume total responsibility for the next thirty days, and to give her a healthy boost in compensation. Virtually turning over the interest in the company for one month, Grant would not sell a portion of the business, but the decision making would be relegated to Robin. He had experienced brief, intermittent moments of apprehension, but none so strong as to dissuade him from his decision. He planted his feet.

"Robin, I need another month. I need you to handle it while I'm here. Can you do it?"

"Really! You're staying a whole month? Is everything okay?"

"Yes, everything's fine. I just need some more time away."

"That's the last thing I expected you to say; I thought you would be back before now."

"I would have if it weren't for Jacobi."

"Grant, that's so cute," she said sniffing. "You have to stay: he's your son! Awww! I'm so proud of you. We have everything under control here. Last week we picked up two more consistent runs that are under contract for a year. The best part is they coincide with two other runs we're already making. We have the capacity, so we don't have to buy any more equipment or make any hires. We only make more profit."

Grant felt better after his conversation with Robin. He knew could trust her to run the business; she was too competitive to let it fail.

Grant spent the rest of the day trying to figure out the best way to gain access into Jacobi's life without creating havoc. Katie was the linchpin. He had to figure out how to get near her without getting burned. He drew a circle on a blank sheet of paper. He wrote Katie's name in the middle. Around the circle he wrote down attributes of Katie he remembered from when they had met in university. On the far right side of the page he duplicated the same activity, listing all the characteristics he had witnessed and gathered from the townspeople concerning her now. In the center, he placed another circle filled with the overriding characteristics that were true both now and then: intelligent, passionate, involved, innovative, strong, empathetic, caring, loyal, friendly, and giving.

The first five seemed to be true and consistent; however, the second five seemed to be true but only consistent when they did not involve him. He realized he had a special place in her heart, probably right next to pedophiles and rapists. What a mountain he had to climb! *I've got to figure out how to make her not hate me,* he thought. *I've got to show her that I am on her side—that I am on her team. That's it! I'll join her in what she is passionate about, what she loves, and then we really will be on the same team!*

He did some research on teaching, sure that he could come in as a substitute or something. The laws were not as stringent as he thought. Since he had already earned a degree, Grant could qualify to teach any subject as long as he went through a few education courses, passed a test, and was certified under a probationary license. This was going to be easy.

The first thing I'll do is go meet her at one of her special groups. I'll keep playing ball with Jacobi at the court, and I'll meet with Katie at her pregnancy crisis group. And, so he did.

That evening, Grant went back to the school after the day had ended. The meeting time for the pregnancy crisis group was around 6:30 p.m., so Grant showed up early, as usual. The security at the school in the evening was minimal compared to during the school hours, so Grant walked right in. He made it past the scene of the epic battle between the Mountain Mauler and Raggedy Ann and kept walking. *Eerie*, he thought, *a place of learning that is such a place of violence. What's wrong with these people?* As he turned right at the first dark hallway, he saw the door ajar with the light on. He came to the door to find Katie, stretched up onto her tiptoes, pinning a letter to a bulletin board above her head. She turned quickly, and the magnanimous smile melted bitterly from her face.

"What are you doing here?" Katie interrogated.

"I am here to volunteer."

"For what?"

"For the crisis pregnancy group," Grant stated.

Katie blew through her nose in mock laughter and it came out like an elongated snarl and scoff. "Oh no, you're not! Who do you think you are? Don Quixote riding up on his trusty steed to battle pretend dragons and slay windmills?"

The literary allusion was lost on Grant, as was the reason for Katie's hostility.

"I'm just here to help. This is what I do; I help find solutions to problems. Why are you so resistant to me?" Grant asked.

"Tell me, Grant, what good have you done? What kid have you protected? What son have you raised? I did my research. You have never married, never had kids, never done anything for anyone. You have built an empire for yourself and you haven't shared any of it."

"Don't pretend you know me. You don't," he said glaringly.

A young pregnant girl began to walk through the door inquisitively, but when she saw the look on Katie's face, she slowly backed away into the hallway.

"Grant!" Katie barked. "You never came after me, you never came for your son, you never helped us, you abandoned me, and bastardized your son! And now you wonder why you are not received with open arms! Get out of here!" She stomped her foot. "Get out of here, you worthless jerk, you uncultured swine, you vagabond harvester—looking to plant your seed and harvest your crop without ever having worked the field! Get out!"

Grant knew Katie's theatrical display was to make him feel infinitely small and to prevent her from cussing a blue streak in the presence of one of her students. *Nobody talks like that—coping mechanism if I've ever seen one.* He held her stare for a moment, then turned and walked out the door.

Rejection

"Everything in me wanted to drill her into the wall with my fist!" Grant emoted, while a vein in his forehead looked as if it were about to burst. "But it would be like punching a mirror; in the shattering glass, *my* self-image would be broken!" Grant ranted at Ronald as they sat beside the court. "I have never wanted to hit someone so bad in all of my life. I can't hit a girl, so what do I have to do? Walk away! Like a little boy! I didn't leave her! She left me! I didn't abandon anyone; I didn't even know. Of course, now, after it's all over I know exactly what to say, but when she was yelling at me I just stood there like a statue and took it."

"More like a whipped hound!" Ronald remarked, chuckling.

"It's not funny," Grant replied, gravely.

"Sure it is, son, you walkin' in dere like you know whatcher doin' and runnin' out with ye tail tween yer legs. It'sa hoot!"

"Whatever," Grant said rubbing his eyes and silently conceding.

"Whatever's right, boy, whatevern' it takes . . . 'member that, whatevern' it takes."

"How could I forget?" Grant asked, rolling his eyes.

Just then, Jacobi came back to the court. It was early, just after dawn, and he was the first one to the court, as usual, with the exception of Grant and Ronald. Grant walked over to greet him, but Jacobi appeared uncharacteristically cold.

"I don't need you, you know?" he said.

"I never said you did," replied Grant in a frustrated tone.

"Well, I don't."

"Okay, I am here to help you, not for anything else," Grant responded.

"Help me!" Jacobi said with mock laughter. "How are you going to help me? I am better than you at basketball, and you haven't even been here for the last thirteen years. You don't know me, how are you going to help me?"

Grant turned to walk away, throwing his hands in the air, but then he stopped, and slowly turned back toward Jacobi. A warm breeze blew across the court, and then disappeared into the woods silently.

"What do you know about lanes?" Grant asked quietly.

"I know how to drive the lane, fill the lane, dominate the lane. What else is there to know?" he asked condescendingly.

"I mean shipping lanes, what do you know about shipping lanes?" Grant asked.

"I don't know what you're talking about," Jacobi
responded.

"Well I do. I know everything about shipping lanes, and I
know that over time they get tired and overused. If
someone creates a new road or a new passage, they can
create a new lane. And a new lane means quicker delivery,
which results in a satisfied customer, more profit, and
provides an opportunity for new businesses to plant new
facilities and make new money along that lane."

"I play basketball; I don't deliver freight."

"How often do you see someone drive down the middle?"

"What?"

"In a game, how many times do you see someone drive
right down the middle, right down the heart of the lane?"

"I don't know . . . once, maybe twice."

"Right, they may catch the ball in the middle, but people
don't *drive* down the middle, especially kids, because
they're scared. They think everyone is guarding the middle,
but nobody guards the middle—they just protect it. You
should make them guard it. In your next game, try it out;
drive right down the middle, watch the defense collapse
around you; see what it does for everyone else."

"I got to start warming up," Jacobi said absently, and he
dribbled down to the basket.

What the heck? Grant thought. *I try to do something right, and I get smacked in the face. I do nothing at all, and I get left alone. Maybe I should just do nothing . . . like everyone else around here.* Then he caught himself, and walking off the court, he spoke to himself aloud, "I'll die before I do nothing. I am going to do something. The first thing I'm going to do is stop thinking these stupid thoughts about quitting. I am not a quitter!" In the distance, he heard Jacobi pounding the ball against the backboard, alone.

Later that day, Grant walked into the administration building for the county schools. He tried to apply for a substitute teaching position, but they told him that they took applications only during the summer, and that he couldn't start until next fall. Three conversations, three fouls, and he would be sitting the bench for the second half.

He went to bed that night knowing that thirty days wouldn't be enough. He would be in for a long summer, and probably a long year. It would take that long for him to make some headway with Katie, get into the school system, watch Jacobi play ball through his eighth grade year, and know his role. Deeper into the mine shaft he walked, willingly, but now at least he had a light on his helmet.

Acceptance

A few days later, Grant decided to go back to Coal Miner's Fodder to visit Dale. He brought Ronald with him. As they were leaving the village, he saw a group of boys playing football on a flat, green tuft of land beside the road. In this mountainous region, there weren't many unused pieces of flat ground, so this one had been claimed for football. Grant saw one of the boys knock a heavyset boy down to his hands and knees. While he was down on all fours, a smaller blond-haired boy came and jumped on his back, planting both knees. The heavy boy's arms buckled, and he collapsed to the ground with a wail.

Ronald made Grant stop, and he ran over to the kids. Grant just hung back, but he could hear Ronald berating them after consoling the injured one. He encouraged them to work hard, keep playing, and keep it clean. Grant thought, *If I did that, they would throw rocks in my face, but if Ronald does it, they act like sheep.* Ronald came back, smiling warmly, and said, "New kid, not from 'round hyear."

"Figures," Grant replied. "Hospitality!" He snorted.

"They jus' don't know how to handle differn't. They learned from their daddies, who learnt from their'n, so that's jus' what they do."

Grant sipped his coffee as they rode along, content to sit and think without talking anymore. Ronald fell asleep.

When they arrived at Coal Miner's Fodder, Grant noticed something different. As he walked through the makeshift lot, he heard a bunch of men whooping and hollering and a clanging sound.

"Sounds like old Dale done got 'em some pits!" Ronald said.

"Some what?"

"Some horseshoe pits, son, ain't you never thrown no shoes, boy?"

"No, but let me guess, you have?"

"Few times, nothing fancy, though . . ."

Grant soon found out Ronald was a liar. When they went around the back of the restaurant, a crowd of men and boys were throwing horseshoes, begging Ronald to join. Half of them seemed to know him, even though Ronald and Grant were two hours away from home. Ronald shook hands and hugged and joked with the men, while one of the guys asked Grant to join, too.

"Mines are closed today . . . had us an accident yesterdee—safety regulations," said one of the men.

"Was anyone hurt?" Ronald asked.

"No, jus' our wallets," said another.

A huge man with shoulders as wide as a doorframe walked over. "Now look hyear, boys, let's get dis game started so I can show old Ronnie hyear who's da boss," he lisped through his missing front teeth.

Everyone laughed, a few of them nervously. Ronald started warming up, and then the games began. He threw perfect ringers, over and over. He shot some with his eyes closed, some left-handed, and a few underneath his leg. Dead ringers, *clank, clank*. Double ringers, *clank, clank*. All the while the huge guy with the missing front teeth, Billie, became angrier.

"You're a cheater, Ronnie!" he accused.

"At horseshoes?" Ronald asked. "Sheeeeeet! You're drunk, and it's not even noon yet. Get en ere and get ye some biscuits and sober up, boy."

Billie stayed and watched the next game, harassing most everyone who played. Grant kept a close eye on him, but Ronald seemed perfectly content. *Clank*! Another ringer.

Finally, Billie and a few of his buddies walked through the back into the room where B.G. performed. Ronald and Grant went around the front, and met up with Dale inside. The place was nearly crowded, but this time it was mainly men—home from the mines today. Ronald and Dale obviously knew each other, and shook hands, clapping each other on the shoulders like old buddies.

"How ya' been?" Dale asked.

"Good, jyou?" Ronald replied.

Grant noticed a marked difference in their accents. Both men obviously had some level of education, although it didn't show in their grammar, but Dale's speech was more polished while Ronald's was thicker but somehow less encumbered.

"How'd you meet this old boy?" Dale asked.

"Play'n ball, just like usual."

Grant and Dale shook hands as Ronnie kept talking. "You'll never believe who dis is," he said. "This hyear's Jacobi's daddy."

Before Dale could say a word, Grant said, "Look, I didn't even know that you knew him. I didn't even know him myself. I was just trying to find my son and see what happened."

Dale paused for a moment. "Well, what happened?"

"I met them, I talked to them, he and his mom, I think they both hate me equally—well, maybe she hates me just a little more—and now I'm here."

"What are you going to do?" Dale asked, chuckling.

"I'm just going to stay. I'll figure it out."

The Low Crawl

"Sometimes you gotta low crawl," Dale said. "Not like a cat in heat . . ." He and Ronald looked at each other and laughed. "More like a dog."

"I don't get it," Grant said as he leaned forward, almost hunching over the table, shifting his eyes from Dale to Ronald, then back to Dale.

Dale paused as a waitress Grant had not seen the first time he visited the restaurant dropped off a bucket of biscuits and three tin cups for coffee. She filled them and excused herself as all three of them politely thanked her. Then they turned back to their discussion.

"Now, yer a good guy, but sometimes you gotta low crawl, like in the mines. You gotta get down on yer belly, so ya don't hit yer head, and get deep in the muck and mire to get to where you can do some work. The work don't start by gettin' on your belly, you just gotta do that to get to where you can do some work."

A loud crash came from the other room, and some shouting. Grant followed Dale and Ronald into the stage room with the bright light, and found Billie kicking some poor guy in the ribs. The guy was curled up on the floor with his back pinned to the wall while Billie kicked the life and blood right out of him. He bellowed as a kick to the ribs forced the air from his lungs, and the sound held Grant motionless, but not Ronald and Dale.

Dale ran right up behind him and yelled, "Billie!" As Billie turned around, Dale smashed his face with a Mason jar. The glass exploded, shockingly loud, and the impact knocked Billie up against the wall, but Dale kept rushing him. As Billie bounced off the wall, Dale grabbed him around the neck with his right arm and pulled it tightly with his left. He threw his hip under Billie and turned, swinging Billie high in the air, tethered by his choke hold. Billie's legs and feet crashed into one of the rocking chairs and sent it splintering across the room. Dale landed on top of Billie with a tremendous thud, and squeezed his neck until his face turned purple. Billie tried to flop and lurch, reaching up to grab hold of Dale, but it was too late, for Ronald ran up, grabbed Billie's legs like a wheelbarrow, and stomped right on his crotch. Ronald left his foot there, pulled back on Billie's legs, and leaned back. Billie's hands reached down instinctively to protect himself, and Dale gave one big squeeze. Billie let out a gurgle and was out like a light.

Ronald told Grant the back story on the way home.

"'At man Billie kicked to the ground said Billie kept sayin' he was a lookin' at his woman, but there weren't no other woman in 'er but one of da waitresses. I guess ol

Billie thought that waitress was his, or every woman is his or somethin," Ronald mused.

"Dale should have hit him with one of those cast iron skillets from off the wall," Grant said.

"No, that'd killed him, and Dale's seen enough dyin', and don't want to see no more."

"But choking him out and stomping his crotch wouldn't?!" Grant laughed as he glanced sideways at Ronald. They had helped carry Billie out of the building and left him for his friends to handle. In the meantime, Dale attended to the man Billie had attacked. Refusing the hospital, the victim was cleaned, fed, and taken home by Dale personally. With Dale gone, Ronald and Grant helped clean up the restaurant, said goodbye to the staff, and decided to go home.

"What do you mean?" Grant asked. "About Dale seeing enough dying . . ."

"Well, 'bout thirty years ago, Dale was 'ere when da mine collapsed. He had a crew in 'er, and the shaft caved in. Some of 'em boys died cause they was in 'ere for over thirty days. One of 'em boys killed hisself, in 'ere, drove hes own head ona pickaxe. Couldn't take it, they said. Screamed and screamed till he bled out. They say it took 'eours. Only thing that got 'em out of 'ere was B.G."

"B.G.? What did he do?"

"He's a miner, and a good one at that. Back when he was a youngin' he used to play ball some, too, and he's a scrappier than a buncha half-starved wolve's pups. Anyways, B.G.'s always been tellin' stories, whole family does. And 'at's what he did. He told stories to keep 'em boys live till someone could dig 'em out. It took over a month to get 'em boys out, but they did it, and everyone said Dale and B.G. is what kept 'em alive . . . but Dale said B.G. is the only one who kept 'em sane."

"So that's why they're friends?" Grant replied, curious.

"Partly," Ronald responded. "'Ere's more to it. After 'em three boys died, one from the collapse, one from pneumonia, and the othern killed hisself, Dale took it real hard. He'd come from a family of miners and moonshiners, but he'd never been a real drunk. Till then. He started drinkin' erey night and day. All the women round hyear loved him, so he started goin' home with a differn't 'en erey night. None of da men would stand up to 'em cause ereyone knew Dale never lost a fight, never. He plumb left his wife and kids for booze en other men's wives till B.G. gotta hold of 'em."

"What did he do, to 'get ahold of him?'" Grant asked.

"I don't rightly know; it's kinda like local folklore . . . legend. He caught 'em comin out of some other man's house one night and convinced him to come home with 'em. Next day, Dale come out all blubberin' and stammerin', holdin' a Bible. Now, I don't know what he done, but B.G.'s a storyteller. I'm thinkin' he got ol' Dale in 'ere and told him some stories that got him so twisted up he didn't know what to do. Or maybe, he got him so straightn'd out he knew zactly what ta do. All I know is what I been told, and that B.G. went home with Dale, watched him 'pologize for what he'd done, and Dale stayed with B.G. until Dale's wife let 'em back in the house. After that, Dale's wife made him promise to quit da mines, the booze, and the women— and he did. He'sa changed man. Changed 'at night he spent at B.G.'s house. He started goin' to church ever' Sunday and took his girls with 'em, too. Then they started this restaurant and worked as a family ere' since."

"So, B.G.'s a religious man?"

"I don't know 'bout B.G., not sure. I jus' know Dale is, and now B.G. lives with him. Stays right 'ere at Coal Miner's Fodder, tellin' 'em stories."

"That's bizarre!"

"You know B.G.'s nephew plays ball with Jacobi, don't cha?"

"Yes, I've met him. They call him Dynamite, but I thought he was his great-nephew," Grant replied.

"Same differnce! Boy's an entertainer just like his uncle, 'cept he's a poet, and he's got a mean daddy."

"Well . . ." Grant trailed off and remained silent until they arrived at the cabin. *What am I supposed to say to that?*

Chapter 8: Forgiveness

Grant did the low crawl. He kept showing up at the court and playing ball with Jacobi. He quietly acquiesced all the decision making power within his company to Robin, and Grant focused on Jacobi—and Katie. He had lost about sixteen pounds; he didn't feel like eating or weight training for the past three months. He kept up his running, but mainly he played basketball, worked with all the other boys who came to the court, bought them shoes and clothes and jerseys, read books, and volunteered anywhere Katie volunteered. At first, she rejected him, so he quit talking to her. He just showed up and started working. When the events were over, he left, without ever saying a word.

Grant's dad, Mr. Erlosung, kept his distance at Grant's request. Grant's mom, however, peppered him with questions. She patrolled for information about her grandson. The conversations grew shorter. Grant pulled away. He loved his parents, but he couldn't lose his focus. Interruptions are the nemesis of concentration.

Jacobi grew some over the summer. He was now a good inch taller than Grant and had just turned fourteen. He played on traveling teams, at the school, and anywhere he could get an opportunity. Grant came to watch him play, but he always sat alone, away from Katie. Word had spread that Grant was Jacobi's father, and it was the town scandal, or that was what Ronald told him. Everyone knew Jacobi had grown up without his dad, so why it was so scandalous when Grant showed up? He didn't know.

He and Jacobi talked at the court by the white building, which Grant found out was the church, but they hadn't really become close—they were just cordial. Grant kept showing up, kept helping out, kept working with Ronald on helping Jacobi improve his game, and kept reading books on relationships and family. One word, which he hated, continued to show up in the books: *forgiveness*. Every time Grant thought about Katie, which was often, he boiled with frustration. Forgiveness was not an option, but he needed her to tolerate him, so he could have a real relationship with his son and not be so ostracized in this community.

And then it happened.

It was mid-August, and it was hot—oppressively hot. The humidity hung in the air draping the trees, ground, and roads with thick musk. Walking up the mountain was like trying to swim in hardened bacon grease, but not nearly as delicious. The humidity clogged Grant's pores as he played one last game with Jacobi for the day. Covered in grime and sweat, they were both filthy and playing intensely when Grant farted going up for a layup. Jacobi burst into a fit of laughter, and that made Grant laugh even harder. Apparently, he'd had too much to eat the night before while celebrating his probationary teaching certificate and new job as a pre-Math I teacher at Possum County High School. Watching each other laugh only exacerbated the comedy, and soon Jacobi doubled over. He was crying, and so was Grant. In their laughter, Grant realized that they laughed just alike.

Ronald, keenly aware of what was happening, decided to disappear. A warm breeze blew through the dank air. Grant stood, covered in sweat and dirt, and walked over and gave Jacobi a hug, and to his surprise, the boy—his boy— hugged him back. *No test*, thought Grant, *I don't need a paternity test to know this is my boy.* As Jacobi moved aside, Grant saw her walking up the hill, Katie was almost in front of him. *Oh, God!*

While she stood in the sweltering heat, sweat beaded up and dripped from her chin. Her radiant face and porcelain skin were weighted with perspiration, and she looked Grant right in the eyes with determination, then down and away at her feet. As Grant walked toward her, slowly, she raised her head and her pink lips pouted a bit as she rolled the bottom one with her teeth. Her hair was pulled back with a few wisps falling about her ears, and the top of her tiny circular glasses was fogged near the thin-wire frame. Grant was lost in her beauty, but his reservation tugged at his soul, holding him like quicksand.

"Jacobi, I need to speak with Grant, please. Can you give us a moment?" Katie directed her son.

"Yes, ma'am," he said warily.

He walked over to the basket and began to shoot. Katie motioned with her hand, and she and Grant walked off the court to the other side of the building. Grant stood like a tree lost in a forest—surrounded by everything he wanted, but unsure how to connect with it. Katie looked him in the eyes; his heart stopped.

"Grant," she said, "I'm sorry." A small tear intermingled with the sweat on her cheek and ran off her face falling to her chest and soaking into her shirt. Her eyes reddened, and she paused, like a hurt child, gasping for breath before the next wail, "I'm sorry for how I've treated you, what I've done to you, what I've said to you, and I . . . I . . . want you to forgive me." Tears streamed down her face.

Grant, momentarily overcome with compassion, consoled her, "It's okay, it's okay. Look, it will be okay."

Katie wiped her face on her shirt and looked up at him, only to see it was not okay.

The words "forgive me, forgive me, forgive me" rolled around in Grant's head, and he stepped back and looked at her with disdain and scorn.

"Forgive you?" he grunted. "I hate you." His face reddened; his eyes and veins bulged at his scrunched brow. His jaw clenched and his head started to shake violently. He let out a guttural yell, just to unclench his face and neck. "Do you have any idea what you've done to me, what you've taken from me? You left me, and I looked for you! I couldn't find you! There was no address, no way to contact you, and you just left! And I didn't know what to do, so I waited, and then I left, or did I go back? I don't know! So I left, but I couldn't forget . . . and then, fourteen years later I get a letter from you telling me you have stolen my son from me! My family, my dreams! My dreams!" He poked himself in the chest with such force he thought he might shatter his own sternum. "So I come here to be treated like some deadbeat father, when I never even had the chance to be a father! Then you play the single-mom card as if I abandoned you! You abandoned me, and you took my family with you!"

As Grant raged, Katie cowered. He had never been so angry, so consumed with hate and rage. This was different than the alcoholic's rage so common in mining country;

this was pure internal combustion, overflowing, erupting from every orifice.

"This place has been hell, and without so much as a kind word you want me to—"

Grant felt himself lurch forward and his head flew back from the unsuspecting jolt. Jacobi was crawling on top of him, screaming and punching, trying to hit him in the face, but Grant was too quick. He flipped Jacobi over his back and harshly threw him to the ground. Jacobi's breath escaped with the impact. Up Grant pounced, ready; he looked at Jacobi and then at Katie. It was over. He was done. He turned his back on them both and walked away.

Katie ran over to check on Jacobi who jumped to his feet.

"I'll kill him!" Jacobi said. "I'll kill him."

She touched her son, cupping his face as she had done when he was a small child. Pulling his face down close to hers, she whispered, "He's just hurt, Jacobi, he's just hurt." Jacobi tried to pull back, but Katie held on tightly as only a mother can. By the time she turned back to see Grant, he was nowhere to be found, but she called out after him anyway.

And in the distance, among the trees and within the clouded forest of his mind, Grant heard a voice calling his name. But he kept walking.

Grant arrived at his cabin and took a seat at the circular table he had made his desk. The screaming had not provided him any catharsis; it had only served to make him angrier. He kept replaying it in his mind. Katie, her face and fear, Jacobi, his hurt and anger, and he, standing there aware that it was all over, all for nothing. As Grant sat, he felt his frustration arise within him, and he began shaking again.

Catharsis

Grant tore through the doorway in an impassioned blaze of frustration. Sprinting, he abraded the clovers, jumped the creek, and uprooted the grass with his shoes while using all the force his legs could exert. Once he reached the edge of the yard, he was on his toes at top speed. Leaping onto the gravel road, his gait became ever quicker and lighter. Arms swinging, knees gliding forward, stride outstretched, Grant maxed out his speed and oxygen as he reached the apex of the hill. His heart rate climbing ever higher, he focused his mind on his current task, avoiding the pain.

Jacobi

Jacobi walked back onto the court where he had grown up. His mom had walked away after he asked for some time alone. He had become interwoven with this place, this hallowed ground, his place of rest and peace, but now it had been molested, adulterated. The days and nights and weekends practicing here were a resonant memory, a piece of him, from whence he came. But today was different. The court was still the musty red clay it had always been, with the bungled chalk lines perpetually blurred by dust or washed away by rain, but Jacobi was neither nostalgic nor immutable. He was ablaze.

Grant

The pain, the burning sensation in Grant's mind, was ever present. The pain of loss and self-loathing, of apathy and fear, of rejection and failure, culminated in this run. He thought of his previous life and the void in his soul. He pushed forward as his pulse mounted in his temples. He could hear his heart in his head and feel it in his ears. His eyes blurred and lungs roared, but the pain did not diminish. The pain pulsated in the cage of his chest and mounted in the cells of his body. He could not escape, no matter how hard he ran.

Jacobi

Stomping across the court violently, Jacobi switched the ball back and forth between his legs with each step. A cloud of dust rose as the ball slammed against the dirty court and ricocheted back into his palm. He ended his assault on the earth at the left side of the basket, and he began his never-ending drills. Off the left side with the left hand, against the board, through the net, into his hand, then back up on the right side again. He repeated this drill over and over and over. Each time he jumped higher, with more vigor and more sweat. This was an old drill, nothing new here except the anger. The anger that burned and did not dissipate, the anger that consumed but did not burn, the fire that presented no ashes, left no residue, but choked out smoke from its smoldering embers was inside him.

Grant

Grant reached a downhill slope and his pace quickened. He burned through strides at an uncontrollable speed. He strode out onto the asphalt highway, and he felt his oxygen deplete, his legs cramp, his throat burn with fire, and tears stream down his cheeks, but he kept running. He was dangerously close to blacking out; he knew it, but he still kept running. Why wouldn't the pain subside? Why wouldn't the pain of his body overtake the pain of his mind? His speed increased. Music thumped in his ears as did his pulse. That eternal bass thumping, cymbals shattering, and voices screaming.

Jacobi

Jump right, up and in. Jump left, up and in. Jump right, up and in. Higher and higher, more and more, yet Jacobi still couldn't clear his mind. His face was red and hot, his hair moppy and sweaty. The humidity was thick and tangible, yet Jacobi continued jumping. He switched to the left side. He drilled the ball high off the top of the backboard on his way up, and caught it at the apex of his jump. He did this again and again. He moved to the right side, and continued the drill. He jumped higher and higher, mastering his timing so he could launch the ball at the beginning of his jump and rip it out of the air at his highest height. Down he came again, right back up, over and over. His face was heated and his body weary, but he still jumped.

Grant

Grant was running toward a dead end and did not know how to stop. The road before him seemed endless, but he felt so restricted . . . he couldn't get it out. It, that irascible, nebulous pain plaguing him. It, that indeterminable fear chasing him. It, that ubiquitous defeat owning him! Everything blurred as the sweat and tears burned his eyes. As he streaked around a long, downhill, leftward curve, his legs began to give way. His arms began to flail and roll as if he were groping at the air to propel himself forward or slow himself down. Fear seized him. He couldn't stop, but he couldn't maintain. His feet began slipping and his bodily functions gave way. In a sudden thrust of compulsion, Grant slipped from the edge of the road, vomiting and crashing simultaneously; his chin bounced against the pavement, almost severing his tongue. And then all was black—and blue.

Jacobi

There was fire in his eyes, fire and sweat. Each landing ground his gritted teeth even harder. With a clenched jaw, snarled face, furrowed brow, he jumped again and again. He let out a visceral roar, his voice nearly cracking at the end. "I hate him!" he screamed, and his thigh muscles screamed right back. His body was not as buoyant as it had been earlier; the coils in his legs had loosened. He missed the ball as it bounced high off the left side of the backboard, and his rage intensified. Swiping the rolling ball off the ground, he turned in disgust and ran back toward the rim. He began his assault on the backboard—and himself— again. Up and down, side to side, each jump harder than the one before, but then something loosened in his head. The left side of his neck, the back left side, shot a quick, pinching pain to the base of his skull. He kept jumping. Jacobi felt something like a small pellet, maybe a pebble, rattling in his skull with each jump. Up and down, side to side, tightness in the chest . . . he couldn't see straight.

Grant

Grant awoke choking on blood and the smell of urine, feces, and vomit. He wished for death, but it evaded him for another day. He was alive and squirming in radical pain. His teeth ached and his eyes felt as if they were leaking burning dust. He couldn't stand, and he dared not, for he hoped that death would come quickly . . . but a tormentor stood before him. A rescuer, one to torment Grant back to life, held his hand and spoke loudly, "Can ya hyear me? Do ya know who ye are? Are ya okay?" And all was black again—and gray.

Jacobi

Facedown, Jacobi pushed the ball against the ground as he lay almost prone, and fired himself up off the ground. A modified push-up, with the ball acting as both propulsion device and impact absorption, was Jacobi's new form of exhaustion. Up and down, and up and down he pushed. The race in his mind would not let him stop, but his body cried for mercy. Jacobi cried, too, but not for mercy. He cried because he couldn't stop: the pain, the frustration, the exercise, the hate. He just kept going.

Grant

Grant awoke in a bathtub screaming as an old man poured cold water over his body. The tub filled with icy water, and Grant began to convulse. He reached for the side to pull himself out, but he slipped and cracked the back of his head against the side of the tub. Down he went again, for the third time . . . he was drowning.

Jacobi

Up and down, up and down, legs in, legs out, Jacobi
pushed and pushed and pushed. He couldn't push the
ground away, and he couldn't fly. No matter how hard he
pushed, he only got weaker. The pushups became shorter,
the jumps became lower, his form grew sloppier, his
headache increased. That little pebble rolling around in his
cranium grew in size. His neck hurt, as did his shoulders,
back, calves, and hamstrings. Acidity built in his throat, but
he could not stop. The burning in his eyes was a mix of
sweat and tears. "I can't stop!" he screamed as he jumped
up and began jumping once more.

Grant

Grant awoke again to the crashing sound of thunder. His head felt like a pick had been shoveled through his brain, and the noise was unbearable. He held his hands to his head and pressed. *What was that noise?* he questioned, and then he heard the thunder crack again and saw the lightning. The rain pelted off the tin roof, drowning out almost any other sound, but Grant cried out, "Water, water, I need some water!"

Jacobi

Jacobi's vision became hazy. The peripheral was a gray, blurred mass. All Jacobi could see was straight ahead, like looking through fogged binoculars. He moved back to jumping, sweating, screaming, gurgling. Acid built in his throat, but he didn't stop. The ball had long ago rolled away. He was just jumping, pounding his hands against the backboard and then returning to earth. Rage flowed through the veins protruding from his temples. His eyes nearly closed, and his pulse reverberated in his brain. Seeing was a mystery, and it went unsolved. Nothing was left but blackness and rage. Jump, jump, jump, raindrop, jump, jump, jump raindrop. It began to rain. Mud began to form under the goal, and the jumping continued. The rain cooled, but Jacobi

didn't feel it. He didn't feel anything. He no longer felt the rage, he became it—or it became him. Jump, jump, jump, crash.

Grant

Grant lay quivering in an unknown bed, yelling, "You could have killed me! You could have killed me!" He could move, but he didn't want to because he felt his brain may ooze out if he did. His tongue was swollen, almost useless, and the water barely slaked his thirst. His ears popped, and some pressure released; he opened his mouth to breathe, and he fell asleep.

Like Father, Like Son

Jacobi's legs slipped out from beneath him, and he fell jarringly hard, face first, into the puddle of tears and rainwater. As his face smacked the ground, the softening of the rain kept him from breaking a bone. The past, the past, it had caught up with him now, and he lay—the left side of his face in the mud. If only the rain could wash it all away . . . maybe one more jump—then darkness.

Hangover

Grant awoke two days later feeling slightly alive. He had been nursed back to health by the old man and his wife: the Halcombs they called themselves. Ronald came over and spent some time with him, poking fun at him for passing out and crashing on the rocks. He had another visitor too— Katie—she had come that morning after hearing about his staying at the Halcombs. She didn't know Jacobi had a similar, albeit less dangerous, experience. When Jacobi came to, he just walked home, showered, and went to bed. He didn't receive quite the same fanfare as Grant.

"Hello, Grant," she said as she walked in the room, and Ronald sneaked out as he always seemed to do when Grant thought he needed him the most.

Grant shivered. He sat up in the bed, fully lucid, and looked at Katie, drinking her in. Here before him was the mother of his son, who had worked up the nerve to ask for his forgiveness— as if he owed her—and the one whom he had berated. He had screamed at her and thrown her son to the ground. *Why was she here?*

"I'm sorry . . . I'm sorry for what I said, for what I did," he said. "It's my fault. I'm responsible for all of this. I screwed this all up and that's why I acted like a jerk. I was afraid."

She sat in a little chair beside the bed and quietly whispered, "It's okay, Grant, it's okay." And it really was okay. She tried to continue talking, but her emotions overcame her and she paused to breathe. Exhaling slowly, she said, "Grant, will you come to church with me on Sunday?"

"What? I mean, yes, but—" His mind caught up with his words. "Yes, I'll be there on Sunday."

"Good. You won't have time to come soon, so I would like it if you came with me now."

"What do you mean I won't have time?"

"Oh, you'll see," she said. "Rest up, and I'll see you Sunday at 9:30."

"Okay, bye, Katie," he said as she walked out the door.

"Bye, Grant," she whispered as she pulled it closed.

Oh my gosh, she is beautiful! he thought as she left the room. *But why did she invite me to church? And then say I wouldn't have time for it later? Weird. She came all the way over here to talk for one minute, and just to leave? I don't get it.* He looked up on the chest of drawers by the door, and atop of it stood a plastic rose, encased in glass, with the words "Family is Forever" painted on the wooden base.

Amazing Grace

Sunday morning, Grant got up early to go for a run. This
was his first day back running since his little episode. He
still hadn't seen Jacobi, and he was nervous about seeing
him today. As he ran, he came upon a black snake crossing
the road. Taking it as a bad omen, he turned around and
hustled home. Having no idea what he was in for, he
showered and shaved, and dressed in olive-colored dress
pants, a blue shirt, brown, shiny shoes, and suspenders,
along with a blue, white, and brown horizontally striped tie.

When he arrived at the church, he realized the error of his
attire. It was still August, and hotter than a sunburnt
seatbelt buckle. He walked up to the church to be greeted
by a balding man with a nasally voice.

"Welcome to da house of tha Loward-a! I'ma Reverend
Smalley and I 'sume youra Grant'a!"

They shook hands and exchanged pleasantries, but Grant
didn't ask how the reverend knew who he was. It was
church; everybody knew.

Katie arrived, dressed coolly in a patterned strapless
dress, a neck full of pearls, pearl earrings, a small hat, and
white gloves. The redness of her lipstick matched the large
ribbon on the bodice of her dress. She had not worn her
glasses. Jacobi, on the other hand, wore shorts and a shirt

with three buttons and a collar, white of course. *He's smart*, Grant thought, and the three of them sat on a bench together. The church began to fill with several people speaking loudly and cackling. The smell of body odor was pungent, but Grant pretended not to notice. One thing he did notice was that most of the women wore dark dresses or skirts that almost dragged the ground. They were covered nearly head to toe.

The men filed in and took their seats, too, and it all seemed to be a well-orchestrated routine. One man, with a tremendous nose and forehead, stood up to lead the group, and they all stood to their feet. Grant looked around warily. The man started in a deep nasally tone.

"Aaaaaaaaaahhhhhmmmaaaaaaa‖ziiiiing graaaaaace‖hoooooaaawww sweeeeeeeeet ta souunda‖daaaat saaaaaved‖aaaa wreeeetch‖liiake meeeeeeeeee!"

Grant stood, breathless. When the man finished his elongated cry, the whole crowd followed the line, again, in the same, slow, sonorous tempo the man had used. *Eternity pasts quicker than this*, Grant thought. He began counting the time on "Iayaee wontce was lost, buut now . . ." and counted to forty-two before the man stopped, and then the crowd followed. The circle was definitely unbroken.

When that song finally ended as well as the next two, the new moon phase began. Some men gathered up to pray aloud at the front of the church, and they spoke in their broken English, but with a twist . . . now it sounded older, more religious.

"We thank thee, o' Lowarda, for thine bountiful harvest ye have placed upont us hyear, and a we give thee reverence forn thine goodness. To thee, we offern' our thanksgiving and our praise, from our grateful abundance, amen!"

The men walked to the end of the benches, which Grant had heard someone call a pew, and began passing a plate down the row. One man would rap his knuckles against the side of the plate before he handed it to the next row. People put in bills, coins, and slips of paper, but Grant just sat there for a moment. When he saw the plate coming his way, he quickly dug into his wallet, pulled out some bills, threw them in the plate, and passed it on.

A lady stood up and began telling how her son was on drugs, "that old dope," and he needed prayer. At that point, Grant contemplated some of "that old dope" himself. *This is ridiculous*, he thought. *It's more than one hundred degrees in here. These people are dressed in clothes to the*

floor, moaning out wails, and throwing money in plates!
How much longer is this going to last?

Finally, the man who had met him at the door stood up to speak. At least this much Grant remembered from church when he was young, until the man started speaking.

"Well-ah, friends-ah, if ye, if ye, have y, y, ye, Bibles with ye today, turn to John chapter one-ah! And the Bible says-ah, 'In a beginningah, was the Word-ah . . .'" and he went on like that adding 'ah' after every phrase. "Ya gotta be saaaaved-ah," he bellowed, and "ye gotta loooove one another-ah!"

Grant would have "looooved" to walk right out of there, but he didn't. When he thought reprieve was likely, his plans were foiled again. Another younger man stepped up to the podium and began to speak. Although he spoke with an accent, his delivery and speech were much more palatable and reasonable. He quoted some verses from some books named Isaiah and James, and one verse from Matthew.

After this younger man sat down, the singer stood back up and led everyone in a song where they repeated "Just As I am" over and over and over again. A few people went down to the front to pray, and Grant prayed, too—to wake up from this nightmare. Then church was over, and most of the people crowded around the front door outside to smoke or spit or talk.

Grant waited until he, Katie, and Jacobi had walked out of earshot, and as politely as he could said to Katie, "What was that?"

"That was church," she said.

"No it wasn't," Grant responded, "or not like I remember it. How are you supposed to know the songs, and why do they last so long? It's like they think if they hold out the notes longer, then it's more sacred or something."

"You know the songs by following the leader, silly. It's called 'lining up.' Have you never read *To Kill a Mockingbird*?"

"No-ah, I haven't-ah, I can't read-ah," Grant said mockingly. He could tell by the look on Katie's face that he had taken it too far.

"Grant, be serious," she requested.

"Okay, I'm serious. Thanks for inviting me to church. I definitely *learned* something."

All the while, Jacobi remained silent, walking along with his mom and Grant. At this juncture he took his opportunity. "Mom, after lunch I need to go work on my game," he stated.

"That's fine, dear," Katie responded, and then she popped the question. "Grant, will you join us for lunch?"

With a frog in his throat the size of his fist, he said, "I'd love to."

They walked the sweltering half-mile to Katie's home and dined on hot white bean chili, corn bread, salad, carrots, and peas. As they talked, Grant had many of his questions answered. He could sense that Jacobi was still hurt, and that Katie was still sensitive, still guarding something. She typically visited her parents, who lived about two miles away, on Sunday, but not this Sunday. Grant asked about Hatchet and her parents. Hatchet turned out to be her cousin, and his name was Vern—short for Vernon. Her cousin had started using drugs at eleven, and by fourteen he was a complete burnout. He got the same girl pregnant twice in the same year. After the second child was born, she ditched him and the children, and then his parents kicked him out. Furious with his sister, Katie's dad took Vern and his two kids in to help raise them.

That Katie ever came from such a family floored Grant, so he asked politely, "Katie, what makes you so different . . . different from the people around here, different from your, well, I mean—"

"My family?"

"Yes," he replied, thankful she had supplied the word.

"Well," she began, "I would say reading, but several people around here read. You would probably be surprised how literate this area is. Many people here have read the Bible multiple times, as well as commentaries, and several of the classics. My old childhood friend, Elma Jean, reads more than one hundred books a year, but she still thinks very much like most everyone else. I have thought about this a lot, Grant, and the difference between the others and me is I believe what I read. I don't believe everything I read; I just believe that the ideals in books are possible. I believe it's possible to love a person truly, to have courage, character, hope, and ingenuity. I believe people can change, and they can change the world. I believe that fairies can exist, as does G.K. Chesterton, and I believe in struggle, passion, peace, and sacrifice. I let the ideas I read in books inspire me, and these ideas make me focus on something other than myself, and that's the difference."

Her wisdom astounded Grant. *No wonder everyone says she's a brilliant teacher*, he thought. The lunch ended with Jacobi not having said a word the whole time. Katie was coming around, but Jacobi was fading away. After helping with the dishes and sweeping the floor, Grant told Katie good-bye, and thanked her multiple times for lunch. As he

walked out the door, Jacobi whizzed right by him, headed
for the court, and Grant tagged along.

Grant could physically feel the separation between them.
He took a deep breath through his nostrils and
approximately three hundred feet from the house said,
"Hey, Jacobi, turn around please."

Jacobi whirled around and faced Grant. His glare was
fierce.

"This might not mean much," Grant said, "but I'm sorry.
I am sorry for throwing you off me, I'm sorry for not being
here when you grew up, and I'm sorry for not knowing how
to treat you now. It's my fault. You're a great ki—man."

Jacobi looked up and out of the corner of his right eye
while clamping down on his bottom lip. His eyes seemed
on the verge of tears, from rage or relief Grant didn't know.
Jacobi turned his back and continued walking, this time
dribbling the ball he had brought with him from home.
Grant knew everything wasn't perfect, but he had smoothed
it over the best he could—for now.

Finally

"School has changed since I was in high school; that's for certain," became Grant's mantra for the week of in-service training. A "growth mindset" seemed to be a euphemism for this new journey on which he was about to embark. He had thought he was going to teach math, not patrol hallways and bathrooms, direct traffic, counsel emotional students, break up fights, call on parents, write multiple iterations of lesson plans, discipline strategies, and rituals/routines, all the while attending professional development courses, setting up his classroom, making copies, and creating "engaging" lessons.

"I thought the teacher was supposed to 'teach,' not entertain," he complained to Katie one day when he stayed in his classroom past an 8 p.m. meeting with other math teachers to discuss how they were going to get their students to engage in the lessons. "Why can't I just teach the lesson, and if they fail, they fail?"

"You can, and they will. Or you can meet them where they are and celebrate the progress as you build them up. Think of it like this: Should you be measured on the same scale of parental efficacy as a dad who has spent the last fourteen years with his son?"

"Uhh . . . no?" He felt the hammer cock, and he waited for it to fall.

"Then you can't do that with students. Sure, they have been in school for years, but some have disabilities, all of them here have economic disadvantages, and, most importantly, most of their parents don't care. The parents don't value education—so neither does the kids—but what they do value is entertainment! So give them what they value, and build them up."

"That seems like a lot of handholding and circus performing," Grant said, relieved by her response.

Katie turned on him. "Grant, do you want to have a relationship with Jacobi?"

"Yes! Haven't I made it clear?"

"Yes, you have, but I'm the only one with any sweat equity in him. I raised him, myself, but I'm not only giving you a chance to get to know him, I'm holding your hand. When you're not around, I'm bragging to Jacobi about you. When you are around, I'm dropping not-so-subtle hints as to how you can get to know him. In order to get someone where you want him to be, you have to meet him where he is, and, yes, sometimes you have to hold his hand."

Her passion was so evident that Grant knew the conversation was over. He said no more, but Katie did.

"While we're on this subject, let me explain something to you. I have built my life around my son. I teach, so I can spend time with him; I read books on basketball, so I can connect with him; and I introduced him to Ronald, so he could develop Jacobi's God-given talent. You might believe," she paused, "that I stole some of those years from you. And I'm not going to deny it. But, Grant," and she looked deep into his eyes, "I gave you one of the most wonderful, talented, well-rounded kids ever—in the middle of one of the most exciting parts of his young life! I love him with all my being, Grant, and to share him with you rips my heart out . . . but I do it because it's right . . . and I can't change the past."

Dumbfounded, Grant struggled out, "Thank you, and I'm sorry if I have been insensitive. Thank you for . . . Ja—" he looked down at his feet, "for caring."

Grant went back to the cabin he had rented for the year, and went to lie down. He wondered about Robin and his company—he hadn't spoken with her in more than a month. He thought about Jacobi, then school, then basketball, then Katie. Waves of exhaustion rocked him; the thin line between being awake and asleep became ever so tenuous, but his eyes popped open. He knew he must do it; he had been avoiding it, even avoiding thinking about it, for the past month. Alone, in the solitude of his mind, Grant chose then and there to forgive Katie. The past was behind him, and, yes, he still bore the scars and felt the pain, but he would no longer blame Katie. He would love her—whatever that meant. He rolled over and slept the deepest sleep he had slept since childhood.

Chapter 9: Ball

The next day was chaos. On the first day of school, the kids came down the hallway laughing, bouncing, playing, but they also came pushing, shoving, cussing, and fighting. Grant stood outside the door to shake hands and greet his students, but many of them just walked on by. Some sneered, others ignored, and a few shook his hand politely—mostly the girls. He tried to start his first class.

"Good morning, ladies and gentlemen!" he called. The boisterous behavior continued. "I said, good morning, ladies and gentlemen!" he called again. He clapped his hands loudly and demanded, "Okay, everyone take out your pencil and paper!" They looked at him as if he were a lunatic as they continued talking. He realized: nobody had a pencil and paper. He passed out the supplies, as the volume level and his irritation increased. "Write your name on the top of the paper in the upper left-hand corner," he called. A few of the girls began to write their names while several students just let their papers fall to the floor. At that moment, a few of the boys, who were bigger than he, began to play cards in the back of the room.

Grant never gained control. He didn't even take roll by the time the bell rang . . . and he wondered why he had ever chosen to do this job. *Jacobi's not even here*, he thought, and then he remembered—he had done it for Katie.

His goal the rest of the day was to take roll in each class, and he was successful. By the end of the day, he wondered how he would ever get through this year, let alone see any of Jacobi's games. Sitting at his desk nervously and running his fingers through his hair, he made an immediate decision: *I'll get fired before I miss a game.* For the first time he could remember, he had completely chosen a relationship ahead of an occupation. *This isn't easy to do,* he thought, *and I don't know why. I don't need the money, so why is it so hard for me to pick time with Jacobi over time spent here?*

Grant packed his stuff and headed for the middle school. The population of the area wasn't big enough to have two separate buildings, one for middle school and one for junior high, so it was all housed in one building. Jacobi, an eighth grader, would have classes in the southern part of the school, right next to the gym. *Time to finally watch Jacobi play school ball*, Grant thought, and he couldn't wait.

When he arrived, the basketball players were all sitting outside on the curb together. A smattering of students seemed to be impatiently waiting on their rides, but, curiously, all the teachers were outside, too.

"What's going on?" Grant asked after he jumped out and hustled over to Jacobi.

"Bomb threat," Jacobi replied angrily. "It happened twenty-two times last year, and it started again today, on the first day of school. We sat in our second-to-last period class when the principal came over the loudspeaker and announced to exit the school."

"That ain't how it happened!" another boy chimed in as he stood up. "It was like 'is, we were in between classes walkin' down the hall, whena alarm went off 'n eryone started screamin' and runnin' out da buildin'."

"No," another one started, "we's in da gym, when 'is kid come runnin' through, screamin', with dynamite strapped to his chest. We all ran out after 'at!"

Then Dynamite stood and said:

> The bombs were dropped, but faking,
> The kids ran out, escaping,
> Taking their sanity and life with 'em,
> 'Cept, um, their dignity is still in there a-quaking.

He rattled off his lyrical tale, as the principal walked over.

"Boys, going forward, all practices will be held down da street, till we get this under control."

Jacobi rolled his eyes and whispered under his breath, "If we get it under control . . ."

Practice

For the first two weeks of school, the boys practiced on the outdoor courts in the summer sun. The middle school coach, Coach Combs, wasn't happy with the circumstances, but he also had the most phenomenal athlete in the area on his team, so his sour feelings quickly abated. He was intensely competitive, even if his appearance didn't broadcast it. A cap always covered his graying hair, and a untucked t-shirt and some loose fitting athletic pants undergirded his pot belly. He loved game day, but he loathed dressing up. What he didn't loathe was winning. He had the best win-loss record of any middle school coach in the area, and Jacobi might just be his ticket to that ever-elusive position as a head high school basketball coach.

Daily, Grant would go to school, teach, leave as quickly as possible to watch Jacobi practice, and then run Jacobi back to the high school so he could play with the high school team. Jacobi served a dual purpose at the varsity practice. Although he couldn't play in varsity games, he made the varsity team better by forcing them to play with and against someone of his caliber. Although he was a much better player than anyone on the varsity team, the competition was much stiffer than it was on the junior high level.

Grant didn't have to take Jacobi back and forth between schools, actually Katie let him. Jacobi didn't care much, as long as he made both events. He and Dynamite were the only two eighth grade boys officially permitted to practice with the high school team, but right now, they only attended open gym.

They couldn't have real practices at the high school yet because it wasn't close enough to the season, but they could have open gym. The open gym forum allowed anyone to play, but it was largely populated by the high school athletes and a few local kids who didn't play on the team for one reason or another. Typically, kids that didn't play on the team came and ran their games the width of the court on one side, while the high school team did likewise on the other side. Since junior high ball wasn't nearly so regulated, Coach Combs ran practices in the offseason, so Jacobi played somewhere constantly.

On the third Friday of the school year, while traveling from the middle school to the high school, Jacobi finally broke their mundane conversation. "Thanks for taking me to open gym." He sat for a moment, awkwardly, and then continued, "If you want, you can come up to the high school tomorrow for the regional three-on-three tournament. It starts at ten."

"I'll be there," Grant said, surprised. "I work there, remember? I was already planning on being there," he said, hiding his smile.

"Thanks. It'll be fun."

Nothing more was said. They arrived at the gym, and as they approached the doors, a clank and then a distinct but hollow reverberating sound broke the silence. When Grant stepped in from the light, he saw the backboard shaking and a line of boys anxiously waiting their turn.

"Why do they do that?" he asked.

"What? Pop the rim?" Jacobi questioned. "That's my favorite sound," he said with a smile. "It's a rite of passage," he said, stealing a line from his mom. "When you can pop the rim, you become a man."

Rite of Passage

The next day, Grant arrived at the gym a few minutes late. He had taken longer than he intended to get out of the shower and dressed after his morning run. After getting dressed that morning, he had sloshed coffee on his bag that contained all of the math papers he needed to grade. Once he got that mess cleaned up, he realized he had stained his shirt, so had to change shirts. By the time he got out the door, he was late.

When he walked through the door, he saw Jacobi was already on the floor with his friends Dynamite and Spencer. Typically, Dynamite ran the point guard position, Jacobi played the two position (on the right side), and Spencer played the three (on the left). Today was different; Jacobi was lined up at the top of the key. Jacobi's team was awarded the ball, the whistle blew, and Jacobi fired the ball to Dynamite on his right. Dynamite whipped it right back as Jacobi rushed directly down the middle of the lane. He caught the ball, jumped, cocked it back with two hands behind his head, and threw it down with authority. Grant heard the rim pop, loudly.

The tournament scoring regulations established that the winners took the ball out (make it, take it), and after the first two points were scored, the scoring team did not have to pass the ball in. They could dribble off the check, and that's exactly what Jacobi did.

The other team's big man, a high school student who was about six feet five inches tall, checked the ball to Jacobi, and Jacobi blew right past him again, this time with a layup on the left side of the rim. On the next play, Jacobi drove down the middle with his left, and when the defense collapsed around him, he kicked the ball out to Spencer for a 3-pointer. The ball ripped the net, and just like that Jacobi's team was up seven to zero. Grant saw the pattern.

They played eight games in the tournament, and Jacobi kept driving right down the middle. He seemingly scored at will while also setting up Dynamite and Spencer for easy shots. They won the first game twenty-one to six, and the rest of them weren't much closer, with the exception of the final.

In the championship round, they played a team from Crick County who had a six feet eight inches tall senior. He could shoot, jump, dribble; he could do it all. He made Jacobi sweat, and work for it, and for the first time, Grant saw Jacobi hesitate. Normally, Jacobi drove to the basket like a runaway train, but against this guy, he would hesitate, drive or pump-fake, and then shoot. It worked, but not well enough.

The last game was tied at twenty-one when the Crick County senior posted Jacobi up. He didn't pause. He spun quickly left off Jacobi's body and slid down the baseline with Jacobi in hot pursuit. He faked on the other side of the basket and Jacobi, trying desperately to block the shot, flew by. The big man jumped and placed the ball in the goal softly to end the game and the tournament. The two teams shook hands, and congratulated each other, but it was obvious that Jacobi was incensed. He had scored 126 points that day, but it still wasn't enough. Leave it to Spencer to throw some ice on the fire.

"Hey there, Dynamite!" he taunted coyly. "Over there's your girl a-waitin' on ya!"

"I know," Dynamite responded.

"Whut, she knock the music outcha? Are ye all lizard-brained?"

Dynamite sang back in reply:

> When I felt the flutter in my chest,
> My breast knew, I best rest the rest
> Of my body, for I'm naughty and
> Forlorn, but don't want to hurt nobody,
> It's gotta be love with which I gaze,
> Not desire settin' my heart ablaze

> Or I'll raise my banner to the sky,
>
> And die, alone without somebody.
>
> Without my heart's behest,
>
> Without my heart's behest.

"What's 'at mean?" Spencer asked him, but Jacobi responded.

"It means if he runs over 'ere like a fool followin' his emotions, he'll probably do something stupid that'll keep him from ever gettin' to know her. He may just hurt her, which would hurt him."

"Cool," Spencer said.

Grant laughed at the boys, and knew he was in for a fun fall. When they walked out the door together, Grant commented to Jacobi slyly, "English teacher's son, huh?"

"What?"

"Nothing . . ." Grant smiled, and let it go. Jacobi was still solemn, but Grant continued to laugh.

Continuation

Every week Grant watched Jacobi play and practice, and often they would get in little games back up at the church. No additional bomb threats occurred at the school after the first week; however, Grant had reluctantly broken up eight fights already at the high school. Six of the eight fights involved two girls, which he couldn't understand. Why were they so violent? He also couldn't understand why he had so many high school students who were well-manicured, but he couldn't find one adult, other than Katie, who was still attractive.

How odd, Grant thought, *why work so hard to be good-looking and fashionable in high school, just to let yourself go when high school is over? High school is only about five to six percent of your lifespan.* He couldn't imagine how these kids stayed attractive with all of the stressors. Every day could be a fight. Every day kids came to school drunk or stoned, or both. Every day some guy or girl cheated with his or her best friend's girlfriend or boyfriend. Every day was like sandpaper to the fingertips. Just being around it made Grant feel more depraved. But he wanted to help.

He spoke to Robin again and let her know his plans. He had already turned over the reins of running the company to her, but now he wanted to sell a portion, forty-nine percent.

Robin's job was to line up potential investors, which she did, and get them to buy in, which she did. Soon, Grant would be the majority owner of the company, but not the only play caller. He had his own plays to call now.

Get Off Me!

During the first game of the season, Jacobi went off for seventy-two points. Grant kept replaying the final scene in his mind. Coach Combs was screaming, "You can't dribble through a press! You can't dribble through a press!" like he always did (according to Jacobi) when the other team ran a press and trap, and Dynamite was dribbling through the press, like he always did when the other team ran the press.

Whirling around a double-team in the corner just before the half court line, Dynamite spotted Jacobi streaking down the other side. He took two more running dribbles with his left hand and then launched the ball up high on the left side of the rim. Like a sailboat cutting through the water, Jacobi split between two defenders and soared into the air. He caught the ball just before his left arm hit the rim, and quickly crammed the ball home with his right hand. Almost the entire crowd grimaced in shock, and then erupted in cries of "Ohhhh!"

About three minutes remained in the game, and the score was eighty to twenty-six. The other team's coach called a timeout, lined his players up, and walked them off the court. Coach Combs, who didn't believe in taking out his best players even if the game was well in hand, called out, "Oh, don't be such a sore loser, John! At least come back and finish the game! You're the one runnin' the press when you're down by fifty!"

The game was over; however, the season had just begun.

Jacobi's team played great at home and just as well on the road. They were totally dominant, as expected, led by Jacobi who averaged forty-eight points per game, twelve rebounds, eight blocked shots, six assists, and five steals. Grant watched him tiptoe sidelines on coast-to-coast scores, soar high above defenders on alley-oops, crossover double-teams and leave them standing breathless as he rifled the ball through the rim, and, most importantly, rally his teammates to play their very best.

Dynamite averaged seven steals a game himself as well as twelve assists—mostly to Jacobi. While Spencer usually hit a few 3-pointers per game, Harold, Johnny, Kerry, and J.J. all filled their roles respectively; but the twins, Homer and Junior, usually fought over who got to sit nearest to the cheerleaders at home games. Nine members in total, they were always a hootenanny, and Grant began to enjoy all of them, especially Jacobi.

When they traveled, Grant enjoyed it best. The boys were in rare form away from the school. After the last game, while the boys were singing victory songs on the ride home, one of the boys yelled out, "Dynamite, you run your hand up Laura's shirt yet?"

Dynamite jumped over the seat and landed on top of Harold, and then scrambled over and held Junior down. Harold grabbed Junior's arms, while Jacobi swung over and grabbed his legs. Dynamite stuck his armpit right on Junior's nose and rubbed it all around, taunting him all the while.

"Armpit sweat drippin' in your eyes. Armpit sweat drippin' on your chin. Armpit sweat up your nose. Armpit sweat's now your friend."

The other boys jumped in and started to give Junior a cherry belly, but Dynamite made them stop. He distracted them by dancing around and clucking like a rooster, until the driver told them all to sit down and shut up.

Grant laughed and laughed and looked over at Coach Combs, who was sound asleep. At least somebody was behaving quietly.

The games and weeks sped by quickly. Only yesterday, it seemed that Grant had just been getting his feet wet at school, and now the boys were playing twice weekly and they were creeping up on Christmas break. Grant had found his niche on the team; although he wasn't a coach, he was a manager.

The dads usually weren't allowed in the locker rooms, but Grant had become an exception. As a school employee, as well as an attendee at every practice and every game, Grant received some special privileges. After the fifth home game of the season, and just before Christmas, Grant walked into the locker room to congratulate Jacobi on scoring sixty-two points that night along with grabbing twelve rebounds. When he came into the locker room, what he saw immediately frustrated him. The boys stood around Kerry, making fun of him for his underwear.

"'At boys got skid marks all down the back his draws!" Junior said.

"They's probably his daddy's underwear, they so big!" Homer added.

"Yeah, 'ont you wash 'em thangs? All yeller and nasty!" J.J. poked.

Grant looked down, and sure enough, there were poop stains on Kerry's underwear. He would have laughed at the "skid marks" comment, too, had the reality not been so sad. Kerry stood there in underwear big enough to be his father's and old enough to be his grandfather's, not saying anything. Indecision paralyzed Grant. But not Jacobi. He burst out of the shower room, wrapped in a towel, yelling.

"Look, jerks! I heard you making fun of Kerry. You're all a bunch of pansies! It's not his fault his family can't afford to buy better underwear! Look at you, none of you have any money, but you still want to make fun of someone else?"

"Yer right, we ain't all got rich daddies like you!" said Junior.

Before anyone could act, Dynamite was all over him. He pinned Junior up against a locker, pressed his face right up against Junior's, and said, "You got anything else to say, boy?"

Dynamite's eyes were blood-red, and his skin reddened from his head down through his shoulders. Junior started to cry, and Jacobi pulled Dynamite back. *It was a good thing, too*, Grant thought. *Dynamite seems like the kind of kid who could hit someone three times a blink.*

As the boys separated, a few looked at Grant warily, and Grant noticed something. All the boys had terrible underwear except Jacobi. They were all poor. He also noticed something else: all over Dynamite's back and the upper part of his legs were scars, as if he had been repeatedly slashed throughout his life. Grant shuddered, and suddenly felt it would be best if he left.

Breaking Glass

A few days later, Grant questioned the coach. "Coach Combs," he said, "how are the boys' practice uniforms and shoes so nice when their regular clothes aren't? I've seen several of them wear their basketball shorts and shoes to school. At least that's what it looks like on the days I've shown up before they change for practice. It seems like they only change their shirts."

Coach Combs, not sure whether to answer a question or agree to a statement, responded, "Charitable contributions. I give some money for 'em boys' practice gear, and so does some others around here."

Walking away, Grant knew the coach's answer was partly true. All the boys had the same shorts and shoes as Jacobi, and Grant knew where Jacobi got his gear: Katie.

The next day, the day before Christmas break, Grant carried in four large trash bags full of items and dropped them on Coach Comb's desk. "Special donation," he said, and the coach looked up, shocked.

Coach Combs began to pilfer through the bags. One bag held mounds of newly packaged and assorted underwear, shorts, athletic shorts, and athletic socks in multiple sizes. Another had a myriad of t-shirts, graphic printed shirts, and basketball jerseys. The third had dress shirts, pants, belts, and socks of all sizes, and the fourth contained shoes: running shoes, dress shoes, basketball shoes, and casual shoes.

"Give these to the boys, including Jacobi," Grant said. "Don't dare tell them where the clothes came from because I know how people around here are about their pride, and they won't take them. They'll rape and pillage each other and the government, but they won't take a thing from someone who they think believes he is better than them. It's lunacy! Give them to the boys, tell them 'Merry Christmas,' and keep the change."

As if on cue, an envelope with a wad of cash fell onto the coach's desk from inside the bag full of shoes. Grant smiled and left the office. He went home that day after Jacobi's high school practice smiling happily. He didn't care if anyone noticed, if anyone knew, or if anyone expressed gratitude. In fact, he would rather that they didn't; he was just glad to give.

When he arrived home, he saw one of the curtains blowing awkwardly through a front window. All the windows in the cabin were broken. Just as he started to think he could embrace this place, someone, some moron had to go and do this! He stood on the porch, seething. Inside, a few of the rooms had been ransacked. The glass in the cabinet doors had been broken, and words were carved into the wood, words such as *rich boy*, *deadbeat*, *faggot*, and *fairy*. Of course they were all misspelled, only adding insult to injury.

He checked his bedroom—no intruders. The top drawer to the nightstand had been left hanging open, empty. His second watch had been stolen, along with the cash he had remaining in the drawer. He checked the other bedroom, and no damage had been done. Only the mattress had been flipped, and all the drawers to the furniture had been opened. Grant walked back out to the kitchen to take a closer look at the cabinets. A warm breeze blew through the broken window, and Grant turned around, startled.

"Ronald!" Grant composed himself. "I'm sorry, I don't know what happened! Everything was fine when I left this morning!"

"Don't worry 'bout it, Grant, hain't cher fault. Sons of—"

"Grant! Ronald! Are you okay?" Jacobi called as he ran up to the house.

He had never been to Grant's before, and Grant wasn't sure why he was there now.

"Yea, son, we're jus' fine! Watch yer step so ye don't get glass stuck in ye," Ronald warned.

"Should we call the police?" Grant asked.

"Yeah . . . sure," Ronald said with his eyes closed.

Grant spotted something different in Ronald this time. He had seen fun and joy, determination and courage, excitement and anger, but never this.

"I guess you had better tell Hammond."

Jacobi and Ronald both looked at Grant. Ronald said flatly, "Hammond's dead. He died two year ago. Left me this place. He's my brother-in-law. My sister died a' cancer two years afore, so when Hammond died, he left 'is place to me."

They stood quietly for a moment, as the winter wind began to blow through the windows, and thunder cracked in the sky. It wasn't cold, just cool, and blustery both outside and in. Finally, Ronald said, "Grant, you take Jaki home now. Come right back and we'll work all 'is out tanight."

So Grant took Jacobi home, as instructed, and found out some more details on the way.

"How did you know something had happened at the cabin?" Grant asked.

"Dynamite told me," Jacobi replied. "He told me that somebody did something, but he couldn't tell me who. After practice, when you dropped us at mom's house, we didn't go in. Dynamite asked me to walk him home, and he told me on the way there. Once Dynamite went inside, I went to find Ronald at the basketball court. He was up there working with a young kid on his crossover when I caught him. I told him what I heard, and what I suspected, but then I also told him I had to go home before I could go to your place. Since I didn't go inside when you dropped us off, I hadn't talked to mom. I ran home quickly, told her where I was going, and took off running toward your place. Mom caught up with me and dropped me off at the bottom of the hill, so she could turn around at the wide spot, and I ran on up. When I got there, you and Ronald were already there."

Grant sat quietly processing. He didn't know who to believe at this juncture, so he decided he didn't have time for cynicism. When Grant and Jacobi arrived at Katie's home, Grant spoke briefly to Katie, who invited him over for Christmas. Grant later hurried back to the cabin to find Ronald alone, rocking in a rocking chair on the porch, with tear-stained cheeks.

Chapter 10: The Rainy Season

It was the first day of Christmas break, and the rainy
season had begun. Unseasonably warm, the wind and the
rain whipped through the region, soaking the mountainous
terrain and creating mudslides. The black earth slid roughly
into the red clay, making some of the roads impassable and
ruining the switchbacks. Most people deemed it a great day
to stay inside by the fire, but not the boys, no, not the
Possum Creek Junior High basketball team of Possum
County.

At the next holler over from where Jacobi lived, between
his mom's house and his grandparents', was a large piece
of flat land where the boys could play. It used to be a cow
pasture until the owners had moved away a few years prior.
Now, some of the locals let their sheep and horses graze on
it, and a few people used it to garden. It was like a
community property, although it seemed as if every
community member fought over it, claiming it to be
rightfully his.

The boys entered the holler with sawed-off pants and
rugged, sleeveless shirts, walking on bare feet. The mud
squirmed between their toes and suctioned to their heels,
making an abrupt siphoning sound as each heel popped
free. Boisterous hakan cries, dank fog, musty sweat, and

rain, pulsing rain filled the air. The boys took their places ceremonially, and Dynamite was the first to dig. He quickly scooped a fistful of mud and let it fly. The mudslinging had begun, and the local politicians would have been proud. Kerry circled around, rifling slider after slider. The muck exploded with a glorious spread as it gooped Jacobi's back. The war was on, but victory was murky. The muddier each boy became, the happier he grew.

Mud pies soaked necks and ears and arms and legs. From thirty feet away, Harold clobbered Johnny right behind the right ear with a doozy. Johnny fell face first in the mire and was engulfed in the backsplash. Spencer found a pile of nearly spherical black sludge balls. He knew they were horse droppings, and he grew excited, but ever quiet, as he furtively gathered his ammunition. The dense downpour combined with the previous days' humidity had softened the turds just enough for them to be squishy.

Spencer dashed to the left side of the field, hunching lowly. As he neared J.J., Spencer erected quickly and discharged a naughty missile of feces that smacked J.J. on the right side of his face. J.J.'s mouth opened in shock as he took the blow and fell backwards with a jolt. He had closed his eyes just in time . . . but not his mouth. As J.J. got up laughing, he looked directly at Spencer and smiled a big, toothy, speckled grin. Spencer crumbled to the ground in a puddle. He was so hysterical he was crying. He hid his face in his hands, but the heaves of laughter shook him wonderfully, and he knew he had just witnessed the most hilarious moment of his life—all idioms aside.

Grant watched the whole thing from the other side of the holler. He had taken a break and left Ronald at the cabin napping. Grant had wanted a diversion from the sadness, the disappointment. They had hired two men to replace the front windows. Each window had been tarped over to keep out the rain. Ronald replaced the back windows with the new ones Grant had bought, and Grant tried to help him. Grant then had stopped at Katie's and found out what the boys were up to. He had shown up just in time to witness their glorious battle.

When Grant saw the boys all soaked and covered in mud, he laughed along with them, but not when they all started tackle him sloppily, knocking the umbrella from his hand. Before he took them home, he made them walk up the holler and ask to hose off at one of the neighbor's. They found an old couple near the top of the holler who had a water hose and agreed to let the boys use it. The couple sat on the porch laughing as the boys sprayed each other with water in the pouring rain.

While taking the boys home, Grant stopped at J.J.'s house first. A single-wide trailer with a rusted skirt and two hound dogs hiding under the porch was very typical for this area. J.J. ran off with a smile and a wave. Harold, Johnny, and Spencer all lived in the next holler over, and they had Grant just drop them at the mouth. They raced up the holler on foot, Spencer outrunning the other two, and disappeared in the distance.

As Kerry directed them toward his home, Grant noticed the homes becoming shabbier and shabbier. Many of the trailers had gaping holes in the siding, garbage in the front yards, and loose boards serving as bridges from the holler roads across the creek and into the yards. When they arrived at Kerry's, Grant noticed the stick-built house was missing several pieces of siding and part of the roof. Insulation dangled from beneath the weather barrier board. No exterior lights were visible outside the house, and no lights were on inside either. A lone candle flickered in the window, iridescent against the darkness inside. Driving farther down the road, Grant saw a well, on the other side of Kerry's home, with a bucket and a crank for drawing water, not too far from the outhouse. He stared intensely, and then shook his head in disbelief.

Arriving at Dynamite's was also eerily arresting. The boys goofed jovially upon arriving, but Grant felt a foreboding presence he couldn't quite identify. Just off the highway, the home looked almost picturesque from the outside. An immaculate garden bloomed to the left and a gray barn stood haughtily on the right, with the neat, cream-colored home right in the middle. Smoke billowed from the chimney, rising above the oxblood-red-painted tin roof that starkly contrasted the dark mountainous backdrop that loomed over the home. On the front porch, Dynamite's mom sat in the porch swing, floating back and forth. Dynamite ran up the puddled lawn, jumped onto the porch, turned, waved, and sat next to his mother and two sisters. The picture was perfect, too perfect.

Grant took Jacobi home and promised to see him on Christmas evening. They shook hands good-bye, as always, and Jacobi entered the house. With a sigh, Grant realized that maybe their fight by the court would last forever in Jacobi's mind. If so, Grant deserved it. He went back to the cabin where he and Ronald spent the rest of the day replacing the windows, one by one.

Christmas

On Christmas day, Grant arrived at Katie's home around 3:00 p.m. He wanted to be sure her family was gone—he couldn't stomach Hatchet on a day like today, or any day. Katie greeted him at the door, dressed in an elf's outfit, complete with pointy slippers. Grant looked for some mistletoe, but he had no such luck. It was easy to adore Katie, now that he had forgiven her, but he still struggled at times. About once a week, he would find himself getting furious at her in his daydreams, and he would have to sit down, talk it out with himself, and choose to forgive. Her cuteness made it easier.

Grant brought over a boatload of presents. He showered Katie and Jacobi with gifts, which Katie readily accepted, but Jacobi did so only with reluctance.

"Don't you like the shoes?" Grant asked.

"Yeah, they're great. I love basketball shoes, all kinds . . ." Jacobi responded.

Grant still sensed tension.

"Do you like the watch?"

"Yes, it's perfect . . ."

"Good."

Jacobi looked at Grant with a dead expression and said stoically, "I didn't get you anything."

"I didn't expect anything," Grant said in return. "I'm just glad to be here."

"I did," said Katie bouncily, "I got you something!"

Surprised, Grant accepted the package, tore off the paper, and opened the white large box. Inside was a copy of *To Kill a Mockingbird*, and beneath it lay a shirt and an item wrapped in brown paper. Grant pulled out the black t-shirt and extended it to read the white block letters. Much to his chagrin it read "WORLD'S GREATEST DAD!" Grant stuffed it back down into the box quickly, feigning a smile and shooting a sideways glance at Jacobi. He then opened the brown paper and discovered a plastic red rose, encased in glass, with "Family is Forever" inscribed on its wooden base.

Grant looked at Jacobi, and he could feel the frustration surging. He said, "Thank you, Katie, I really appreciate it," but he could see Jacobi leaving out of the corner of his eye. Jacobi walked down the hallway, shut the door to his bedroom, and Grant heard the lock click.

Katie looked at Grant quizzically, saw his frustration, and looked down the hallway at Jacobi's room. Grant saw a wall being erected around her heart when she looked at him with a deep sadness then rushed after Jacobi. She stood knocking at the door, and Grant took it as his cue to leave, so he recused himself, and left.

That night, Grant found a mud-stained, tri-folded piece of paper in the back of his vehicle. He opened it and the words were barely legible. Down the center, in scribbled-stained ink it read:

The songs of my heart have traversed such pain
As to pass flowing over thoughts of thee.
Without which, I pray for to die, fain
I cannot maintain the ones I now see.

Do not leave me nor forsake me now here,
But ever be a new lover to me,
For my heart breaks to think you so, so near,
Giving your heart to another fondly.

I have lost my heart's appetite once to
Things which I have lov'ed so dearly past.
Only to grow in wild wonder of you,
My maiden muse, my life's one true at last.

You hold my love in your heart's two small hands;
It will never drift like Time's shifting sands.

After a few moments of pondering, Grant realized it was a love poem from Dynamite to that chestnut-haired girl he had seen at the three-on-three tournament. As Grant sat staring at the cabinets with missing doors, the poem, and the encased rose, he saw that love and hate will make people take extravagant actions. He decided, that night, to have one object of his affection, one rose for his eyes, and one vision to cast beyond the shadows of today and out into the future. And it was Jacobi. He had come here for his son, and his son only.

Grant's heart bowed silently in his chest, broken for Katie. His eyes were dry and chafed, for he had lost her once in the wind of the night, but now he was willingly giving her away. He made a choice then and there. The pain was unsustainable, and this place was an oppressing force. His mourning would cease tomorrow, and he would choose to overcome the depressing atmosphere with grateful dreams and hopes. He had turned long ago, but now he would turn his world with him, but for tonight . . . he would mourn.

His visions of Katie's beauty kept him mesmerized, his dreams of wealth and prestige had kept him working, but his visions of his son kept him fulfilled, and the thoughts of losing him, again, kept him up all night.

Chapter 11: Hope

The next day, Grant awoke early. He had his normal four cups of coffee, read from his current book on successful relationship building, and then donned his running gear. When he opened the door, he frowned. The rain hadn't stopped for six days. Due to the holiday festivities, Grant had sworn to take the week off from running, just as he always did, and then pick it back up after Christmas. He hadn't even thought about how the rain would interfere with his running because he had been so hyper-focused on the cabin, Jacobi—and Katie.

Determined not to let the rain stop him, nor depression to take route, he put on his rain gear. When he stepped off the front porch, he slipped on slick, black muck and landed right on his back. The mud and water splashed on his mouth and face while some dropped in his nose. He gurgled violently. Frantically, he scrambled up, determined to run. He stepped forward, and his left leg shot straight back, sending him lurching forward, falling on his face and sliding like a child on a Slip'N Slide. Two steps, two falls, too much.

Grant still went for a run, kind of. He walked. He walked in the rain, through the mudslides, over the hills and through the knee-deep puddles. He wasn't going to let rain stop him. He even talked himself into visiting the church again, though it could kill him.

After a long hot shower and breakfast, Grant got dressed, grabbed his rain parka, some rain boots, an umbrella, and a Bible. He had never read it; he just took it so he didn't feel so awkward, and since there were two of them in the cabin. He was not sure if they were Ronald's or Hammond's, but he figured neither would mind his borrowing a Bible, especially not Hammond.

Once he made his way into the church, he took a seat in the back. Shortly thereafter, in walked Katie and Jacobi. Katie looked like a Christmas angel, and Grant stared, hard. Then he remembered his decision. *Of course it would be like this*, he thought, and he looked away. All throughout the service Grant did everything he could to avert his eyes from Katie. He looked at the floor, the ceiling, counted the pews, twice, read the bulletin, counted the number of letters in the bulletin, multiplied them by five, then ten, then fifteen. Before the last verse of "Just As I Am," Grant ran out the double-door entrance. "Those people probably think I'm running from God," he said to himself softly. "They don't know that I'm running from me!"

Grant did not see Katie throughout the rest of the holiday season, but he did see Jacobi. Practice was grueling throughout the break, not so much for the junior high team, but for the varsity team. Apparently, Jacobi could "play up" on the varsity team if they made the playoffs. He couldn't play during the regular season because that would count toward his four years of varsity eligibility, but by some loophole, he could play on the varsity team during the playoffs. Likely, it was just a way for teams to sneak in ringers at the end of the year.

Jealousy exuded at the varsity practices, but Jacobi pulled it off by being dominant on the court yet kind and diplomatic off it. Many of the varsity players recognized Grant from school, but none of them were his students—since he taught freshman and sophomores in Pre-Math I. The team was going to play in an out-of-league tournament in two weeks, and they needed to be prepared, so the coach scheduled extra practices. Because the tournament didn't involve the scholastic league, eligibility was not an issue. Most teams still took their normal roster, with the exception of a few kids who were academically ineligible. The Possum County Badgers were going to take Jacobi.

Before the big tournament, Ronald thought it would be a great idea for Jacobi and Grant to get away. Of course, he didn't share all the details fully with them.

"Now, boys, get yer stuff; we're headed up to Coal Miner's Fodder today."

Get Away

It was Saturday, and Jacobi had practiced all week long, running two-a-days between the junior high and high school teams. Going to Coal Miner's Fodder sounded like a great idea to him, and then he heard, "And pack ye an overnight bag, too. We'll be stayin' the night."

Grant looked at Ronald, and Ronald looked right back at him. They had all three met at the church to discuss the big tournament where Jacobi would be showcasing his talent. Due to the perpetual rain, they would be not practicing on the outdoor court for a long time, so they met at the church to discuss strategy—and work on balance drills.

Ronald was all about balance. Everything he taught had to do with balance, and rightfully so, since it was what transformed him being from a clumsy kid to a star basketball player. Balance and his belief that he could do it, self-determination, were what he preached.

"Now look hyear, boys, I said we'rea goin' up to Coal Miner's Fodder today! We'rea gonna get the right thangs in and the wrong thangs out."

Grant and Jacobi looked at each other.

"You boys think I'ma stupid?"

"No," they said in unison.

"Then why are ye lookin' at me like I'm stupid? Getchyer stuff and let's go."

First, they went to Katie's to pick up Jacobi's things. Ronald had already spoken with Katie, and she knew all about the trip well beforehand. A packed bag was on Jacobi's bed when he walked into his room. Although he seemed wary, Jacobi still said, "Thanks, Mom!" and gave her a big squeeze and a kiss.

Grant tried not to look at her at all, but she was endearingly gorgeous standing there in her pajamas and glasses.

"This is going to be one long haul," Grant said to himself.

"What?" asked Jacobi. "It's only a couple of hours."

Embarrassed, Grant said, "I know, and it'll be great," and in his mind he repeated, *You can do it, you can do it, focus on Jacobi, not on Katie, don't focus on Katie, Katie, Katie, Katie . . . stop it!*

On the way there, they came upon a poor, soaked man walking beside the road. Patrick was his name, and he didn't have any possessions except what he carried on his person. Struggling with a severe speech impediment, he told Grant and Ronald that he was trying to get to some place that sounded like "Levita," but they couldn't make it out. Ronald characteristically invited Patrick to come along with them to Coal Miner's Fodder. Patrick agreed.

When they arrived, something was definitely different. Where Dale had originally placed the horseshoe pits was now what looked like a standing rooftop. Someone had moved enough earth to build the horseshoe pits into raised mounds. Then they had placed railroad ties all around the pits and dug trenches to irrigate the water away. A building, like a vehicle bay or a covered bridge, shielded the area that held the pits. Constructed of wood, all of it, from the posts that held it up, to the roof, the horseshoe pit home was a gazebo of beauty. Inside, three strands of lights ran from end to end: one right down the middle and one down the left and one down the right. The building was exactly twelve feet tall internally. On the outside were heavy curtains to block the rain, as well as exterior lights mounted to the roof. At this point the curtains were drawn and tied back, so everyone could see right into the pits when they arrived.

"Tournament," Ronald said. "A horseshoe throwin' tournament."

Grant and Jacobi looked at each other again, this time with a little excitement. They went inside and found a seat, waiting for Dale to join them. Gracie came over and took their order, delivered some coffee, and flirted with Jacobi heavily. *He's only fourteen*, Grant thought, as he watched Jacobi handle it in stride. Jacobi barely seemed to notice, but Grant was practically drooling. *Stop it! Why is every little distraction such a big deal now?* And then he remembered his work. He no longer had his work to keep him distracted . . . not his company, not teaching . . . he had been on a break for nearly two weeks, and he was cracking up.

Dale arrived at their table with some towels for Patrick, and then he took him to the back to get a change of clothes.

"I gave 'em all the stuff he'd need to get a shawr back 'ere, and I encouraged him to get cleaned up, shave, brush his teeth, and all 'at," Dale said when he returned to the table.

"What made you think of this, Dale?" Grant asked, pointing out the window.

"Well, ya' see, I didn't really. It was more like ah . . . B.G.'s idea. He saw how crazy da men was all gettin' with the mines bein' flooded 'n all, so he suggested that we give 'em somethin' to do. So I did. I had 'em dig out all those pits, raise the dirt, lay the railroad ties, build the coverin', and irrigate the mound. They's miners so they know how to dig and build and cover stuff up. They know all 1'bout lights, too. Ran all 'em lights 'emselves, and the electricity. Once we got it built, we put it ta use, and got 'em all in there throwin' shoes. Some of 'em have even been bringin' their boys up hyear, seein' they're on break 'n all. Can't call it Christmas break, no sir, might get ye'self in trouble if you go callin' it Christmas break. Gotta call it 'winter' break cause you don't wanna offend nobody, specially somebody who don't do—" Dale broke for a pause. "Sorry, boys, sometimes I get all worked up 'bout stuff like 'at!"

"Really," Ronald said with a big smile, and they all laughed at Dale's expense.

Gracie brought the food, and it smelled wonderful. They waited on Patrick, politely, but that didn't stop them from polishing off two buckets worth of biscuits. When Patrick arrived, Dale asked to pray; everyone agreed, so Dale began quietly. His prayer was simple and profound, not showy, but sincere. *Here is a man who has sincerely changed; he's not just showing off and sincerely wants to help people,* Grant thought. *I can get behind that.* For better or for worse, at least Dale was authentic.

Patrick returned and ate ravenously, having second and third helpings of everything. Ronald didn't fall too far behind, while Jacobi ate and ate and ate but mainly just the pork chops. He eschewed the gravy, and was very careful to cut the fat away from his meat. Grant ate carefully and conservatively, too, on his first helping, but on the second he went ahead and ate all the bacon, eggs, gravy, biscuits, ham, and butter he could handle. With a few cups of coffee in there for good measure.

Afterward, they went outside to begin the horseshoe competition. Grant felt like a literal tub of lard. Jacobi was nice and limber, Ronald was . . . well . . . pretty much a savant at any physical sport, and Patrick was effusive. Patrick, off balance and out of sorts, was intensely excited to play. He seemed as if he wanted, like a child, to fit in desperately. Ronald made him feel right at home.

Pairing up, Ronald with Patrick and Grant with Jacobi, they entered the tournament. Twenty-four teams took part, and it was double-elimination. In the fourth round, the team with the lowest number of points scored in the consolation bracket would have to move up and play in the final four of the championship bracket, leaving eight remaining teams in the consolation tournament. Some of the men complained about the format of the tournament, but Dale didn't seem to mind. Forty-eight games would take place if there wasn't a double-elimination final round.

Jacobi and Grant warmed up while Ronald coached them.

"Now, boys, it's just like shootin' free throws. Ya gotta bend yer knees, keep yer back straight, get that shoe to flip one good time, and develop that rhythm. You gotta feel that rhythm to play shoes. It's in ye, ye just gotta translate it to the shoes." Ronald had his eyes closed. "Now, boys, put ye hands over yer hearts—ye feel that rhythm? Not the beat now, the rhythm. The beat changes if ye get excited, but the rhythm, she never changes, less 'ers problems, or yer dead. We don't have no problems now, hyear, and that heartsa beatin' so you shore hain't dead, so let's getta pitchin', boys!"

And "pitchin'" they did. While Jacobi and Grant worked on their rhythm, Ronald nailed double-ringers. *Clank! Clank!* Jacobi and Grant found it, their rhythm, together. During their second game, Jacobi hit a double-ringer, then so did Grant. They caught each other's eye, and Grant winked.

"Just like shooting free throws!" Jacobi called.

"Just like making sales!" Grant returned.

The sounds reverberated like banjo strings over mountain air, and Grant danced around after each score. When they broke for dinner, Jacobi and Grant inflated the tales of their best shots.

"Then I hit that one right on top of my other shoe," Grant said. "It was like a horseshoe double-stack. You couldn't measure the distance from the stake with a micrometer!"

"What about my shot that hit the top of the stake, bounced back, hit the other shoe, and knocked them both on? Heck, when it first hit the stake, it knocked the other guy's shoe off!" Jacobi topped.

Grant kept the verbal tussle going for as long as he could maintain it while they sat down for dinner. They ate again, but this time Grant didn't eat so much. Filled with gravy and regret from lunch, he decided to abstain from overindulging on dinner, or "supper" as they called it there. Once they finished, they went back outside for the final few games of the night.

As mosquitoes grew to be the size of palm leaves, and rain continued to fall, Grant and Jacobi finished their last round, then sat on the porch to watch Ronald and Patrick finish up. Patrick steadily got better; at first he couldn't even get the shoes to the opposite pit, but now he had even hit a ringer or two. Ronald still hit both left-handed and right-handed, under-the-leg shots, and even an occasional football hike. All the while he talked, talked, talked. He never said anything to discount the other team; he just said things to encourage himself and Patrick.

"We got that rhythm now, boys, wesa hittn' now. Can't stop a freight train, toot! Tooooooo! Hit dat stake, Patti, hit it good. Eww, boywas, I can feel that rhythm now! Double shot comin' up right chyear!" *Clank! Clank!*

Ronald and Patrick went undefeated, while Grant and Jacobi lost their first game, but won the remaining games that day. Tired and happy, everyone crowded up in the stage room to hear B.G. tell a story about Dynamite Red playing shoes.

"And he hit that Quietus right 'tween the eyes!" B.G. called. "Put a knot on his noggin so big that it'd get sunburnt in the fog! That's where the game all started . . . aftern' Dynamite hit that Quietus with the rock, they tied 'at Quietus up and let the horses kick 'em to death. One of them horse's shoes come off, and landed right around that knot. That gave Dynamite the idea, and him and Seymour started pitchin' shoes that day. It's how it all started, boys, and if I'm lyin' . . ."

"I'm dyin'!" the crowd called back in unison.

After the performance, the miners went home through the soaking, tired rain. Grant and Jacobi shared a room at the restaurant while Ronald and Patrick went off with Dale to his home. Smiling as he lay down for the night, Grant glanced over at Jacobi, who was shooting invisible basketballs through invisible hoops. Even in another person's bed, Jacobi visualized shooting, *swish, swish, swish*, with no *clanks*!

In the middle of the night, Grant awoke to a familiar gurgling, a rumbling, rolling down his abdomen, deep into his loins. He cramped up, seizing his breath and feeling the blood rush to his forehead. He raced through the bathroom door and exploded on the pot. Sweating and breathing heavily, he vowed never to do it again; never, ever, ever would he eat like that again.

St. Patrick

The next morning, Patrick was gone. Sometime in the middle of the night, he had escaped from an unlocked cell. Dale's place offered safety, comfort, and belonging: all things foreign to Patrick. To him, it was like a cage to a deer; he was a mighty buck made to roam and run at his leisure. To Ronald, it was like watching a mouse run out of a cheese factory into a cat sanctuary.

"I gotta forfeit, boys," Ronald said as he met Jacobi and Grant at their breakfast table.

"Grant, too," Jacobi joked, "after the way he was in the bathroom cryin' last night. I thought he was going to die!"

"What's wrong?" Grant asked, looking up from his second helping of gravy.

Grant's tone, although inquisitive, was foreboding, and his brow was slightly furrowed, so Jacobi listened intently.

"Well, Patti took off somewheres last night. Can't find 'em."

"Should we go looking for him?" Grant asked.

"Naw, we did some 'ere round the house. Guy like 'at, he don't want to be found. I feel sorry for 'em; feel like if he could jus' get a few days in him, a few days a someone treatin' him right, teachin' him, he could change. Well, I guess 'ats 'at. I'll just coach y'all."

Not quite knowing how to respond to the news about Patrick, Grant began focusing on his own circumstances— his chance to be a father. Grant knew there was hope yet. Jacobi hadn't run; he had stayed. So had Grant. The tough part was not the working—the tough part was the staying.

"That would be fantastic if you could coach us!" Grant said to try to distract Ronald, but he knew there was another problem. Jacobi was right, Grant did feel like he was going to die, but not because of his stomach. It was his arm. His right arm, specifically his bicep and forearm, was so sore he couldn't straighten it out. It was the pits.

They went back out to the pits, and the rain had stopped, temporarily. Jacobi and Grant started warming up, and Jacobi started to throw. *Clank! Clank!* On his first two shots. Grant decided to give it a go. He knew he needed to throw with some extra strength—with heart—since his arm was so stiff. He threw what he thought would be a high and lofty shot, with a perfect back flip and into the stake, but, alas, he fell short. The shoe left his hand sideways, landed on edge, rolled across the dirt, and clanked against the railroad ties that were set up to keep the rain out and the shoes in.

"What was that?" Jacobi asked, laughing.

Wincing in pain, Grant said, "I can't straighten my arm; it's too sore. I haven't lifted weights in eight or nine months, and I killed it yesterday!"

"C'mon, don't be a wimp!"

"I'm trying," Grant said. All of these fantastic horrors started running through his mind. He had just started making a connection with Jacobi, and now he couldn't even play the man for a game of horseshoes! *The kid's going to hate me*, he thought. *I have got to do this.*

Stirring up the encouragement inside him, he tried to throw again, and again, but he couldn't even make it to the pit. Ronald, after talking with Dale briefly, and messing around with some of the other contestants, made it over to Grant's forlorn lane.

"Wha's wrong, Grant, can't ye thrown no more? Is ye arm sore from yesterday?"

Grant had a flash of hope. *Ronald knows everything about this kind of stuff—basketball, horseshoes, balance— he might have some trick up his sleeve.*

"Ronald! What do you do? What do you do if you haven't played in a while and you get really sore?" Grant waited in anticipation.

Ronald turned and looked at Grant with a bit of compassion and a twinkle in his eye. "Never happens. I taught m'self to throw left-handed, so I wouldn't never have 'is problem."

Grant dropped his chin to his chest.

Grant tried learning to throw left-handed that day, but it was an utter failure. He swung his arm back, stepped forward, and slapped himself right against his leg as he awkwardly tried to throw the shoe. While he grabbed the back of his leg, the horseshoe ricocheted off the ground—right into his other shin.

Jacobi's play carried them, and Grant was too determined just to drop out. The staying was the hard part. He could have let Ronald take over, but that would mean he would have to give up, and deal with a bunch of raving coal miners accusing them of cheating. So he played on.

Billie was back, but he didn't talk much, except for the occasional condescending comment. As they continued to play, and Grant started to lose, Billie started to poke fun at him more and more. Dale walked over and stood beside Billie, quietly, and the comments ceased.

Like a vulture in an abandoned slaughterhouse, Jacobi attacked the first game. Determination emitted from his eyes, which appeared a darker shade of green today. He wore shorts with frays at the bottom and a black Coal Miner's Fodder shirt Dale had given him. The shirt said *Pig*

Out! across the top of his chest and was black with a white pig bursting through an open gate as a farmer chased it with an uplifted pitchfork. Grant watched his son. The dark shirt, the shaded area under the horseshoe port, and the determination made Jacobi's eyes look dark. Grant couldn't help but notice: Jacobi reminded him so much of himself, and Katie, and his own father, but surely not Katie's father! Jacobi hit another double-ringer, and then smiled across the lane at his dad.

Now it was Grant's turn, and he diligently tossed his first shoe left-handed. The horseshow flew straight, and flat, and wonderfully short. "It was the pits," Grant complained, "they were raised too high!"

"You didn't say that yesterday," Jacobi said with a smile. "Maybe it's all the gravy you ate, or maybe you blew all your strength away last night in the bathroom . . ." He could barely finish his sentence he was laughing so hard.

Walking together, they accidentally brushed shoulders. Neither of them said a word; they just kept walking and laughing. They had won their last game, now it was time for the final four.

Fourth place. They took fourth place in the tournament, and everyone was happy, except Grant. He thought Jacobi would be upset, but Jacobi had been laughing and throwing and goofing off with Ronald, and now he was joking with Grant. Grant looked over at his son, who sat on a railroad tie as the final game came to a close. *He isn't mad*, Grant thought. *He's happy, he's relieved, he looks just like he does when he's playing with Dynamite.* With that knowledge, Grant decided he could choose to be happy, too.

Homeward bound, the three of them gathered up their belongings and wished Dale and Gracie good-bye. With their items intact, and their hearts full, they began their trip home—only after Grant visited the restroom one last time.

The rain picked up again as they crossed the countryside, so they moved slowly. The mountains deepened in color due to all the rain. The trees all mushed together appeared a shade of dank blue, in spite of the time of year. Interspersed with the sad blue and chalkboard green color were patches of brown dead leaves, tree trunks, and branches. It was near dusk, and the sun was slipping behind the mountains to close out another day.

"Well, Jaki, tell me what ye learned for ye tournament."

"Can I think for a minute?"

"You mean from the tournament," Grant interjected.

"No, I mean for 'is tournament." Ronald looked at Jacobi. "Sure can, you can thank for two minutes if ye'd like!"

"Okay, I got it," Jacobi said, then paused dramatically. "I learned that men are drawn to competition."

"Why do you say that?" Grant asked.

"Everyone there was a man. Most of them have wives and kids, but they were playing horseshoes instead of spending time with their family. The mines are a competition, making money is a competition," Jacobi continued with raised brows.

"This kid is brilliant!" Grant interrupted as he looked at Ronald.

"Hold on dere now, son, let'sa see how smartchoo are. How can you apply whatchoo learnt to basketball?"

"Easy. I have to make the other team think they are my friends. If they like me, they won't compete as hard to stop me; they'll just compete with me. It's like playing with Dynamite. We go at each other, but we're friends, so we don't want to hurt each other. And we also want to see the other one play good—I mean well."

"How ya gonna convince the other team 'at you're their friend?"

"I gotta talk to them outside the court. I have to talk to them during warm-ups, congratulate them on how they played this year, tell them 'good shot' when they score, help them off the floor. I have to treat them like we are friends for them to believe we are friends. It's the competition they love, not the winning. If they feel like they're on my team, my side, and I'm winning, then they're still winning."

"Good boy!" said Ronald.

Astounded, Grant said, "Okay, Mr. Combs," with a stressed, feigned admiration, "what else did you learn?"

"Everybody runs from something."

"Explain."

"That Patrick guy, he ran from food and shelter. It doesn't make sense; he needed it, but he ran from it. Remember that Billie guy you told me about on the way here, the bully? Well, he ran from losing his reputation. He knew that if he didn't show up, he'd look like a weakling, so he showed right back up at the place where he got his tail whipped. He even tried to act tough! Until Dale shut him up. You're running from talking to mom after she made us both mad at Christmas, and, Ronald, you're running from slowing down. You're afraid that if you do, you'll stop."

The vehicle was silent for about four minutes, and then Grant asked, "Okay, Mr. Big Stuff Ballplayer, what do you run from?"

"Losing."

For about thirty minutes the vehicle was silent again: Ronald had fallen asleep and so had Jacobi, but Grant still had one more burning question. Perplexed by how intelligent Jacobi seemed, and still trying to find his niche, Grant pressed to discover how he fit—as a father or friend. In the darkness, he slowly turned to Jacobi and whispered, "Hey, Jacobi, are you up?"

"Um, yes, I'm up."

"Let me ask you something: If you run from losing, then why weren't you more upset today when we lost?"

"Because I didn't lose, Grant," he said, and he fell right back asleep.

Chapter 12: Ball Me Up

Christmas break was over, and school was back in
session, and so was basketball. Only two more games
remained for the junior high team, but the high school team
had to play until the rainy season was over. The kids at
school were restless, from the rain, from the break, and
from the math. Grant had stood his ground on learning, but
he had given up on trying to teach the curriculum. It was
pointless.

"Factoring polynomials, are you kidding?" he asked his
department head. "These kids can't factor, period. Half of
them can barely divide, so how am I supposed to teach
them to factor polynomials? Heck, three of the kids in my
fourth period class can't read. They can't read! I'm
supposed to teach them how to do math when they can't
read? No, this is what I'm doing. I am teaching them the
skills they need, so they can move on to the next step. They
are grouped by what they know, and they get small group
lessons, and guess what . . . I make them look up their own
lessons. I give the students the terms, and I have them find
them; they read them, and they ask me questions when they
need help. Nobody leaves my class until their whole group
is done with that day's assignment, and that's it. The kids
who can't read, they do word problems every day. Each kid

takes a turn trying to read a problem, and then they work together on figuring it out. If they can't read it, then they ask me, or look it up, or ask a classmate."

"But what 'bout the integrity of your gradebook?"

"It has integrity. If I name an assignment 'factoring trinomials' and only two kids in the class can actually factor trinomials, then only those two kids get that assignment. The others get the grade for the assignment I give them, and it goes in the gradebook under factoring trinomials. They don't even know what that means anyway."

"Then why don't you teach them?"

"I will. Right after I teach them that if you have zero, and you keep borrowing from the other numbers around it so you can get where you need to be, you still deplete all the other numbers. Then, I'm going to teach them that if they have zero, and borrow eleven, they now have negative eleven. See, here you teach them that if they borrow eleven, they have eleven, but that's not true. Somebody always has to pay, and if they borrow eleven, they have negative eleven, because they owe eleven. They have to learn to build to eleven, not borrow to eleven."

"I'm lost," she said.

"I know," Grant replied, and he walked out of the teacher workroom down to the coaches' offices.

"Coach Procrete!" Grant called into the office of the high school basketball coach. "What's the likelihood that you guys will make the playoffs?"

"We'll find out right'cheer after the tournament. We'll see how 'em boys do in the tourney, and I'll be able to predict how they gonna do for the rest of the year."

"Have you talked to Coach Combs about when you're going to need Jacobi? They have their last season game the weekend of the tournament."

"Procretes don't talk to the Combses . . ."

"Okay, so what are you going to do about the tournament?"

"I need da see how 'em boys do at the tourney without Jacobi anyways, cause that's how they're gonna finish the season. Once Jacobi gets done with his game, he'll come over hyear to our game—well, not hyear, but to the tournament. Haven't ye talked to his mom? We's already had this discussion."

"Erlosungs don't talk to Combses either," Grant said with a smile and a wink. He thanked the coach and walked back toward his classroom.

Just Stay Away

The second-to-last game of the season was played at Possum County Middle School, and it was a packed crowd. The Trotters, the junior high team, were playing the Peaks in a cross county rivalry. Grant was sure that half of the stands were drunk, but he didn't mind. He was there to watch the boys.

Dynamite and Jacobi were electric. Jacobi tipped the jump ball out to Dynamite, who ripped it out of the air and went flying toward the basket. He cut between two defenders and flipped the ball underhand to Jacobi, who floated from far outside the lane on the left past a defender, and scooped it up and in, finger rolling it right into the basket.

The press was on, and Jacobi stole the inbound pass, and threw a no-look pass, two-handed, straight over the top of his head to Dynamite, who drained the three. The crowd was on its feet. The room filled with energy, and the boys bounced all over the court.

The Peaks missed a shot on the other end, which Jacobi rebounded quickly. Spinning left past the first defender, he bolted down the middle toward half court. Another defender tried to cut him off, but he deftly shifted back left, slinging the ball around his back. He crossed over the next defender, who fell on his butt, tiptoed to the right, and laid it high off the glass. It was like money in the bank—guaranteed.

The rest of the game was like a circus of Jacobi, Dynamite, and Spencer. On one fast break, Jacobi laid the ball up off the glass with his left, and then rising high above the rim yanked it out of the air and threw it through the goal for a shattering dunk. When the Peaks made it down to the other end of the court, the goal still shook from Jacobi's assault on it. In the final quarter, Jacobi drove to the basket eighteen times, mainly down the middle. He fed Spencer for a few 3-pointers, set up Dynamite for some quick jumpers, and had a few magnificent scores of his own. He ended the game with fifty-eight points and thirteen assists. The final score was ninety-six to thirty-three, the highest-scoring game all year, and in all of Possum County Middle School history.

After the game, Grant went into the locker room to congratulate the boys. He noticed that Dynamite had some fresh wounds on his back, but he still managed to play a fantastic game. The others seemed to ignore the cuts, but it bothered Grant. After the team had showered and were leaving the locker room, Grant stayed behind to talk with Dynamite.

"Red, hang out in here for a minute. I have something I want to talk to you about."

Dynamite stayed, but asked, "What djou want—I mean, what do you want, sir? What do we need to talk about? What is it?"

"Hold on, just a second. Let the other boys leave."

"Why do they need to leave? What's the problem?"

Dynamite began to pace around the locker room like a caged rooster. Back and forth, back and forth.

"Dynamite, sit down," Grant said.

"No, sir, I can't. I need to get goin'. What is it you need?"

Grant looked at him with as much compassion he could muster and used his best fatherly tone, "Your legs and back, Dynamite. What's happening?"

"It's none of your business! You mind your own business!" he yelled and ran out.

When he hit the doors, Grant heard him begin another chant in a determined tone.

> We showed them boys today, how to play, the way, that'll make you stay,
>
> On top of the reservoir of stardom, givin' em some Harlem-type pedagogy,
>
> I'll show thee, how Jacobi, can only,

Be the capital, the only one, the son,

Of the sky, who can fly, by another guy's eye, with a
sigh, so high, don't cry.

When he lands, with both hands, through the rim,
get off the stands!

We're the best, you're the rest, and I must confess,
ya jess, better put on ya dress,

Cause you're the madam, of a badger, and we had
yer ego fracture, for our snack 'er . . .

Dynamite's mom ran over and grabbed him to walk him
out. Another man, large and rugged, accompanied them and
Dynamite's two sisters out the door. Grant had seen the guy
sitting next to Dynamite's mom throughout the game with a
menacing look on his face. He didn't show any affection
for her, clap for anything, cheer for Dynamite, or the team.
The one thing he did do was ridicule the refs and the
coaches from both teams. Tobacco stained his chin, and his
eyes were bloodshot-red. He pretty much had
"condescending" written all over him, at least that is what
Grant thought, assuming this guy must be Dynamite's
uncle or cousin.

Katie was talking with the coach on one side of the court,
and Jacobi was talking to some lady and a cheerleader on

the other side. The paper-thin lady talking to Jacobi repeatedly put her hands on him. She pressed against him aggressively, rubbing his back and shoulder, and devoured him with her eyes. She nearly straddled him as he uncomfortably wiggled backwards away from her. *Lot lizard,* Grant thought half rushing that direction. He was confused, but he followed his intuition. When he arrived, the pint-sized cheerleader behind her was standing with her head down, slightly pulling on the lady's shirt.

"Mama, come on, we gotta go. Daddy's waitin' outside, and I'm hungry . . . c'mon, Mama."

"Don'tcha interrupt me, girl, Ima talkin' to this fine, fine young man hyear. Hard worker I see, I'd like to work—"

"Whoa!" Grant yelled. "Your speech sounds a little slurred tonight, ma'am," as he stepped between her and Jacobi, "and inappropriate!"

"Who are ye?" she stammered as Grant grabbed her by the other arm and walked her out of the building. She tried to make a scene, but Grant was quick and forceful, almost unbecoming.

When he returned, Jacobi stood with Katie, but Grant did not avoid her.

"Hey, Jacobi, you want to spend the night tonight?" he asked, while looking at Katie. "Only if it's okay with your mom." Jacobi had never spent the night before.

Jacobi looked at his mom expectantly, and then turned and said to Grant, "Yes."

Grant congratulated Coach Combs on a fantastic win, waved good-bye to Ms. Combs (Katie), and took Jacobi with him. They stopped at Jacobi's house and picked up some clothes. Then they headed for Grant's home—and for the first time, it felt like home.

Chapter 13: Still a Boy

On the way to his home, Grant realized he didn't really know what fourteen-year-old boys do when they're not playing basketball. He'd only hung out with the boys when they played ball, or had an epic mudball fight. Most of the time they all just goofed off, but Jacobi was different. He was driven. Grant had spent the night with him at Coal Miner's Fodder, but they spent most of their time playing horseshoes. Tonight, Grant wouldn't have the luxury of such distractions. Maybe Jacobi spending the night wasn't such a good idea.

Grant tried to remember his childhood favorites with his father. He thought about their evenings sitting on the back porch, watching the rain, and talking about everything. He remembered his dad usually taught him while they were working with wood, or building, or passing a ball, but never sitting still. Grant didn't like to sit still anyway, so it was even harder for him when he was younger to have a conversation.

Most of Grant's conversations with Jacobi were on the basketball court, or traveling from the middle school to the high school. Now, on the way to his home, he could think of nothing to say. They both looked ahead in silence until Jacobi broke the ice.

"Why did you ask Dynamite to stay after in the locker room?"

"Because I needed to talk to him about something."

"About what?"

"That's really kind of personal, Jacobi."

"Dynamite's my best friend. I know everything about him. Did you ask him about his legs . . . and back?"

"Yes."

"And he told you to mind your business, right?"

"Yes."

Leaning over toward Grant, Jacobi revealed the truth. "It's his dad. His dad beats him. That's a secret. You can't tell anybody, but that's what is going on. We've tried to help him, but he always protects his dad. I even promised to sneak into his dad's room one night and beat him the man with a baseball bat, but Dynamite chickened out at the last minute. That's why he spends so much time at our house. Did you know that he's my best friend, but I have only been in his house one time? We have known each other since we were six!"

"Your mom hasn't turned him in?"

"She did once, but when the people that protect kids . . . the protective agency . . . whatever their name is showed up, Dynamite's dad talked them right out of the house.

Dynamite wouldn't say a word. His dad's really smart, too. He may look stupid, but he never loses an argument. Anyway, he beat Dynamite worse than ever that night, so mom never said another thing."

Grant sat in silence in front of his home for a minute. "Okay."

As they walked toward the front door, Grant noticed a raven sitting atop his home. "You know, my dad used to call those birds 'swans of blood.' I never understood why."

"My mom usually starts talking about Edgar Allan Poe when she sees one," and they both laughed while walking through the front door.

Inside, Grant tried to manufacture some conversation while setting out some things to eat. "Did you know that bluebirds aren't actually blue? It's the structure of their feathers that makes them look blue."

"Like the ocean is not actually blue, the sky makes it look that way," Jacobi said. "Funny how we can see water clearly a million times, but when we see it blue, we say, 'Water is blue.' Why don't we believe what we know is true instead of what we see once? Or at least try to discover the difference?"

Grant could see this wasn't going to be the type of father-and-son conversation he was used to—the kind where his dad divulged the knowledge as he bumbled around trying to pick it up.

"You want some deer jerky?" Grant asked. "I got it from one of my student's dads."

"Who?" Jacobi asked.

"Darrell Collins, that's the dad's name anyway. He came to my classroom—"

"Sure, he makes the best deer jerky around!"

". . . to talk with me about Donnie," Grant continued. "He said he couldn't get Donnie to take school seriously, but he didn't want him to end up dropping out like he had done. I told him to pay Donnie."

"Pay him for school?"

"That's what his dad said! I said, yes, 'Pay him for school. He works the mines to get paid, have Donnie work the books to get paid.' The next time I saw him was a month later, and Donnie had improved in all of his classes, and his dad gave me three pounds of this jerky."

"I'd say that's a deal! He sells this stuff for a pretty—" Suddenly, the thunder cracked, and the floodgates opened.

"Well, no lawn darts tonight," Grant joked.

"Lawn darts? What are lawn darts?"

"You've never heard of lawn darts? I was just joking, but I'll show you," Grant said and hurried off to his room.

When he came back he had two large hula hoops in his hands and threw them down in the living room of the cabin. He looked at Jacobi, who had an inquisitive look on his face. "They're for my kids at school; the hyper ones use them when we play math games or to give them something to do when they are really antsy." Jacobi looked at him with his eyebrows raised. "They're not for me. It's not like I run around in here practicing my hula-hoop tricks."

"Then why are you so defensive?" Jacobi asked.

"Shut up," Grant teased, and then took Jacobi with him to the back porch. They grabbed two broken tree limbs that had blown onto the porch, took them inside, and cut them down to about two feet in length. Grant pulled two plastic cups out of the cabinets, and filled them with some modeling clay.

"Vocabulary," he said. "Math vocabulary." Jacobi rolled his eyes.

Grant took the sticks, jammed them down into the modeling clay, secured them, and then dumped a whole bottle of quick-drying glue on top of it. He allowed it to sit for about twenty minutes while Jacobi polished off the bag of deer jerky. When they were both ready, he had Jacobi stand on the other side of the room.

"Throw this dart, and if you get it to stand up in the circle, you get four points; if it lands in the circle but isn't standing, you'll get two points. If you miss the circle completely, we'll call it an airball. That's not the official set of rules, but it works for indoor play."

As they lobbed the makeshift darts back and forth, Grant felt the tension subside. He could breathe easier, and he could speak with more candor.

"So how did that crazy mom make you feel?"

"That happens all the time," Jacobi said.

"What? You have women practically attack you all the time?"

"Not exactly like that, but it happens all the time. Usually, they want me to date their daughters, and they will do anything to get me to do it. Anything."

"Pardon me for being ignorant . . ." Grant said with false humility. "But why? You're a good-looking kid and all, but c'mon."

"It has nothing to do with looks; it has to do with dollars. They see me as their daughter's lottery ticket. Some of them are just gross, and think I'm *their* ticket out, but most of them are trying to do it for their kids. They know I'm bound to get picked up by a college, and if their daughter comes with me, then she gets out."

"Why don't they take them out themselves?"

"Not enough gumption, I reckon. They're looking for an easy ticket, and that's me."

"What makes you so sure?"

"It's been happening since sixth grade. It really picked up last spring, just before you came. I went to our major university, in the state capital, and played some scrimmage ball up there. It was a big deal all around here, and both coaches and both principals went. I got to play with the college team during an intra-team scrimmage, and I was pretty dominant. I had twenty-three points by the fourth quarter, and they had to stop the game when the center came unglued after I dunked over him. They ran me out of there before that guy could kill me!"

"What? So you dominated some top college players?"

"Yes, then the word came back here, and everyone started talking about me going pro, and all the money, and fame, and then all the mamas came out of the woodwork. Before, it was just so their kid would be popular. Now, they look at me like a lottery ticket."

"How'd you know what to do? What do you do?"

"Ronald told me it would happen, and we have a strategy. I never go in a room alone with a girl, and I never spend the night at a friend's house if he has a sister. That's why most of my friends come to my house—that and mom's house is a little nicer than most people's around here.

"I noticed. Tell me about this college visit. I trust you, but if you're that good, then why didn't you handle that big center during the three-on-three tournament?"

"First of all, he's not a center; he's a forward. He can play guard, too. Sometimes he plays center because he's so tall, but he moves like a guard. Second, he's one of the best players around, and when I say around, I mean in the nation. He is one of the top most recruited—"

"Most heavily recruited players."

"Yes, thank you, he's one of the most heavily recruited players in the nation."

At that moment, Jacobi landed his two darts simultaneously in Grant's circle, and the darts were standing up.

"Hey, you can't throw them both at the same time!"

"Why not?"

"I don't know . . . you have to go in order. Okay, back to the player from Crick County. You're telling me that one of the best basketball players, one of the best high school basketball players in the whole nation, lives within fifty miles of this place?"

"Yeah, why's that such a big deal?"

"Do you see any top-notch businesses here? How about entrepreneurs, corporations, schools, anything? Heck, even the football and baseball teams are pitiful. Why would I expect there to be good basketball players here, when there's nothing else successful?"

"Dale seems pretty successful!"

"That's two hours from here . . ."

"Everyone here plays ball. Look at all the old men who come up to the church to play ball with their kids. What about all the kids who come to open gym to play, but don't play on the school team? Most boys are raised playing ball, and they play until they're old . . . like the old deacons from church. We're raised on basketball."

And moonshine, Grant thought, but he didn't say a word. He was actually growing to like some of the men he met at the games, although he couldn't really understand their thinking, or speaking for that matter.

"All the old men can still shoot the long ball. You've seen Ronald play. He's better than all the kids at the high school, and he's old and disabled."

Grant landed two more darts. "Okay, okay, so people in this area either play ball, coal mine, or eat and drink a lot."

"C'mon, most of the people here have been good to you. Ronald has been, mom really has been, I have been, and the team and Coach have all been good to you."

"Yep . . . watch out, you're gonna lose!"

"No, you'll choke first!" Jacobi replied.

"Okay, let's be serious for a second. I have one more question for you. On the way back from the horseshoe tournament, you said that you run from losing. What are you actually afraid of?"

"Seriously, I'm afraid of people crowding me. I hate it. I hate big crowds all pressed against me, touching me. I don't mind them watching me, but I don't want everyone pressed against me. I don't like being in the stands. Once, when I was a kid, I got hurt playing in a game and all my teammates crowded around me. It made me feel crazy, but they had to do it because the coach told 'em to. I'm afraid of big crowds."

Grant picked up their darts for the last round. Jacobi had won two games and so had Grant. They were both tired and sipped on water to stay awake.

"Last game!" Grant announced.

"What are you afraid of, Grant?" Jacobi asked in return.

"Honestly, I'm afraid of not being as good as my dad."

"At what?"

273 | Michael D. Ison

"At everything. His job: he worked for a distribution company, worked his way up with a very minimal education. He became the manager, then the plant manager, then the vice president, and then he left that company and started his own distribution company that ended up buying out the one he worked for previously. He's good at woodworking; he can build anything, fix anything, restore anything. He knows all about birds, and stars, and music, and on and on and on. He's good to mom, too. They've been married for forty-one years, and they are still happy, and he's a great dad. He's really better than me at everything."

"If he's such a good dad, then why hasn't he been down here to visit? Why haven't I met him?"

"I asked him not to come. I told him I would let him know when to come because I knew he would come down here and interfere by trying to fix things."

"So he's not good at keeping his nose to himself?"

"That's not the problem. He'd probably counsel everyone into a better place and we'd all be thanking him for it. The problem with him coming here would be that I wouldn't deal with stuff myself . . . and this is my deal, Jacobi, I have to learn how to deal with it."

Grant landed his last two darts to win the game. He collapsed into his rocker and said, "Finally!"

"Finally, what?" Jacobi asked.

"Finally I beat you at something."

"I let you win," Jacobi replied with a smirk, and he walked to the bathroom.

When he came out, Grant said, "Do you want to go for a walk? I love to walk late at night."

"In the rain?"

"No, you're right. I forgot. Well, I'm going to head for bed," he said, wanting to retire before it felt awkward again. "You can set up in the guest room. Do you need anything?"

"Just some more water, but I'll get it. Good night, Grant."

"Good night, Jacobi," Grant said and closed the door to his bedroom. His hinges didn't creak.

Hanging On

The next morning, Grant dropped Jacobi off at his house. He stuck around to talk to Katie and pulled her aside. Although it was terribly wet outside, the rain had stopped, and the sun peeked through the clouds. They stood on the porch, in the sunlight.

"I know I have been distant since Christmas, and I'm sorry. I appreciated the shirt and the family rose, really, it kind of caught me off guard, though. Then Jacobi got upset, and I didn't handle it well. I'm sorry. I reacted poorly in that moment . . . and since then."

"I understand," she said, "it was a lot of pressure."

"If I've been awkward, it's because I didn't know what to say, and I've been trying to focus on Jacobi. I need to figure out where I fit with him. You understand, right?"

"Sure," she said, with her eyes almost closed and her lips slightly pursed.

Grant chose not to push the issue any further, and he went home. He spent the rest of the day cleaning up broken branches and running. He went for a run, twice, and tried to avoid the mud.

On Sunday, Grant attended church again, and he still hated the singing. He decided he would start coming later, and skip the singing. He did like listening to the young guy preach, but not the old one, though he still didn't understand why both of them said "ah" after every sentence—even when they read the Bible. He knew he needed it, the church, but he couldn't pinpoint why. Something needed to change, something lingering and latched to him like an indeterminable albatross. Grant knew it existed, but he couldn't identify it. The only time it left him, stopped gnawing at him invisibly, was during church. Church wasn't the anecdote though; it was his thoughts that momentarily changed . . . when he got lost in the phantastic dream of actually living like some of the characters about whom he had heard in the sermons—without fear.

Facing Fear

The last game of the season ended in a blur. Jacobi and Dynamite took turns showing off, and Dynamite played better than Grant had ever seen. He stole the ball from practically everybody, even the refs weren't safe. He ended the game with nine steals, eight assists, and twelve points. It was his first time to score double-digit points. Jacobi scored forty-eight.

After the game, Coach Procrete had his assistant see if Dynamite wanted to "play up" in the tournament. Apparently, the assistant was told to stay for the junior high game, to make sure Jacobi made it to the tournament. His instructions were: "If that Dynamite boy keeps a playin' like 'e has been, you brang him, too. If he gets more 'an five steals and five assists, I want him hyear."

And the assistant coach obliged.

"Dynamite, you 'ont to play with the high schoo' ta'nite? Coach told me ta bring ye if ye stole it more'n five times."

"I'm not sure," Dynamite replied. "I've gotta, um, I've gotta ask . . ."

"We can't wait all day, son. You gotta chance to play for the big team ta'nite. You 'ont it or not?"

Dynamite hesitated. He looked at Jacobi while Grant's wheels started to spin. Why was he so hesitant?

"Cowards die many times before their deaths," Dynamite said. "I'm in."

Dynamite and Jacobi were extremely excited, and couldn't stop talking about their big day. Katie took them to the next county to the place of the tournament, Crick County. Grant followed suit, and was just as excited as the boys.

On the varsity level, Jacobi usually played two positions: the two guard and point guard. Against this team, he played the two guard and made them pay. After scoring twenty in the first half of his first varsity appearance, he came out in the second with his guns blazing. He hit three 3-pointers in the first four minutes of the second half. When the defense moved out to double-team him, he started to give and go. Grant's favorite moment was when Jacobi, who was double-teamed at the 3-point line on the right side, fired a two-handed overhead pass down to J.J., who was on the block in the post. Jacobi ran right around the defenders on the right, and accepted the quick pass back from J.J., who then moved aside, as Jacobi extended fully out, flying in for a two-handed slam. He swung far up on the other side of the rim, let himself pop off dramatically, and landed softly in a squatting position on the floor. The other team's coach dropped his clipboard on the ground, mouth agape, and grabbed his head with both hands as if he were clutching a toupee.

If he continues playing like this, Jacobi might be the most heavily sought after basketball player in the nation, Grant thought. *Ronald would know*. Grant decided to talk to him tomorrow after the tournament. It was a shame he hadn't come tonight. Jacobi said that Ronald used to come to all of his games, but he had backed off this year; he said Jacobi needed to get used to playing without him there. Grant found that odd, especially with Jacobi being only fourteen, but he wasn't going to question Ronald—everything that man did worked.

The Looking Glass

That night was especially clear. The stars were windows of heaven, casting down glory onto the naked world. Jacobi played like a champion, and Grant had never been so proud. Katie took both boys home, Dynamite to his, and Jacobi with her. Grant went to the cabin alone, but his enthusiasm was so amplified he couldn't sit still. He decided to go for a run.

Though the mudslides were still thick reservoirs of wet, sloppy filth, the rest of the ground was relatively dry. The shape of the mountain caused most of the water and topsoil to roll away. Grant jogged along the road until he reached the base of the mountain. Following the railroad track, he came upon the highway that would lead him past Dynamite's house to the next holler over. He never made it.

On the flat ground, he really picked up his pace. Blowing past Dynamite's house, he heard a scream so shrill it stiffened his neck and sucked his breath away. The sound were as if a bleating calf had just been skinned alive. He heard another scream, quieter, and a muffled gruff voice rasping in the darkness. Not sure whether to flee or stay, Grant stood still for a moment. His curiosity pulled him forward, dragging him through the screams, though his heart wrenched away, away toward home.

The screaming came from the barn, and by this time Grant was sure he knew what it was: Dynamite. Creeping along affront the house, through the grass and up to the barn, Grant felt a gnawing trepidation, alive and squirming inside him, telling him to leave, but he pressed on. When he reached the double doors, his fear held him. He was able to peer through a little crack, and in the sliver of sight was Dynamite, stark naked, tied up, facing the wall with blood oozing from his back.

Furiously, a man was whipping him, cussing him, screaming at him, beating him mercilessly with a thin tree branch. They called it a "switch" but it never seemed to switch anything--except love to hate. With ravenous blows and anger, the man beat Dynamite until the switch broke into a nub, and then he picked up another. He continued to beat him, beat him, beat him, as if he were lacerating the devil right out of him. He raged again: "You go cross county without askin' me, and ye gonna get beat! You run that filthy mouth a yours, and ye gonna get beat! I taught you respect, boy; you don't run whare ya think ya want, you go whare I tell ye! Dynamite! Ha! Yer name's Diana! Listen at ye screamin' lika girl . . . 'Oh, Daddy, stop, Daddy, stop, please don't whip me!' Cryin' like a baby! Call for ye mammy, baby, call for ye mammy!"

As Dynamite's father wailed on him, Dynamite floundered nakedly against the barn wall and back into the raining switch. Sweat soaked through the back of his father's shirt, and beads rolled down his face. He spit on his son, and then hit him again.

Grant stood looking through the crack for a lifetime, but it had only been a few seconds. Filled with rage, he grabbed the door to yank it open and bolt in, but his rage was pacified, overcome by something stronger, something deeper, something weightier. *What if I can't do it?* he asked himself. *What if I rush in and can't save him? What if he takes me out, too? What if this causes him to get beat worse? What if he kills Dynamite, me, and his wife once he knows that I know . . . What if? What if?*

Grant slowly backed away from the door. He ran. He ran away from Dynamite's pleading screams, from his tears of agony. He ran up to the road, and away from that home, that home of hate. He could still hear Dynamite screaming into the night, and his last poor bellow was drowned out by the self-deprecating screams in Grant's own mind. And then there was silence. All Grant could hear was the sound of his own feet hitting the ground, his breathing, and his heart beating recklessly in his chest. He couldn't hear Dynamite any longer, and he couldn't hear himself.

He ran ferociously. He ran through the woods, up the holler toward his home. He ran forever, and he ran wildly, until he slipped on a pile of mud and leaves, falling, sliding on his hands and knees. He collapsed in the mud, with his face in his hands, wailing, crying out, "I hate myself! I hate myself! Oh, God, kill me now! Kill me now!" But He didn't.

Grant went home and wished for death. How could he face Dynamite now—if he were still alive? How could he face himself, or Jacobi? He looked at himself in the mirror, and he punched it. His image shattered like raindrops, as he knew it would.

Alone in His Own Mind

Grant did not return to the tournament the next day, or to
church the next, or to school for the two following days.
Jacobi came to visit, but Grant did not answer the door.
Ronald came over and unlocked the door, but Grant met
him forcefully and stormed at him to get out. His bloodshot
eyes were crossed, deep purple circles lay beneath them,
and a fierce look of mindlessness was scratched across his
face. Ronald locked the door, but he did not leave. He
stayed. He stayed, and he rocked in the rocking chair on the
front porch, and listened. All the while, the warm breeze
blew in Grant's mind.

Ronald's Turn

Ronald knew. He had heard from Jacobi that Dynamite had not been to school, either. Ronald had threatened Dynamite's dad before, and said that if he ever caught him, he'd kill him, but he never did. Dynamite's dad showed no fear, no sign of being intimidated by Ronald.

"You don't know, old man, ye don't know nothin'! Don't come round hyear 'cusin' me of beatin' my boy! I take care of my family . . . and I'll kill you if I see that stupid face again!"

They both stood and stared—neither backing down—until Dynamite came outside and saw the stand-off. He grabbed his dad and begged him to come inside. That had been more than a year ago, but the violence never stopped. And Ronald had not forgotten.

When Grant finally let Ronald in, on Wednesday, Grant sat in his chair rocking back and forth saying, "I can't forgive myself. I can't forgive myself . . . I hate me, I hate myself, I want to die, I want to die!"

Ronald stayed another night, and on Thursday, he finally had enough.

"Grant!" he said. "Stop feelin' sorry for ye self and get up and do somethin'! Yer in here cryin' 'I can't forgive myself, I can't forgive myself,' but if ye don't, you'll kill yerself. You don't need to die, ye need to live! Ye need to do somethin' right, and make amends with Dynamite and yerself. Do it!"

"I don't deserve it! Dynamite didn't deserve it!"

"Yer right, ya don't! But if ye don't do it, you'll never move. Forgive yerself, knowin' that the forgiveness will give you the ability to move, and then you'll make it right."

Hung Over

Grant couldn't do it. He sat in the chair, rocking, blinded by fear and hate.

On Sunday, Grant finally broke. His feelings were numb, but he had to do something, or he would die. He scraped himself off the bed, still covered in dried mud, snot, and blood. Like an early-morning throat punch, the standing sent him reeling. The wave of pain that rushed to his head knocked him right back in his chair. He had only moved from the chair to the bed to the bathroom to the chair in the past week. He felt as if he were hung over—hung over a railing and all the blood had rushed to his head. Again he stood, weak and unstable because everything had atrophied, including his appetite. He forced himself to eat, shower, and shave. Then he went back to bed, exhausted, with plans to burn those clothes.

Chapter 14: Game Time

The next week, Grant returned to school. He never looked Katie in the eye, and he disconnected from his students. He taught his lessons, and then he went home, skipping Jacobi's practices. After four days of continuing like this, Grant talked to his father—and talked and talked and talked. He was like a dam erupting. His father listened patiently, for what seemed like hours, intermittently asking questions for clarification, but never interrupting. When Grant reached the part in his story about Katie giving him the shirt and the rose, he heard Mr. Erlosung audibly gasp.

"What is it, Dad?"

"Grant, what did you say? What did you say that base said? Are you sure it was a red rose encased in glass, with a wooden base that said 'Family is Forever'?"

"Yes, Dad. Why?"

"Just keep going, Grant, finish the story," his father encouraged.

Grant continued with the story but then stopped at Jacobi's last game.

"So what happened after the game?" his father asked expectantly.

Grant had made Jacobi sound so magical, so majestic, that his dad—like any good grandparent—couldn't wait to hear the rest of the story, embellishments and all.

"Dad," he said, "you're going to hate me when I tell you the rest of this story, but I'm going to tell you. I have to tell somebody."

"Grant, tell me!" his father said. And so he did.

Grant revealed all the details of the story: Dynamite's beating, how he had run away while Dynamite wailed into the night, and his own wish for death. He wept bitterly again, and he begged his father not to hate him for being so weak, so opposite of him.

"Grant, I have to tell you something, and I need you to listen. Don't question me, just listen. When I moved here, I was a woodworker. My father was a woodworker, and his father was a woodworker, and I made keepsakes from wood. I started a business, hand carving items— trinkets for people to have in their homes. I later met your mother, and I started building a life for us. Grant, I hand carved roses. I hand carved roses out of a butternut base, painted the rose red, placed a glass bulb over it, and carved "Family is Forever" into the base. These were specialty items, handcrafted by a master hand carver, not like the cheap ones you've seen where you are—no plastic. But it's the same model, and what you're seeing is my idea. And I lost my shirt. I lost everything. The demand was high, but my output was not. I couldn't keep the business afloat, so I had to sell it out to some cheap manufacturer who wanted to mass produce everything. When I sold out, I was so far in debt I couldn't recover. I lost the house I had purchased and everything I owned. I even pawned off all of my tools."

"Okay, Dad, I get it, you—"

"I'm not finished! Your mother and I were not married yet, but I had lost our home. She was still living with her parents, and I couldn't handle the failure. I didn't think she would wait. I hated my failure; I hated myself. Grant, I've never told you this, never told anybody this for over forty years, but I tried to kill myself," and his father started to choke up. "I tried to hang myself, and I couldn't even make myself do it. Your mom found me standing on a chair in the basement of the butcher shop where I worked with the noose tied, but too afraid to jump. She talked me down, and I checked into a hospital." His throat began to clear.

"When I got out, I had a massive amount of debt, no home, and no job, but your mother stuck with me. She inspired me. I got the idea to go to work for the company that provided materials to the butcher shop, and that's when things started to improve. I refused to let myself think negative thoughts, just as the counselor at the hospital taught me, and I worked my way out of debt. Grant, it took me three years until I could marry your mother, but we made it. We got pregnant with you after just a few months. By the time you were five years old, this was all a distant memory."

"Dad, why didn't you ever tell me?"

"Because I didn't want you to live in fear. I didn't want you to live in fear of what you might do."

"Dad, you recreated yourself, and you were extremely successful, why would that cause me to live in fear?"

"That is not what I meant. I did not want your fear of failure to drive you to do what I did or try what I tried. You might have been successful. I wanted you to believe that failure is only temporary."

"Dad, that still doesn't make sense."

"I did not want you to get any negative ideas. I did not want you to try what I did . . . Grant, do you remember what I told you about the blue jay and his feathers?"

"Yes, Dad. I tried to tell Jacobi, but it wasn't quite the same. He seemed to already know about the blue structure thing."

"No, Grant. Do you remember what I told you about the blue jay dropping his feathers? Grant, focus—I need you to hear me. A blue jay does not lose what makes him unique if he just drops his feathers. He loses what makes him unique when the feathers are crushed. Grant, it doesn't matter if you drop feathers . . . it's going to happen. It matters *where* you drop feathers, and for whom you drop them. Don't let this one instance cause you to lose what makes you unique. You dropped some feathers. Go pick up your feathers, move them, and drop them where they belong, before they get crushed."

Furious

Katie was furious. That Friday, she raced into his classroom just after the final bell had rung. She walked up, determined, grabbed Grant by the back of the arm, squeezing intensely, and turned him around to face her. She got up on her toes and right into his face.

"Listen to me!" she barked. Grant was all ears, and bulging eyes. "You haven't spoken to anyone for two weeks! You skipped a week of school, and only kept your job because we're so desperate. You haven't seen Jacobi, asked about Jacobi, or even checked to see how he did in the tournament! He's had two weeks waiting to see if the varsity team is going to make the playoffs, and you haven't been there! You didn't even tell me you wouldn't be taking him to practice! Nothing! What's wrong with you?"

"I'm sorry. I just couldn't. Some bad stuff happened and I couldn't deal with—"

"Couldn't deal with it! How do you think your son is dealing with his father, whom he didn't know for thirteen years, disappearing? He told me how he came to your house, knocked on the door and windows, and all you could do was shoo him away! Who does that? To his own son? Get over yourself!"

She let go of his arm and began to pace around the room. Tears flowed down her face, and her lips trembled. The bases of her palms were bright white where she had dug her nails into each of them, and she placed her hands behind her back stiffly.

"For the past week and a half, he has been taking it out on me! You disappear, and he takes it out on me! What am I supposed to do? Maybe I should shrink up and crumble because I can't handle it; except, I would never do that because I actually love my son!"

Grant looked away, but Katie circled right into his gaze and said, "Look at me! He's broken and he's hurting, and he's hurting the other people around him now, so you better do something to fix it. If you thought I was going to let you off the hook, let you get away with it, you're wrong. I'm going to push you until you either become a man or you leave! Do you understand?"

Before Grant could respond, she started right back in on him.

"His grandpa is dying. He doesn't need this right now, but it's happening. Dad has pneumonia, and compounded with his other ailments, he's not going to make it. He has twenty-four to forty-eight hours at the most, and then he'll be gone . . ." She broke into even more tears.

Grant didn't dare try to comfort her or touch her. She was too volatile at this moment.

"You need to step up and be his dad right now, while I tend to my dad! Pick him up tonight and take him to your place. You take care of him, cook for him, spend time with him. Do whatever you have to do. Listen to me, he's going to be with you for a week, and you'd better be a man. Every day you eat breakfast with him, understand?" She started to calm down. "That's the most important time you can spend with him, in the morning. Bradbury said that first hour was 'a philosophical hour,' but I'm telling you it is a relationship hour. I've been doing it since he was born, and it works. It lets him know he is first. You need to do this . . ."

Her chest heaved beneath her flushed, tear-stained face.

"What time will you be picking him up?" she demanded, as the anger flooded back.

"Six," Grant responded.

"Good!" she said. "And don't be late."

She stormed out of his room and back down the hallway. As her heels clacked, Grant heard her crying audibly again, louder than before. He knew she wasn't crying for her dad this time; she was crying for herself—she felt like she was giving her baby away.

At that moment, Grant had a realization. Katie's parents were the reason why she had never married, why she had only dated sparingly after she left college. She confessed she had been on a couple of dates, when Jacobi was six, but it never worked out. Katie blamed the lack of quality men, which Grant did not deny, but she also busied herself by volunteering constantly as well as caring for her ailing parents. Although she lived in the next holler over, she could often be found at their home in the evenings. He wondered if they ever "became ill" because they thought she might leave again. He had taken for granted that her logical answer was the true one. After all this time, he realized that the truth of her actions could be found in her emotions.

Breakfast—Again

Jacobi spent the weekend with Grant, and Grant cooked every meal, washed every dish, and did all of Jacobi's laundry. Jacobi was evidently uncomfortable and hurt, but he did what his mom asked him to do. Grant could see that if the circumstances were different, Jacobi would have put up more of a fight, but since his grandfather was dying, Jacobi wasn't going fight.

Grant took Jacobi to the hospital for a couple hours and waited outside. The trip took three hours, there and back, so they spent the weekend traveling, cooking, cleaning, and in much silence. Grant did get Jacobi to tell him about the tournament, but it was a brief description. His team took second place, losing to Crick County. Andre, the big man from Crick County, was devastatingly good. Andre's assignment was to guard Jacobi the whole game, and he held him to twenty-two points—the least Jacobi could remember scoring—ever. On the other hand, Andre scored forty-four and had fourteen rebounds—against a double-team! After that, there wasn't much more conversation from Jacobi.

Wake Up!

At 8:02 a.m. on Monday morning, Chester died. The way Grant heard it, Chester woke up, asked his wife and his daughter to sing "When the Roll Is Called Up Yonder," and he passed as they called. He struggled for his last breath, and then nothing. Grant caught a glimpse of a raven flying off the hospital window into the darkness of the mountain and disappearing into the lonely trees. Grant and Jacobi arrived to the hospital at 8:13 a.m.

A problem emerged. Jacobi was supposed to play his first varsity game that night. On Saturday, the Possum County High School boys' basketball team had clinched a place in the playoffs, and the first game was on the upcoming Monday. Although Jacobi would only be able to play due to a loophole in the four-year eligibility system, the school policy still dictated that a student at least attend half of the school day to be eligible to play in an event that same day. Of course, it was on everyone's mind, everyone's except Katie's it seemed.

Grant surmised that she had been so wrapped up in taking care of her mom and dad: trying to figure out if her mom would now live with her, what they would do about Vern and the kids, and how things were going with Jacobi and Grant that she had forgotten.

"Oh my gosh! I totally forgot!" she said looking up at Grant. "How could I forget that he has to go to school today so he can play tonight? Why didn't he mention it? Why did he have you ask for him? Oh, I'm so sorry!"

Throughout the weekend, Grant had begun to strengthen his resolve to do what he felt was right, no matter how difficult. In this instance, it was to talk to Katie about Jacobi—just after her father died. He asked her, just moments before, if he could take Jacobi to school so that Jacobi could play that night. Her inconsonant phrases betrayed her emotional conflict in the moment.

"Jacobi, sweetheart, you know you can ask me these things!" she said while looking at him over her father's dead body. "I know you were trying to be sensitive, but Grandpa would want you to go. You know he loved watching your games, and he would have gone to more of them if he hadn't been so ill. Get to school. I'm sorry, I can't come. I have to stay with Mom. You understand, right?" she asked.

She informed them that there would be a wake at the church, and they could come after the game. This was news to Grant. He had never heard of a wake, nor of "sitting up with the dead," and especially not for three days as Katie described. As he walked out the door, side by side with

Jacobi, he made up his mind that he would do whatever Katie asked in the wake of her father passing. Even if it meant "sitting up with the dead."

He dropped Jacobi off at school, went to his school, and walked into the office.

"I'll be teaching the rest of the day," he told Mrs. Clowers. She was the office secretary, substitute teacher coordinator, administrative assistant to the principal, and a list of other roles that included head of the hospitality committee.

The substitute didn't look too upset to see him, and pretty much ran out of the room when he showed up. Kids were playing cards, lying on the floor, sitting in each other's laps doing unmentionable things. Scotty, Grant's oldest student, returned from the bathroom and his right nostril was bright red, just like his eyes. Grant ignored him. He was utterly disengaged at this point, but he mustered through the period, determined to do the next right thing. After a few moments, he called the office and had a disciplinary dean come pick up Scotty. He got the other students on task. While they worked, he mulled over all the advice his dad had given him, all the things Katie said to him . . . he couldn't make it all make sense; it didn't fit. But he played the role as if it did.

That evening, the first game of the playoffs was in Combs County. The Possum County Badgers would face the Combs County Roosters. The Raping Roosters, as they were locally known, was the most violent team around. Anywhere else, their name would have brought shame and reproach, but they wore it like a badge of honor. Jacobi wanted to tear it off and take a few feathers with it.

Before the game, Jacobi did everything he could to be friendly toward the Roosters. He spoke to them, he talked to their coach and their fans during the girls' game, he even messed around with their mascot, but he received only rude treatment and intense disrespect. One of the boys from the other team, who had really short hair on top, but long, straggly hair in the back, spat right in his face.

"H'aint got no time for yer kind round hyear, boy! Getchye self over ta yer side fore poppa rooster comes da getch ye." He reached down and grabbed his crotch, as if it were some type of provocation to Jacobi.

Jacobi backed away slowly. He turned to find Grant saying, "Well, I see you have met the lame cocks! Don't sweat it. They're just insecure. They're afraid you might make them choose one hairstyle, when they want both!"

At that, Jacobi and Grant both laughed, trying to reduce the tension. Later, Grant caught a shocking glimpse of

Dynamite. He hadn't heard anything from Jacobi, and was sure that neither Jacobi nor Dynamite knew what he had witnessed that night he peered into Dynamite's barn. He hadn't expected Dynamite to be at the game, but then again, Grant was ascribing a thirty year old's recovery time to that of a hyperactive thirteen year old. During the first half of the girls' game, Grant willed himself to speak with Dynamite.

"How you doing, Red?"

> "Great, so you better 'preciate, the state,
> of the weight, when I state, how we'll win state, and—
> "

"You can't rhyme *state* with *state*, Dynamite!"

"I just did," Dynamite said. They gave each other a high-five, but Grant proceeded to the stands with a pit in his stomach.

The Rectum Roosters, as Grant renamed them, took the court for warm-ups. They didn't look nearly as athletic as the Badgers, but they looked mean. Their heads were nearly shaven on the top and sides with long, luxurious locks in the back. Each player was missing some type of tooth or couth. Every time one of them jumped, he flailed his elbows. Their layup drill looked more like a wrestling drop-kick drill. But somehow they had made the playoffs, *so they must have some talent*, Grant reasoned.

He was wrong. They didn't have any talent. They were extremely adept at pain and intimidation, but not basketball. He feared for Jacobi, remembering a time when he, too, had played against a violent team of athletes. It was at a track meet in late spring of his seventh grade year. The other team was known for stepping on heels. They would step on the heel of the runner in front of them, with their spikes, in order to cause an injury that appeared accidental. Grant was running the fourth leg of the 1600-meter relay, when a kid from that team stepped right on his heel just after he received the baton. He tripped and landed face first on the track, smacking himself in the eye with the baton. Mr. Erlosung came irately rushing out of the stands to defend his son, and now . . . Grant, the son, was the nervous father.

From the tip-off, Jacobi played wisely and intensely. Defensively, the Badgers ran a zone, so Jacobi played off the position of the ball more so than he did the position of the opposing player. This allowed him to intercept errant passes, of which there were many, and create fast break opportunities for his team. Blowing past defenders like a scalded dog, he ripped down the floor tenaciously and either finished strong or gave it up for an easy finish for his teammates. Always after scoring, he turned quickly and hustled back to the other end, with his eyes wide open for any attempts to molest him.

The coach had Jacobi run the point, and that's what he did—run. He had his team hustle down the court on every possession—looking for the quick score—and avoiding the opportunity for the Roosters to needle them when they set up their offense. On one possession, Jacobi streaked down the floor like an illegal coal truck hauling helium balloons and headed straight for the basket. From the other side of the court, a Rooster came flailing like a chicken with his head cut off. Their arrival coincided: Jacobi's by air, and the Rooster's by land. The Rooster tried to flail Jacobi out of the air, but he caught a knee to the temple, which Jacobi had delivered, that sent him crumbling and careening off the court. Some of the Rooster fans began to rush the court, but Grant beat them to it. Like a freak show wrestler, Grant stood in front of Jacobi, holding a metal chair he had picked up from the sidelines, and taunted some hill-jack to get the rest of his teeth knocked out. Nobody volunteered.

The police escorted Grant outside and reminded him that he was in Combs County, so he better be careful if he wanted to make it home tonight. He waited outside with the team driver—who hated basketball anyway. Grant was proud of himself for defending Jacobi, but he knew it was incomplete. This time, he had been prepared. He had played the scenario over and over in his mind: what he would do if someone at the game tried to hurt Jacobi, how he would defend him, where he would find a weapon. Preparation was key. With preparation, Grant felt like a tycoon—without it, well, a buffoon.

On the way home, Jacobi filled him in on the details.

"Once they got the crowd quieted down, we finished the game. It took like twenty minutes just to get everyone in their seats and to be reasonable."

"Nobody there was reasonable!" Grant interrupted.

"The cops threatened to shut the whole thing down," Jacobi continued, "and I wouldn't have even cared. I was scared! I could take one or two of those boys, but it looked like the whole team, along with their mamas and daddies, were trying to get a piece of me."

"So what did you do?"

"I went right at them! As soon as the whistle blew, I dribbled up the court and slung a pass like I meant it for Jason and drilled one of their players in the face! His hair shot out like peacock's feathers, and he fell to the ground with blood spraying from his nose! I grabbed the ball, hit my layup, and then walked right between 'em and helped him up. One of them tried to say something, but the refs were all over us. None of them tried anything after that, and Coach hustled us out of there as soon as the last whistle blew."

"How many did you score?"

"Forty-nine."

Later, after showering at Grant's cabin and changing, they headed up to the church. On the way, Grant asked Jacobi, "Do you think you did the right thing at the game? Hitting that kid in the face with the ball?"

"I don't know. Ronald wasn't there; my coach didn't give me any advice, so I didn't know what to do. I just acted. I knew they would try to hurt us, so I wanted to let them know we weren't afraid. It wasn't just me they were gunning after; it was all of us."

"Good point," Grant said, and they rode on into the night.

At the church house was weeping, wailing, and gnashing of teeth. The weeping and wailing were for Chester—and attention—the gnashing of teeth was over the sheer quantity of food being consumed. Grant had never seen anything like it. Well, yes, he had; he had seen all the raccoons, opossums, and coyotes running away that day

Hatchet had burnt the trash bags filled with chicken remains. People flocked to the dead like scavengers, not to mourn over them, but rather to feast off of them. It was pure carnage.

Set up in the dining hall and the foyer of the church were tables covered with cakes and pies, fried chicken, fried potatoes, mashed potatoes, scalloped potatoes, cheesy potatoes, everything but baked potatoes was available. They even had sweet potato casserole, covered in brown sugar and smothered with marshmallows, right next to the green bean, spinach, broccoli, and chicken casseroles, wedged next to the shepherd's pie, goulash, and soup beans—the many cauldrons of soup beans—and cornbread.

Grant had discovered soup beans were a main staple at every house. They were simply pinto beans, rinsed with the rocks removed, and cooked for about one hundred years in salt water with grease or lard for flavoring. Often people consumed them with another staple vegetable: ketchup. People also ate collard greens quite a bit, cooked, salted, and drizzled in bacon grease for flavor.

Grant went into the kitchen and saw Ma Jones drowning a perfectly good roast beef with tons of brown gravy.

"What are you doing, Ma?" he asked.

"I'ma smothern' this hyear roast with gravy. Whatsit look like I'ma doin'?"

"Ruining a perfectly good roast beef."

"Ruin' it? This hain't ruint. We can't eat it less we soft'n it up!"

Grant looked around the room at several people with frail teeth, gumming roast beef and white bread soaked in gravy.

"Well, Ma, you better soften it up then!" he said, and reached over to give her a side squeeze. Ma was one of ladies at the church who spoke to Grant without hesitancy. She was always kind, but direct, and she always looked Grant in the eyes—from the beginning. Apparently she could also cook—their style.

Grant began to walk into the sanctuary to see Chester when one of the men grabbed him and handed him a paper plate and plastic fork. "Try 'is, boy, yer gonna love it!"

Grant looked down at the lime-green, wiggly jello, filled with peeled grapes, marshmallows, and some type of nuts. He dumped it in the trashcan after making sure nobody was looking.

The sanctuary was another sight to behold. Several people sat in the pews, talking, cackling, laughing, crying, and effusing a little too much, but near the casket was dead silence. Nobody was paying attention to the casket. Chester lay with eyes and mouth closed, cold and alone at the front of the room, a stick of forgotteness floating in a river of self-absorption. Grant sat down front and waited, sure some type of service would start soon.

After about an hour and a half, he realized this was it: a wake. A wake was sitting around talking, eating, crying, ignoring a dead body, but there was no service, no sanctimony. The evening dragged on forever, and he was tired, and he was sure that Jacobi was, too. He made his way over to Katie to speak with her briefly before exiting.

"He did well tonight. He's a good kid. You should be a proud mom," he said.

"Thank you," she said, running her handkerchief through her hands repeatedly.

He still didn't understand how she came from that family, loved them so much, lived so near them, managed to be so different, and raised a boy like Jacobi. *I guess some things really are inexplicable,* he thought, and he wrapped up some banana nut bread in tin foil for himself. He grabbed Jacobi, and they went home.

As the moon shone down in all of its brilliance, and they crossed over the railroad track, Grant thought of the business, and Robin, and his home so many, many miles away. What was he going to do about all of this? He remembered some advice he had heard several months before, and mixed it all together in the mush pot that was his mind. Jacobi went to bed, and as Grant's head hit the pillow, his last thought was, *I guess some blue jays are called to stay.*

Another Letter

Tuesday was the day of the memorial service, not the funeral. After school and practice, Jacobi and Grant went home together. Jacobi had not prepared well for the week. He was aloof.

"I don't really have anything that nice to wear," he said. "I have some slacks and a dress shirt, but they are too small now. I got them last year for the awards banquet."

"Hold on," Grant said. He came back with a black, thin, pin-striped suit and a white shirt. "A few years ago, it was really popular to have a skinny suit. It had to be thin, fitted, and tight. I still have mine and some tapered shirts. You're a little taller than I am, and thinner in the waist, but it'll do."

Jacobi went to change, and came out with the pants puckered at the waist from being cinched tight by a belt. He put on the jacket to cover his indiscretion and looked across the room to Grant.

"You, my friend," said Grant, "are a stud!"

He looked Jacobi over, his sandy hair and green eyes contrasting starkly with the thin, fitted suit. He looked like a model, except he still had the face of a fourteen-year-old.

"Thanks for letting me wear the suit, Grant. It's nice!" Jacobi said with a mild hint of awareness.

"No problem. If you haven't noticed, I have about fifty. Please, keep it, and we'll buy you a couple of your own next time we can get out of town to a place with a real clothier."

"Clothier?"

"Forget it."

They headed for the church. Something else Jacobi didn't know was that Grant had given Katie the money for the funeral. Money hadn't been set aside for the funeral, the casket, the gravestone, anything. When Katie told him how much they had, which was next to nothing, Grant produced enough funds to cover everything, plus about two years of living expenses for Katie's mom.

The church's emotional ambiance grabbed Jacobi and sucked him in before he even made it through the front doors. He was a ball of tears. Grant, on the other hand, was somewhat appalled by all of the scream-crying, but what was he going to do? He rolled with it.

Inside, a small, sniveling man, who was not crying, stayed nearly hidden in the shadows of the entryway. He was in charge of consoling the people and keeping the doorway free of impingements. His beady eyes, his scraggly, gray and black, curly hair on the sides and back of his head, and his shiftiness were enough to cause Grant alarm. As the miser took coats and hung them, he also pilfered their pockets for any valuables. Grant saw him pulling his hand out of a lady's coat pocket, and gave him the evil eye. The thief held up a memorial service program in response, as if his little sleight of hand technique would exculpate him from his crime. Grant walked over and whispered discretely, "Keep your hands to yourself, and I'll keep mine to myself."

Two days and two times I've stood up to someone for something other than trying to cheat me in business, Grant thought. *I'm making some progress*. He gazed to the front of the room. Standing over Chester was a big, rotund man. He leaned over the casket, draped above Chester, with his arm resting on the open lid. He wore a sleeveless t-shirt. Grant saw his armpit hair close enough to tickle Chester's nose, and, as the big man mumbled and sobbed, Grant saw sweat run from the tip of his armpit hair and splash on Chester's cheek. *Some battles are worth fighting*, Grant thought, shaking his head and walking toward Katie, *and some are not.*

"I'm nervous, Grant," she said amid all the wailing. "I have to read 'An Ode to My Father' tonight."

"An ode to your father? What's that?"

"It's an ode that I wrote to my father."

"Oh, so it really is an ode to *your* father, isn't it?"

"Yes, and I can hardly keep it together with all of the crying and wailing going on . . ."

At that exact moment, some lady muffled out a nasally cry that would have made the sirens blush.

"Okay, what do you need?"

"Nothing really. Can you and Jacobi just sit up here by me, please?"

"Jacobi already is," he pointed behind her to Jacobi sitting there with his face resting downward in his hands. "I'll sit by Jacobi, and your mom can sit next to you, okay?"

She turned and hugged Jacobi, and Grant realized she was completely frazzled. Jacobi was always her first priority, and today she didn't even notice him. He was on her mind, but stress clouded her vision.

They took their seats while the families of Chester and his wife gathered around. All the women wore thick black dresses that dragged the floor, except Katie. Hers was black, but it was three-quarter length, with straps that covered just the shoulders, and she wore little black gloves with a small black hat. Grant saw a trend.

He knew it was not the right time, but he leaned over to Jacobi and asked, "Why do all the women here always wear dresses that come to the floor?"

With shrugged shoulders and puffy eyes, Jacobi said, "Probably to cover their legs."

"What do you mean? Is it bad if their legs show?"

"Well, probably, but they probably do it more to cover the hair on their legs."

"What?" Grant asked incredulously.

"Yeah, they don't shave their legs . . . or their armpits for that matter. They don't think a woman should cut her hair, any of it."

"Then why do they let your mom come here?"

Obviously irritated at this line of questioning, Jacobi said in an exasperated tone, "Mom's not a member, and she came back here pregnant, remember? They didn't kick her out, but they wouldn't let her join. So, she doesn't have to follow their rules. They all love her now, anyway. I'm sure they wish they could dress like her sometimes, too. Especially in the sum—"

Before Jacobi could finish his sentence, he was interrupted by, "Weeeeellllllllllllllllllllll! Aaaaaamaaaaaaaazzziiieeng graaaaaacc . . ."

Grant sang right along with them, somber spirit and all. He practically burst a blood vessel when they sang "I'll Fly Away." After the singing came the preaching. The preaching came, but it did not go. It stayed. For a long, long time the old reverend preached about heaven and hell, death, and life, the past and the future, but all Grant could remember was the part "but for now we see through a glass darkly."

What did that mean? he wondered, and mulled it over and over, but he never understood.

Katie stood up, startling Grant back to attention. Now it was time for her to read her ode. She walked gracefully to the platform, but stood a little off to the right as the reverend kept his rightful place behind the pulpit. The reverend shifted his eyes toward Katie. Grant was sure there were a few lustful eyes even on this most somber occasion. Katie's bottom lip quivered, Grant looked away, and she began:

Ode to My Dad
Longingly hoping to be held by my father,
Whose hands were so firm and strong yet rough.
His squeeze so tight, reassuring, endearing with
The same hands he used to work the pickaxe
And beat away at the stone and coal. Too

Set before us a meal and put over us a covering
And provide a place for us to dwell in unity.
His hands our protection were,
And homage to them we pay, for
Our life and our laughter were created thus.

O, however we wish his words were.
So firm, so strong, but rough, too.
And never reassuring, endearing with
The same mouth he used to kiss mother
And beat away at my heart and sister's. Too
Break before us our spirit and put over us a cowering
And take a place from us to love liberally.
His mouth our furca were
And horror to it we pay for
Our lives and our laughter were stolen thus.

Criminal! I would be claimed if
I did not represent the true nature
Of a man who practiced love
In all he did do with his hands.
And love true, must be practiced thus.
For words, words fade and dissipate like rain
While work, work's work continues on
As it passes on the true teaching by which
Homes and lives are built.
Without which I could not honor my father thus.

Several women sat with their mouths agape, as did the men, while Katie walked back from the stage to her seat next to Jacobi and her mother. Grant wasn't sure he understood any of what she was saying in her ode—other than her father's hands were strong, but his words were harsh. Nothing had indicated to Grant that Katie's relationship with her father had been so strained, but as Grant would soon learn, relationships were like coal mines. Parts of them were never unearthed and never experienced light. *I don't know if that's really appropriate at a memorial service,* he thought, *to drudge up bitter memories publically,* and by the behavior of the crowd, he felt he was not alone. After a minute, he decided he didn't want to be on the crowd's side against Katie, and agreed within himself to conclude that he just didn't understand. This was a normal practice for him of late.

As the memorial service ended, the night began for Grant. His mind was a jumbled mess, but it temporarily focused when he saw Ronald on the way out the door.

"I haven't seen you lately. Where have you been?"

"I been sick. Those two days a sittin' up there with you, really put a hurtin' on me. Plus, the court's not dry yit, and Jaki's a playin' at the schoo' all the time. We just aint crossed paths. I'ma better now, tho."

"I'm glad you're better, and I appreciate your sitting with me—more than you know." Grant paused for a moment. "Hey! What's the reason behind all of this loud wailing and crying and overblown behavior? I realize someone died, but you would think by their reaction that Chester was everyone's brother." Grant paused again and waded in his sarcasm.

"Let me tell ye a story," Ronald replied. "A king came to a city an aconquered it. When 'e did, 'e put a stop to their dance festival. Said it was stupid. On the eve of dance, the people drug 'm out in tha strait and danced on 'm till he came bones." Now Ronald paused. "Another king came and conquered 'a same city. He gave 'em two days for their dance. On the eve of the dance, they brought the king into the street and offered 'm dere daughters to marry an 'ere sons to be in his army."

"So, when in Rome . . ."

"Cry louder'en 'em Romans, boys, cry louder'en 'em Romans."

"Okay!" Grant said, patting the older man on his thick back. Although Ronald was slightly hunched, he was still stalwart and powerful.

Grant and Jacobi made their way out of the church to head home. Silence was a welcome third party between the two: one, because Grant was so distracted by trying to untangle the mess in his mind; and two, Grant assumed, was because Jacobi was too emotionally drained to speak. Into the house they plodded. Jacobi showered and brushed his teeth after hanging his new suit carefully. He said good night to Grant and went to bed. Grant was sure Jacobi was asleep before his head hit the pillow.

On the other hand, Grant was unsure if *he* would ever be able to sleep, so he set himself up at his table near the front door. A long way away from his standing desk, Grant pulled out some beige-colored writing paper and a black ink pen. This was going to be much more difficult than any contract he had ever negotiated, any deal he had ever constructed, any return on investment he had ever calculated. He was going to write a letter of forgiveness— to himself.

He had read about it months ago in a book about relationships. He had thought it was crazy then. Now, it was the sanest idea he had heard in weeks. He wondered if the inability to forgive oneself was the problem with those crazy Roosters in Combs County, or with Dynamite's dad, or even with Chester who had just passed away, with his harsh words. It didn't really matter that much, he just needed to write.

He sat down at the table and began.

> Dear Grant,
>
> I forgive you for being a piece of trash who couldn't even stand up for a kid while he was being beaten. You're a pansy, but I forgive you! You should be beaten yourself, for being so weak.

Grant took that letter, balled it up, and threw it in the trash. He concentrated, started over, and began again.

> Dear Grant,
>
> I forgive you for your failures. Although you failed your son, his mother, your parents, and everyone around you, I forgive you. You should probably consider getting therapy for your inability to forge a relationship without sabotaging it and destroying everyone in your path. You're pathetic.

That one ended up in the trash, too. To whom could he appeal? He didn't know. He tried to make a list of what he liked about himself, but that list could never overcome his failures. Dynamite's screams were still in his mind. After staring blankly for a few minutes, he looked over and saw the cheap family rose Katie had bought him. Although he detested it, he had set it right in the middle of the table. It gave him an idea.

Dear Grant,

It has been a long time since I have seen you, and I miss you. You are the person I want to be. I remember how you used to walk with confidence and swagger because you knew you were making the right decisions. I remember the time that you stood up to the two guys from Forter Freight who were trying to take advantage of Mike over at Sayer's Distribution. They were so afraid of the lawsuit you promised that they both quit their jobs and skipped town. Mike was eternally grateful. I remember the time in second grade when you stood up to Butch Jenkins when he pushed down Lillian. You punched him right in the nose, twice. He needed it, and she needed someone to stand up for her. I even remember when you were a senior in high school, and you decided you would never cheat on another assignment again—and you didn't. You didn't cheat in college, you didn't cheat any of your customers, and you have never cheated on a relationship!

Grant, this is your assignment, so you can't cheat! I know you hate yourself for not finding Katie, for not being there for Jacobi, and for not defending Dynamite, but you can't hold yourself captive anymore. If you do, you'll never be the father or man you want to be. You are a slave to your own weakness, and forgiveness is the only thing that will

set you free. Can't you see it? You are holding yourself in
the cell! The "free you" does what he wants, what he knows
is right. The "captive you" settles for safety and fear.
Forgive yourself for settling for safety and fear, and let the
real you out!

I will not hold on to my hate any longer. There's always
some heat in hate, and I'm taking the heat off. I will be free
to walk in confidence because I will be walking around as
me, the true me, the me I want to be, the me I am.

Forgiven,
Grant

Although the letter writing was a bit cathartic, Grant did
not feel any huge weight lifted off his shoulders, he didn't
feel a mountain move, and he didn't feel any extra energy.
Now, he felt tired and wondered if what he had written
would make any difference. He felt more peaceful, but he
could still hear Dynamite's screams in his mind.

About twenty minutes later, Grant didn't feel anything.
That was the difference. He didn't hear anything either. No
more screams, no more pressure, no more inner monologue
whispering he was going to fail. Nothing. Just silence and
peace. Rather than falling asleep, Grant was totally
energized. He decided he was going to chronicle his whole

time here—the whole time since he had left home. He would leave it for Jacobi, and maybe—no, certainly—it would help him in a time of need. He moved the paper and pen out of the way, got himself settled, and began to type and dictate everything he could remember.

After Math

A rooster crowed as the sun split the mountain-ensconced sky. Grant's energy—not worry--kept him awake all night. He took an early morning run, in the dark, before Jacobi was up. He made breakfast, and while he was cooking eggs, his mind began its old propaganda again:

Good teachers get enough sleep at night to be available for their students! Good fathers don't leave their children while they run. Good friends don't judge their son's mother for her feelings toward her own father. Good men don't leave a kid down!

The pressure was gone, but the thoughts had returned. Grant said, "I don't believe this. I know who I am. I love my son, I love my students, I love Katie, and I love Dynamite." Finally, he was telling the truth.

Jacobi walked into the room rubbing his eyes, with his hair all mussed. "Who you talking to?"

"Oh, just some idiot," Grant said. "You know, myself . . . my old self, I mean."

Jacobi smiled, drank some orange juice, and went to the bathroom. When he came back out, Grant had breakfast made, so they sat down to eat, together.

During breakfast, Grant realized he had not scheduled a substitute to cover his classes while he attended the funeral.

All the other events had been at night, so he hadn't even thought about today. *So stupid!* But then he reminded himself that everybody forgets. Next time, he would mark it in his calendar, just as he used to do before he was a teacher. He reminded himself nothing had changed; it was just a new job, with the same old application.

After Jacobi got dressed, Grant informed him they would need to stop by the school early so he could see what he could work out for a substitute. They arrived about twenty minutes before school started. Grant booked it inside and spoke with Mrs. Clowers.

"Okay, sweetie, we's got you covered, no sweat," she said.

Grant knew she was lying. There was reason to sweat. They were already low on teachers, Katie and he were out, and so were several of Katie's friends. Not waiting for any further explanation, he rushed back out the locked doors, down the steps, and into the parking lot.

There they stood, the vultures. They had Jacobi surrounded, circling him like a piece of dead meat baking in the hot summer sun. High school girls, they were relentless. Jacobi wore his new suit, a new hairstyle, and a look of confidence. He didn't seem bothered by the attention—in fact, he appeared to enjoy it, but what he didn't know was another flock of seagulls was watching. High school boys, they were defensive. They would fight for their fish.

Before any drama could ensue, Grant broke up the séance. "Jacobi! We gotta go! Girls, get to class before I call Mrs. Clowers and have her assign you Saturday school. I know that's how you want to spend your Saturday morning!"

As the gaggle of fishnet stockings, short skirts, low-cut blouses, and big hair dispersed, Grant rushed Jacobi out of there.

"You remember what you told me about big crowds?"

"Yeah," Jacobi responded.

"You should have embraced that back there in the parking lot. A pack of boys was behind you who were about to have themselves a Jacobi sandwich, if you know what I mean."

"The guys at this school love me; they wouldn't mess with me. Remember, my mom works here? They love to watch me play! They're not that stupid."

"Don't be so naïve! Anybody who gets between a man and his stuff becomes an enemy. The problem around here is all these boys think they own these girls."

"I don't think so . . ."

"Remember the Roosters? To them ownership is everything."

When they arrived at the church, it wasn't heavily crowded yet. Apparently, missing a chance to mourn publically was an unforgiveable sin, so everyone who was able—and some who weren't—would be there. The sniveling little kleptomaniac from the funeral home was there, too, and Grant gave him a look of warning. Grant watched the scowling little man ball up his greedy paws and place them in his own pockets. Grant thought, *He probably robs the dead, too.*

As if on cue, the wailing started. One of the ladies of the church broke into a despairing, unmitigated cry. Several others rushed to her aid, and all of them fulfilled their dutiful obligation: stealing attention. Katie, on the other hand, circled the room, making sure everything was in its proper place. She hugged Jacobi, and even Grant, when they both caught her attention.

Katie's mother looks downright pitiful—exhausted— Grant thought. Still, Katie's mom gave Grant a squeeze on the arm to let him know she appreciated his being there. Without thinking, he threw his arms around her, and pulled her close.

Another wail! This one was different; it was deep and masculine—full of anguish and pain. Grant turned quickly to see Hatchet. *Vern!* He stood, broken, his two kids clinging to his legs, with his body heaving out exhalations of ballooned grief. His hair had been cut, fingernails cleaned, face shaven, and he wore a shirt—a nice one at that. The pain on his face attracted much more attention than Grant's donated clothes. As Vern's body shook, and Katie ran to comfort him, Grant wondered if Vern's cry was from loss or despair.

Beneath all of his intuitive repulsion, Grant felt some compassion for Vern—especially for his children. Chester had been their only hope. Grant decided in that place, at that moment, he would do something. He wasn't sure what, but he would do something. A warm breeze blew.

"Grant, I'ma sorry, but I need ye to move out of the cabin this month, son," Ronald spoke from behind him. "I'ma lonin' it to Vern and he's kids for this year, or till they figure somethin' out."

Grant turned to Ronald. "I'll pay their year's rent . . . today." And the deal was done.

The church filled up with patrons, pallbearers, and pedestrians. Backs and necks were sweaty, shoulders rubbed, and the cool air on the tail end of the rainy season was transferred into a hot box. The singing and the wailing began. No piano, no strings, no harmony could be heard, just a bunch of discordant sounds, until a small man in the far rear corner began to sing out, in a quick tempo, above the rest.

"When the roll is called up yonder, I'll be there!"

B.G. belted it out. He had a mighty voice: melodic, powerful, wonderful. Everyone followed his lead and sang Chester's spirit into the afterlife—or so it seemed. When the song was over, B.G. took his seat, and Grant didn't see him again. B.G. seemed as if he were a phantom exhalation of the mountains, breathed into the church only for the appropriate time, and then sucked back into the great beyond. Dynamite sat beside him, and Grant knew he'd see Dynamite again, and soon.

Unlike everything else, the funeral service was short. The young man preached this time, calling on the audience to consider the gravity of the situation, that death was imminent. Grant swallowed the sermon in one big gulp.

The final portion of the service moved to the gravesite. Clad in winter coats and hats, the crowd moved up the mountain to meet the casket, now closed, holding Chester's remains. The pallbearers placed the casket atop an altar-looking box, and stood around the grave. People jockeyed for position. Now, the older man began to preach, and seemed to beg God to commend Chester on the other side. Out of the corner of his eye, Grant spotted a somewhat familiar scene, and his heart sank.

Two dogs, one lame, began to fight in the cemetery as Grant and the crowd stared wildly. Their fur was mangy and covered with stickers and burrs. Unannounced, the dogs had arrived separately, spotted each other, and decided the cemetery would be a good place to settle accounts. One of the bystanders ran over to shoo the dogs away, and Grant watched as the lame one sprinted lopsided on three legs. She was coming right at them! *Thud!* The three-legged dog ran right into Chester's freshly dug grave.

Smacking her face on the other side of the dirt wall, the dog with three legs had not made the jump. She fell to the bottom with a whimper. Grant blushed visibly, but none of the other attendees seemed to be alarmed. Ever ready, Ronald grabbed one of the straps used to lower the casket, and tossed it down to the helpless canine. She grabbed it with her teeth, locked her jaw, and used her three legs to help propel herself upward as Ronald and Dynamite pulled. Once atop, she hobbled over and settled herself at Ronald's feet. She didn't make another sound.

The remainder of Chester's burial was without incident. Grant was shocked that nobody else died. It seemed like the most entertaining thing to do in these parts, but he didn't see anyone jockeying for a position in the grave. When the roll was called up yonder, they all left and went back to the church. People consumed more food, told more stories, and shed more tears—one last, public time.

Like Two Dogs Fighting

Friday was the day of the next playoff game. Held at none other than Possum County High School, the Badgers would be taking on the Muskrats from Nehemiah County. Now was Jacobi's time to shine, and the light atop the head of the coal miner's helmet was about to explode. Jacobi would ensure that the Possum County Badgers would no longer be fodder for other counties' jokes.

Somewhere between Wednesday and Friday, Grant and Katie managed to have a conversation.

"Since Mama is moving in with me, and Vern is taking your old place, that'll leave their old house empty, except the chicken coop."

"Are you or your mom emotionally attached to the house or the chicken coop?" Grant asked.

"Not particularly," Katie responded.

"Then I'll buy it," Grant said. "As long as you don't mind if I bulldoze the whole thing and have it blasted and grated down about ten feet. Of course, I'll sell the chickens first."

"No, we don't mind. Good riddance to that place. We will take out everything we want."

"You're right. Good riddance. I'll have a two-story log cabin built up there this summer, but in the meantime, I'll get a double-wide and slap it up there." Grant feigned a smile, and Katie laughed at his chagrin.

Katie went and picked up Jacobi and Dynamite from the middle school to bring them to the game. Grant now had another responsibility: he had been asked to announce the game. He accepted, but he wondered if anyone would be able to understand him with his strange accent.

Just before tip-off, Grant got to announce his own son's name as he took the court.

"At guard, six-two, from Possum County Middle School, number twenty-four, your Jacobi 'You Can't Control Me' Combs!" He also got to announce Dynamite as the last man coming off the bench: "At guard, five-seven, from Possum County Middle School, number three, Elijah 'Dynamite Red' Par!'"

Grant didn't have much time to pay attention, but he did notice that Dynamite's father was in the stands. Grant's ears felt as if they were filling with fluid and his eyes clouded black when he thought about him, that evil monster in the stands. Grant turned his attention to the game. The tension was thick and tangible, for Possum County hadn't been to the regional playoffs in forty-three years, and all they had to do was win this game. The crowd was loud and buzzing, and in desperate need of deodorant and mouthwash.

Jacobi hit their defense like shotgun pellets through wet paper. *Bang!* And he blew them apart. Grant could barely keep up with his announcing duties: "Number twenty-four, Jacobi Combs, slices down the right side of the court, leaps, and finishes with a monster jam from high above! Oh my goodness . . . wait, he steals the inbound pass and dunks that one home, too! Ohhh, you're in for a real treat tonight, ladies and gentlemen, as Jacobi Combs has—wha . . . he steals another inbound pass, takes it out past the 3-point line, shoots, and scores! Seven points in almost as many seconds!"

At the half, the Badgers were up sixty-five to thirty. Coach Procrete, unlike Coach Combs, usually took his starters out if he had the game well in hand. He rotated most of them out, but he left Jacobi in because he thought he might break sixty-three points. That was the school record, set by none other than Ronald Combs.

The second half was more of the same. Jacobi's going to the basket, Jacobi's getting fouled, Jacobi's dunking over someone, again. The scene was almost comical, had it not been so embarrassing for the Muskrats. Jacobi scored up to seventy and took a seat to a standing ovation from the

Badgers' side. Jacobi's replacement took the court, and it was Dynamite.

Dynamite, too, hit the ground running. Only five minutes remained in the game when he came in, but he played his heart out. Immediately, he took a steal coast to coast for a layup. Next, he found himself whirling through traffic and assisting Jason, a second-string shooting guard on the varsity team, with an easy bucket. Before too much else could be said, Dynamite had stolen the ball again and put it up and in. The Badgers were up ninety-six to forty-two. Suddenly, Coach Procrete called a time-out and waved the boys over.

"Now listen hyear, boys. I'ma not one much for records and all, but tonight's a special night. Jacobi's already got sebenty, and now we got a chance to break the school record for scorin'. The record's ninety-eight. We's gotta have ninety-nine to break it and a hunered to put the icin' on. We got fiddy seconds. Y'all thank you can do it?"

"Yeah!!!" they all clamored.

Coach Procrete took out Dean, the other second-string shooting guard for the high school team, and put Jacobi back in, leaving Dynamite, Jason, and Jacobi in the backcourt. The coach announced to the whole crowd that the team was shooting for one hundred. The Muskrats coach looked at him incredulously, tossing his hands up, then took a seat on the bench.

Jacobi threw an inbound pass to Dynamite; Dynamite fired the ball back to Jacobi, who tore through the defense right down the middle of the lane, and missed. The ball bounced high off the back of the rim, and a Muskrat seized the rebound and rifled the ball one-handed down the court on an attempted fast break. It wasn't fast enough. Dynamite intercepted the ball and slung it right back down to Jacobi for an easy dunk. Twelve seconds had expired off the clock, and only thirty-eight seconds remained. The Badgers wouldn't trap because that would be unreasonable when they had such a substantial lead, Grant thought, but then again, what unreasonable thing hadn't these coaches tried?

He looked up in the stands at Katie. She seemed a bit perturbed that Jacobi was still playing when the game was so well in hand. *Overprotective mother*, Grant thought, with a smile, and then he turned his attention back to the court.

The Muskrats ran twenty-five seconds off the clock when their forward finally took and missed an easy jump shot. Jacobi seized the rebound and whipped it to Dynamite, who ran like a jackrabbit toward the basket. Dynamite caught the ball, dribbled, jumped, and was clotheslined by the

Muskrats point guard, which sent him flying into the padded wall. The referee ejected the Muskrat and awarded Dynamite two free throws while the rest of the players stood on the other side of half court.

Clank! The first shot hit the front of the rim, but then rolled in. Dynamite had just helped the Badgers break their all-time single game scoring record! One more shot. *Clank!* This one hit the front of the rim head on, and fell to the floor. Dynamite still had two more chances to put the team up to one hundred points. Since he had been fouled while shooting, and his team was in the bonus due to the Muskrats' abundant fouls, he would get two more chances.

He bent his knees, spun the ball back twice, dribbled three times, pulled the ball up by his right ear—as was his custom—extended with great follow through, but he bricked it off the back of the rim. He got the ball again. Again he spun the ball back twice, dribbled three times, pulled back the ball up by his right ear—as was his custom—and slowly turned his head to the left. His dad sat there, stone-faced, contemptuous, while his mom bit her thumbnail. He extended fully, but caught nothing but air. He had shot, an air ball, on a free throw. He hung his head shamefully.

The referee blew the whistle and awarded the ball to the Muskrats. The Muskrats ran the time out on the clock and loosely let the ball roll off the court, but the Badgers fans were ecstatic, the Badgers team was ecstatic, Jacobi and Grant were ecstatic, but Grant could see that Dynamite wasn't. He wasn't present. Dynamite's smile seemed manufactured, and his words were not lyrical, nor inspirational. They sounded flat.

That night, Grant had an itch he just had to scratch. After all the celebration and hoopla, he and Jacobi went back to the cabin. He would have it for only a month longer, so he wanted to make good use of it. For that matter, Jacobi should have gone home to his mom's house, but he didn't. Grant lay in bed with his head instinctively twitching left— his itch. He felt pulled to his running shoes, pulled to the door, pulled to Dynamite—the scratch. He knew better than to resist, so he donned his running gear, sneaked a glance at Jacobi, and headed out the front door.

As he ran, his heart palpitated irregularly. He felt weak, lethargic, dreadful. Just breathing took everything he had, but he had to keep going until he met the highway and heard . . . it. Dynamite's scream rang in his ears, only this time it wasn't internal. Dynamite really was screaming— again.

Unleashing the inner hound, Grant tore down the highway, through the grass, and up to the barn. But something stopped him. A great anxiety covered him, staring him in the eyes, pushing against his chest, daring him to come one step further. With pure fear, he looked through the crack to see Dynamite dangling. His dad was strapping up his free hand, his right hand, to the wall. Dynamite bellowed and flopped, screaming, yanking, begging for his dad to stop. His white skin, exposed, naked, turned bright red with fear and heat. His father backed away.

"No, Daddy, no! NO! Daddy, please, God, no! Daddy! Daddy! Daddy! No!" he screeched as his lungs let out all his air.

"Oh yeah, boy. Oh yeah! Call for your mammy, boy, cause your daddy's gonna give you what you deserve for embarrasin' him like 'at!"

Snap! Grant heard the whip crack violently. He hadn't noticed before, but Dynamite's dad held a long, black whip. Dynamite let out a bloodcurdling scream, and grunted as he writhed against the rough barn wall. Grant did not see when the whip struck, but he saw the skin on the back of Dynamite's right leg, just below his buttock, swell white, flay open, and begin to ooze blood within a few seconds.

A blue jay died in Grant's mind. His senses mushroomed all at once, rushing upon him like a tidal wave. His eyes narrowly focused, although they bulged with intensity.

Dynamite's dad threw down the whip and ran over to Dynamite and grabbed onto Dynamite's naked back.

"That'll teach you to embarrass me again, boy, that'll teach you!"

What was it that the preacher man said? The questions rang in Grant's mind. *What was it? Something about "protecting widows and orphans"; something about "wash yourselves, make yourselves clean"; something about "protecting the innocent" and "giving one of these a cup of cold water." A blue jay would drop his feathers for his son!* Grant didn't feel the heat; a cool wind of compassion blew right through him and snapped into the barn.

Before realizing it, Grant was upon him. He charged through the barn and tackled Dynamite's dad from the back. They slid on the dirt floor, and Grant shoved the man's face against the ground with all of his weight. As the friction brought them to a sudden halt, Grant dug his knees into the ground, and planted his toes. He pulled his right fist back and punched with blunt force repeatedly into the back of that thick skull. In a split second, Dynamite's dad had pulled his knees up under him and was up on all fours.

Then Grant hamstrung him. It hurt worse than Grant could imagine, but he grabbed the man's right foot, pulled it out from under him deftly, yanked straight up past his waist, and lay on it. The toe of the boot dug deeply into the right side of Grant's groin, but Grant had to immobilize him. Again, Grant punched him in the back of the head, and again. Dynamite's dad reached back over his head and grabbed Grant's shirt. Instinctively, Grant punched his shoulder blade, right near the socket. Although the arm snapped away, the force of the impact and the recoil of the leg threw Grant off, right next to the blacksnake whip.

Grant was on his feet like a cat, and flailed the whip. He hit his target right across the back, but with no snap. As he yanked the whip back, he smacked himself underneath the arm he was using to protect his face. Grant bit down on his lip, hard, and recoiled the whip. He couldn't hesitate. Again he flailed the whip, this time with a snap, and cracked his target on the cheek just below the eye, splitting the skin violently. That did it. Dynamite's dad flung his hands to his face in horror and began to cry for mercy, but there was no mercy. Grant whipped and whipped and whipped, until his sweaty hand felt fused with the handle. The screams didn't stop him—he had to protect Dynamite—but the pain finally did.

Wash Me! Make Me Clean!

Grant's arm and right shoulder were like gelatin. He couldn't swing the whip any longer, and Dynamite's dad had long since stopped bawling. He was unconscious, dead perhaps. Grant didn't know, so he stopped. He cut Dynamite's tethers away from the wall. The ropes fell listlessly, as did Dynamite into Grant's arms. Naked and ashamed, Dynamite squirmed away when he felt Grant's touch. Dynamite pulled down an old blanket from a stall, covered himself wildly, and stared at Grant, then his father. Momentarily, he seemed lost in a fog, then he turned to run, but he collapsed, grabbing his right hamstring. Grant helped him to his feet and guided him to the house.

When they walked through the door, the home was anything but welcoming. Perfectly clean and well-manicured, the entire place, even the hearth had been scrubbed. The house felt clinical. Dynamite's mother was aghast when she saw Grant and hastily stood from the couch, panicked. She exuded defensiveness, and it was not lost on Grant.

"Look, before you say anything," Grant said through gritted teeth, "I found your husband beating your son out there in the barn! I need to know what you are going to do. Right now!"

"Oh, Dynamite!" she exclaimed and rushed over to grab her son. She walked him to the restroom. "I'm so sorry, I'm so sorry!"

No doubt she had seen this many times, had cleaned up Dynamite repeatedly, so Grant didn't trust her. "What are you going to do?" he demanded.

"I . . . I don't know yit," she managed through voluminous tears.

"Okay, then the boy's coming with me."

Before Grant could reach him, Dynamite's mother screamed "No!" and stepped between Dynamite and him.

That was the answer Grant sought. She rattled, "I'll call the police on him. I'll call the police on him!"

In her hysteria, she pushed Dynamite back, and he fell. She collapsed to the floor, huddled around him, and glared up at Grant, petrified.

"You call the police," Grant said, "and I'll stay and wait."

Dynamite's mom cleaned and dressed his wounds, apologizing and speaking soothing words to him. The girls got out of bed due to the commotion, but Dynamite's mom sent them right back to their rooms, immediately. Grant sat in the kitchen, listening, wondering how many years and how often she had stood by silently while her son had been beaten. He slipped out the back door unnoticed. He hustled out to the barn, only to see Dynamite's father, mangled, lying with his face in the dirt. A slight movement in his shirt caught Grant's eye, but it was only that of an expanding and contracting diaphragm. Grant felt pity, but not remorse and walked back toward the house.

"I did it," she said as Grant stepped through the back door. "I contacted 'a police like I said I would. Dere on dere way."

Before the police arrived, Grant slid out the back door again, and hid behind the mound of coal. He had cracked the kitchen window ever so slightly so he could hear. He knew perfectly well that the police wouldn't arrest him for protecting the boy, but he also didn't want to advertise his involvement. Obscurity, in these parts, was next to godliness. He listened for the conversation inside.

"Ma'am, we've called 'nambulance. Yer husband's nearly dead. Ned and Scooter are out there right now, tryin' to keep him still."

He was doing a pretty good job of keeping himself still a little while ago, Grant thought sardonically, visualizing the nearly dead version of Dynamite's dad he left in the dust.

"Now, you say you don't know who dun it?"

"No, sir, he was a beatin' my baby, and someone took to beatin' him and 'scaped."

Grant could barely make out her words, wanted to move closer, but waited.

"And ye don't know who it was?"

"No, sir."

"How'd the boy get inside? Who cut the ropes?"

The officer turned his back knowingly, and peered out the sole kitchen window.

"The good Lord must ha' dune it!"

Grant saw the officer turn back to face Dynamite and his mom. He heard him say accusingly, "Why didn't ye stop him?"

Grant rolled his eyes. She was all of four foot seven inches tall and weighed approximately eighty-five pounds. The officer continued with his questioning, "Why didn't ye call us none of the other times he done it?"

"Said he'd kill me."

As the officer continued his line of banal questioning, Grant sneaked to the side of the house near the garden. He hunched down to hear.

"Lemme ask the boy. Who stopped 'im?"

"Fate!" Dynamite replied.

"Who's Fate?" But Dynamite remained silent.

The officer began to raise his voice, but Dynamite would not answer. He threatened to take Dynamite with him, but Dynamite responded, "I'm not a talkin'."

His mom ran interference. "My bowya has sufferd' enough. Please let 'im be! Please just take my husband, and let my bowya be!"

The officer acquiesced, but warned her to be expecting some future visits. Grant perceived the officer wasn't only looking out for Dynamite's best interests.

The air in the house smelled of sulfur. Grant squeezed through the back door as the ambulance and officers left. Nobody had even examined Dynamite, not physically anyway. He told Dynamite he was sorry for what happened and searched for resentment in his eyes. Grant found none. What he did find; however, was a very uncomfortable silence as the ailing son and mother looked up at the man who had just shattered their assailant and stolen their security. Grant felt the silence and the conflict. He let himself out, and walked back home, slowly.

Isaiah 119

Saturday passed without incident, that is, except for Jacobi's deciding to stay another day at Grant's. On Sunday, however, they met Katie and her mother at church. Katie's visage confirmed his suspicion. She knew. Grant had guarded his secret, but word spread far and wide of a man "whippin' 'at old boy up yonder, 'at one who beats 'is kid." Grant felt . . . identified.

Jacobi gathered his belongings from Grant's house after church, including his new suit, and went home to where his mom and Grandma were waiting. Katie met him at the door, embracing him again and again. *She just saw him at the church*, Grant smiled. Grant waved good-bye and headed back to the cabin, alone. When he arrived, depressing solitude confronted him, but he chose to focus on happy memories of Jacobi. While he envisioned their last game of horseshoes, a warm breeze blew, and a knock came at the door.

"I heered ye might be lonely!"

"What are you doing here?" Grant asked, laughing, as he wrapped Ronald in a big bear hug.

"Well, I's up aire 'spectin' the court when I saw y'all leavin' from the church. 'Spretty dry up aire now. You wanna go shoot some?"

"Yes," Grant said. "Yes, I do."

They spent the whole afternoon playing HORSE and talking. Ronald said he already knew what Grant had done, but Grant pretended not to believe him.

"You didn't know . . . if you would've known, you wouldn't have looked at me all stupefied when I told ye!" Grant said, mockingly.

Ronald laughed at Grant's attempt at sounding native.

"I knew, son; I knew . . . I've always known."

"Whatever," Grant said, "just like I know I'll make this shot." He shot a hook shot from behind the 3-point line exactly as he had seen Ronald do many times past. Nothing but net.

From Head to Toe

That night, Grant went to the hospital, the same one where Chester had died. The trip took ninety minutes, and he practiced his speech the whole way. He got the room number, and although the nurses said the patient didn't want any visitors, Grant walked right in and closed the door.

Dynamite's dad lay in the bed, covered in bandages. His right arm was set in a cast and in traction, his neck was braced, and his head was immovable. He had an IV stuck in his left arm, among the lacerations, and his hand rested on the railing beside the bed. He looked up at Grant with fear and rage swirling in his eyes, but Grant looked down on him with raw determination.

"I'm here to talk. You listen!" Grant growled. "If you touch that boy again," he said, pointing his finger, "I'll kill you. Now, I'm not here to fight. I'm here to forgive. You may hate me and you might try to come after me once you get out, but I don't hate you. I think you're messed up, and you need some help, but I don't hate you. Let me tell you, I forgive you, but I will come back for you if you touch Dynamite again."

Without looking for confirmation, Grant turned and walked out, pulling the door closed. He stepped to the right, and with his back against the wall, he crouched down into a sitting position. He could feel the back of his head knocking against the wall as he trembled, and his jaw ached from clenching. After about two minutes, still breathing heavily, he stood up and walked away.

He didn't trust him, Dynamite's dad. Grant knew from experience that if this man returned home, he would play nice for a while, but then the angry monster would raise his villainous hand, and Dynamite would pay the price. Grant decided Dynamite's mom and the judge would have to make the decision as to whether the man could return. He would not be the barrier between the father and son if Dynamite and his dad were to reunite one day.

Chapter 15: Grant'd

Friday was the day of the big game, the regional final, and it was in Cook County. The Cook County Otters gave up their court to host the game between the Crick County Cubs and the Possum County Badgers. There would be no home court advantage.

Grant decided to travel with Ronald and Katie, while Jacobi rode with the team. After school that Friday, Grant went home to change, and then headed toward Katie's. When he arrived, she spoke frantically.

"Mom's having an anxiety attack! Mom's having an anxiety attack! I can hardly get her to breathe," she cried as she rushed back to the bedroom.

Grant waited in the living room listening as Katie soothingly talked to her mom. She finally got her mom breathing, talking, and then responding in monosyllabic words. Grant sighed.

About ten minutes later, she came back in the room and said, "I can't go. I can't leave her tonight."

Grant stood and hugged her as she stained his shirt with tears. Gripping the back of his shirt, she exhaled, "When will this awful year end?"

Her reality hit Grant. This year that had been so terrible but so wonderful to him, had only been malicious to her.

She had lost her privacy, her persona, her father, and now she missed her son. None of the good deeds Grant could do would console her, so he just held.

Slowly, she pulled herself away, and said, "Oh, I'm so sorry, Grant, I'm so sorry." She hid her face from him. He looked away to grant her some privacy while she wiped away her own tears. "Tell Jacobi I love him and I'm sorry. Tell him I love him ten times, twenty-four times," she said. "Make sure he knows it, please."

Grant promised and backed out of the house slowly, but left anxiously. He picked up Ronald and headed across the counties.

"Good news, son." Ronald said.

"What's that?"

"Rumor done has it dat Crick County boys 'a got ta flu!"

"No way!" Grant said, shaking his head.

"'At's what they're sayin'!" Ronald responded.

When they arrived at the gymnasium an hour before game time, it was already packed. No girls' game would be played tonight, just the varsity Cubs against the varsity Badger boys. Dynamite was dressed in warm-ups, but everyone knew he wouldn't play. Word had spread about his dad and him, and it was still pretty evident that he was injured. He was smiling, though, and his mom was already in the stands with the girls. Ronald took a seat right next to them, and so did Grant.

Jacobi ran out on the court with the team to begin warm-ups. He looked flawless, and Grant couldn't have been prouder. Grant squeezed through the crowd and made his way to the sidelines where Jacobi ran over to meet him.

"Where's Mom?" he asked.

"She had to stay home tonight with your grandma—anxiety attack."

As the look of disappointment spread across Jacobi's face, Grant said, "Hey, look, Jacobi, she felt awful. She cried and cried about it. She begged me to tell you she loved you and that she wanted to be here. You know she would have been."

"Oh, I know she would've. I feel sorry for her, staying home to take care of Grandma. This never used to happen, but after Grandpa got really bad," Jacobi ran his fingers through his hair, "then Grandma got sick all the time, too. I wish Mom could be here."

"I know . . . hey, have you heard about Andre?" Grant asked, changing the subject.

"Yeah," Jacobi said, "they're saying he has the flu."

"Why are you so down—isn't that good news?"

"That's terrible news, Grant! I don't want to beat him because he is sick. I want to beat him because I am better than he is. This isn't just about winning; it's about being the best."

"Okay, okay!" Grant said defensively. "He's a senior and you're an eighth grader. Calm down." Grant noticed while he was talking that Jacobi addressed him as "Grant" when he wasn't just trying to get his attention.

He slapped Jacobi on the back, and gave him a hug. The action was a bit unnatural, but he did it anyway. Grant walked jauntily to his seat next to Ronald. Nachos and cheese, pretzels, popcorn, pop, beef jerky, and a mess of other snacks were everywhere. The gym was hot and sweaty and smelly and home. Grant nestled right in.

After the warm-ups came the announcements and the anthem. Grant decided he had been a much classier and more entertaining announcer than the present one. He didn't ask for Ronald's opinion, though. The boys took the floor, and the tip-off went in the Badgers' favor.

Jacobi dribbled up the court, hesitated, put his head down like a maverick, and butted right past Andre for an easy layup on the opposite side of the basket. Andre was indeed sick. The Cubs fumbled down the floor and passed the ball inside to the big man, who dropped it under pressure from the triple-team. The Badgers recovered, pushed it up court to Jacobi, who missed the fast break layup, but Dean, the varsity center, got the put-back off the rebound.

Dean had worked into a starting position during the playoffs due to his tenacity, and it was paying off for him. He and Jacobi double-teamed Andre and kept him all but scoreless. Jacobi, on the other hand, scored at will. In the first half, he had thirteen field goals. Three of them were 3-pointers, and the rest primarily were easy layups. At the half, Jacobi had thirty-three points, including the four he earned at the charity stripe. He also had seven rebounds, four assists, four steals, and an unbelievable twelve blocked shots. Almost every shot Andre tried, Jacobi rejected.

After the halftime break, the Badgers took the court, and victory seemed to be well in hand. The Cubs put on a second-half surge, but it was no match for Jacobi's play. He cranked up the intensity and played like a jackhammer. He just kept smashing away. He intercepted a pass near half court and streaked to the basket, finishing with a ferocious dunk. He jumped from the left side, about eight feet from the goal, leaned forward, almost prone in the air, and smashed the ball through the rim with a mighty jolt. Jogging backwards, he switched directions just past half court. Dean intercepted another pass on the right side of the floor. Dean bounce-passed the ball across the court to Jacobi, who caught it in mid-stride. His defender to the right of him, Jacobi planted with his right foot and exploded off the floor with his left knee and arm high.

The snap was deafening, the anguished cry worse. Something had popped. Something had popped just as Jacobi jumped, and he fell to the floor like a clipped marionette. He lay on the floor, with his face to the ground. His feet kicked uncontrollably. Grant stood from his seat as the coach and the team rushed the floor. The referees tried to hold the Badgers back as more trainers rushed over.

Jacobi was surrounded. Coaches, players, referees, and trainers all stood upon him, around him, covering him. Grant rushed out of the stands. He pounded down the stairs, shoving people out of his way. Food flew everywhere. He ran toward Jacobi, yelling, "Back off, back off!"

The referees tried to hold him, too, but he swiped them aside with a bump of his hip and a push from his arm. He crouched over Jacobi, defensive, angry. The look in his eyes told the story well enough, and nobody pushed him away. He knelt beside Jacobi. "Jacobi, it's me. What do you want?"

"Out," came the muffled reply from the buried face.

Grant pulled his feet underneath him, leaned forward, rolled his son into his arms, straightened his back, and stood with that massive boy leaned against his chest. Unbalanced and wobbly, he ignored cries of "Don'tcha touch 'em —you'll hurt him worst," and "What are ye doin? Are ye crazy?"

He walked Jacobi to the double doors amid the disharmonious cries. Just in time, Ronald pulled the right one open. Ronald looked from the door to the crowd following Grant and said, "Back up, boys!" and they did.

Grant turned left and carried Jacobi through the door feet first, clutching him tightly. He could barely sustain the weight. He had taken for granted that he knew what he wanted his whole life. Now, everything else could wait. The business was sold. Robin was in charge. Robert was right, and Katie could wait. Only one thing mattered: the weight. *Is this my wish?* Grant wondered. Nothing else mattered. Ronald let go of the door from inside the gym. Grant carried Jacobi down the corridor. Into the future they walked, the father carrying the son. As Grant stumbled and Jacobi moaned out a word of thanks, the gymnasium door slammed that chapter shut forever.

Author's Note

Every once in a while, we all get off track. This is one of the most consistent practices in life, but somehow we all seem shocked by it. We've all heard people say, "I would have never thought . . ." or ask, "How could this happen?" The wisest thing someone can do is prepare himself before he gets off track. That's where this novel comes in: it is an example of several characters who are all a little off track. Their goal, as well as yours, is to discover where their track lies, and then to get each other back on it. I hope they do, and I hope it provides encouragement for you to prepare for eventual trips off track and to repair any broken ones. Eventually, the tracks run out, and we all hope to be on the right side in the end.

The second purpose of this novel is to become an English teaching tool. Hours have been poured over creating scenarios that allowed for the use of specific literary devices and certain vocabulary words, grammatical functions, punctuation usages, and additional literary elements. The novel will be deconstructed into a manual whereby English teachers can teach poetry, prose, vernacular, grammar, composition, spelling, punctuation, and more. This model is meant to help eliminate teaching from several disparate sources and to teach within context.

Previously, we used this model to teach English, but it has since been lost, and we have paid dearly. Soon, this will no longer be an issue.

Acknowledgements

I have been blessed to have been inspired and encouraged by many people. Some have stuck by me even when they should have left, and some have offered forgiveness when it shouldn't have been offered. To all I am grateful.

To Evelyn, my daughter: Without you, I would not have written this book, or grown so much. You were my inspiration to get off the couch many years ago, and you still are. I admire your consistency and your loving spirit. I am amazed by your ability to look past the exterior of people and to love them for who they are. If I have met anyone I admire for being dependable, consistent, and true, it is you. I am happy to get the chance to watch you grow and mature into a person I want to be.

To Eliana, my daughter: Without you, I would not have written this book, or grown so much. Your words have been a source of inspiration for me. I admire your positive outlook and your confidence in who you are, your self-respect. I am amazed by how you can look through negative circumstances and see the positive, and I love that you are confident enough in your person to live in the moment. I am encouraged by watching you grow and lead and help. I am happy to get the chance to watch you grow and mature into a confident person I want to be.

To Ethan, my son: Without you, I would not have written this book, or grown so much. Your excitement and energy have been sources of inspiration to me. I admire your willingness to lead and to take responsibility. I am amazed by how you can shake off negative experiences and offer forgiveness. I admire your ability to include others, so that nobody is left out. I am encouraged by watching you develop into a man. I am happy to get the chance to watch you grow and mature into the inclusive person I want to be.

To all three of my children: Life has been an incredible journey. You have given me much more purpose. I almost thought I had lost you, until I found myself, and I am trying to be there for you. Thank you for your forgiveness.

To Mom: Thanks for never giving up. I trust you implicitly. Whenever I come up against a Quietus, I want you on my side. I don't know anyone as trustworthy as you. You're my role model. I love you.

To Dad: Thanks for being the inspiration behind many of the ideas in this novel. You were the real Dynamite Red, and, I wish I had been able to spend more time with you on this earth, but since you're gone, I'll see you on the other side. And you'll see me, too.

To Stephanie, my sister: Thanks for being an encouragement and a role model as a parent and a sister. I am glad that we have grown together as we have aged.

To Allen, my brother: Thanks for being available for advice and wisdom. I look to you to lead the way for our family, and I have learned much from you. You may be the smartest person I know.

To Tony, my brother: Thanks for walking with me through the most difficult time in my life. You taught me about peace and about taking life one day at a time. For that, I am grateful.

To Marvin, my brother: Thanks for teaching me about boundaries and standards. I never would have made it through being off track without instating those principles. My kids and I are both grateful.

To Jeff, my brother: Thanks for teaching me about compassion and grit. You show your love through your work and your resilience is admirable. I look forward to growing together with you.

To Liz, my sister: Thanks for being available for me, for counseling me, for talking with me, and for never giving up on me. You're a true best friend. Thanks for forgiving me when I needed it most. I love you.

To Rob, my brother: I always looked up to you, and I always will. Get used to it! Thanks for encouraging me when I was young and scared, and thanks for encouraging me now that I am old and scared. I am encouraged by how you have kept fighting. You're my inspirational story.

To Robin, my sister: Thanks for being one of the best people I know. Somehow, I didn't realize this when I was young, but now when I think about you, I see you are loving, caring, giving, sacrificial, wise, and trustworthy. I'm glad you're my sister. I admire you.

To Nat, my sister: Natalie! Natalie! Why aren't you mad at me? I guess because you fully understand the principle of forgiveness. You're my best friend. I trust you. I am glad I have been allowed to watch you grow into the woman you have become. Thanks for never giving up on me. You're my hope for humanity.

To Steve Conner, my brother: I love you. You should have been my brother, but you couldn't be because God picked to be a wonderful husband to Stephanie and a fantastic father to all of your children. You are the model of Christlikeness to me because you don't just talk about love, you embody it.

To Brian Grooms, Chad Finton, Matthew Brown, and Jason Brubaker: You guys were my friends from childhood, and hardly ever is there a friend as close as one established in childhood. I love you guys.

To Sarah, my friend: Thanks for showing me what forgiveness means. Thanks for loving our kids.

To James, my friend: Thanks for being good to my kids. If you don't know it, you're brilliant. Let that little light shine!

To Don and Allison Sandoval: Thanks for making my family your family. Don, thanks for being my friend who was near when my brothers were far away.

To Jared Austin: Thanks for being a friend and an editor. I trust you. You are a man of integrity.

To Andy Lee: Thanks for being a friend who always included me. I believe in you and I trust you. You're a great friend, father, and husband.

To Lisa Jones: Thanks for being the model of hospitality and patience with our family. We love you.

To Brad Nuse: Thanks for being a model provider for our family. I admire your giving spirit.

To the following life coaches whom I have never met: Andy Andrews, Andy Stanley, Zig Ziglar, Tom Ziglar, Dave Ramsey, Michael Hyatt, Brian Buffini, Robert S. McGee, Frank Minirth, Paul Meier, Malcolm Gladwell, Charles Duhigg, and many others. I have never met any of you, and I realize that I don't have your endorsement as an author. I just wanted to say thanks on a personal note for giving me inspiration.

To the best teachers: Kari Harris, Dr. Darrell Holley, Tom McCullough, Clint Morgan, and Ron Schaar.

To those for whom I am grateful: Steve and Kathleen Hays, Eric Houtari, K.J. Yoon, Joel and Bridgett Riley, Micah Derby, Mark Littlefield, Jeff and Lou Ann Hawkins, Gideon and Linda Ison, Raymond and Vernie Jent, Phillip Collins, William Haggins, Beckham Jent, Sue Jent, all my nieces and all my nephews, thanks!

Notes:

48110389R00230

Made in the USA
San Bernardino, CA
18 April 2017